In memoriam: P., 1961–73

All of the characters, corporations, religions, nations, philosophies, political viewpoints, events and makeup in this novel are fictional and are not intended to portray anything in the world as we know it. None of the characters represents the author's personal opinions, which are, in any event, not quite yet organized into publishable form.

GENESIS

Dortmunder opened the door and a distant burglar alarm went *CLANGangangangangang* . . . "Hell," Dortmunder said, and shut the door again, but the *angangangangang* went on and on and on. "Hell and damnation," Dortmunder said, while from some distance away a police patrol car's siren went *whoop-whoop wiggle-wiggle-wiggle whooooooooooopp,* the sound rising from the grid of New York City's streets up five stories through the two A.M. air to this quiet blacktopped roof. The burglar alarm kept nagging: *angangangangang.* WHOOP-WHOOP; the patrol car wasn't so very far away after all.

"Goodbye," O'Hara said.

Dortmunder looked at his partner in crime; in this crime, anyway. "Where you going?"

"Florida," O'Hara said over his shoulder. He was already halfway across the roof to the fire escape.

Raising his voice just a teeny-weeny bit, hoping O'Hara could hear him but none of the neighbors would, Dortmunder said, "Maybe you shouldn't do that."

"I'm gone," O'Hara called back, climbing onto the fire escape. "It's too hot around here, I'm going to Florida to cool off." And he disappeared from view.

Dortmunder, as he replaced his burglar tools in the special inside pockets of his black sports jacket, dubiously shook his head. He just had the feeling O'Hara was making a mistake, that's all, which would be his second of the night, it having been O'Hara who'd paused on the way *up* the fire escape to "neutralize" the burglar alarm. Either those jumped wires had failed to do their job or the proprietor of this importer's warehouse had a second alarm system unknown to Mr. Chepkoff, the food wholesaler who'd commissioned this evening's operation. In either event, it was clear now that the recent shipment of Russian caviar three stories below this roof, the object of Mr. Chepkoff's current intentions, would not after all be removed from the premises this evening, which was a pity.

Quite a pity. In the first place, Dortmunder could use the money. And in the second place, he'd never tasted caviar, and had been looking forward to lifting one or two cans from the shipment—Mr. Chepkoff would never know—and trying them out in the privacy of his own home, swigged down with a nice bottle of Old Milwaukee Light beer. His faithful companion May had even brought back some imported crackers to try the caviar with from the Bohack supermarket where she worked, and was waiting up, butter knife poised, for Dortmunder's return.

The WHOOP-WHOOP had stopped now, but the *angangangangang* just went on and on. It was too bad. Dortmunder hated to go back to May empty-handed. On the other hand, he'd hate it even more if he didn't get home at all. O'Hara's decision to go to Florida via fire escape had been a hasty and unwise one, but departing these premises in one fashion or another was definitely a good idea.

Dortmunder sighed. The caviar was so close he could almost taste it—if he knew what caviar tasted like. Resigning himself, he crossed the roof to a spot on the edge near the fire escape, from where he could look down at the sidewalk and at O'Hara, engaged in unsatisfactory conversation with two uniformed cops. Unsatisfactory to O'Hara, that is; even from here, the cops could be seen to be *very* satisfied. Soon they'd find the stolen truck backed up to the loading dock on the side street, and then they would begin to wonder if O'Hara had brought any friends along tonight.

In fact, as two more patrol cars—lights flashing, but no sirens—came to a stop at the curb down there, one of the original cops started *up the fire escape*. A young and agile cop—very unfair, that—coming up two steps at a time, flashlight in one hand, pistol in the other.

Time to go. This building was on the corner of two streets in a southwestern area of Manhattan recently rechristened Tribeca, which means "the *Tri*angle *Be*low *Ca*nal Street," and whenever any section of New York gets a cute new name—SoHo for South of Houston Street, Clinton to replace the honorable old name Hell's Kitchen, even NoHo for *North* of Houston Street—it means the real estate developers and gentrifiers and condominiumizers have become thick as locusts. It means the old handbag factories and sheet-metal shops and moving companies are being replaced by high-ticket housing. And it also means there's a long transition period of years or even decades when the plumbing supply places and the divorced advertising executives coexist, uneasy neighbors, neither entirely approving of the other. When Dortmunder turned away from the cop-laden fire escape, therefore, he looked down a long block of rooftops over who-knew-what. All the way to the next cross-street the rooftops were at the same level, each with its telephone-booth-like structure on top like the one Dortmunder had so innocently opened, giving access to the stairwell. But down those stairs, what might he find? A tool manufacturer, his premises girdled with burglar alarms? A Wall Street lawyer with a pet Doberman pinscher?

Not a cop with a flashlight and a gun, anyway. Dortmunder loped away across the rooftops, a tall bony middle-aged man who ran stiffly, like Pinocchio before he became a real boy, and whose burglar tools went *rattle-rattle* and *clank-clank* in his jacket pockets.

First door, locked, no knob or keyhole, just a blank metal sheet. Drat.

Second door, similar. Third. Fourth. There wasn't time now to jimmy a door, not with that cop on the way, and what were the odds on finding one of these doors unlocked?

Zero.

Last roof. Dortmunder looked back and saw the flashlight beam on the roof above the caviar, drawing white lines on the night, up and down, back and forth. The cop hadn't seen Dortmunder way down here yet, but he soon would.

But this wasn't exactly the end of the block. There was one more building, broad and square, between here and the corner. Unfortunately, it was only three stories high, its jumble of A-shaped roof sections a good twenty feet below where Dortmunder now stood.

Back there, the bobbing flashlight had started to move in this direction. "Oh, boy," Dortmunder said.

What were his choices? (A) Prison. And, since this time he'd be classed as an habitual offender, it would be prison for all eternity. (B) A broken ankle. (C) If that cop's flashlight and eyes were good, prison *and* a broken ankle.

"Might as well go for the whole thing," Dortmunder told himself. The low wall at the edge of the roof was topped by arched slippery sections of tile. Dortmunder climbed over, clutching to the tiles, letting his feet dangle, his arms straight up, his nose and cheeks feeling the rough cool brick surface of the building wall. He could sense every single molecule of air in the vast distance between the worn soles of his shoes and the slanted top of that building down there. "I better not take the chance," he told himself, changing his mind. Maybe he could hide behind one of those stairwell constructions, or find some other fire escape to go down. "Too dangerous," he told himself, and pulled to get back up onto the roof, and his hands slipped.

2

Good heavens, thought Sister Mary Serene, *it's barely two o'clock, my vigil's only half over, and my knees are killing me. But, mercy, think how much better off I am than all the people out in the world, forced to ride subways, talk to one another all day long, earn livings, watch television, eat meat, be distracted from contemplation of the One. For it is the One, the Eternal, toward Whom our thoughts should ever be directed, the One Who raises us above the mundane world through contemplation of Him, and Who, at the end, will lift us to eternal joy in the Bosom of His Peace and His Contentment. The mystery of the One who Is Three and yet One, Who created this world only for the purpose of renouncing it, Who created us in His image but Is Himself incomprehensible and unknowable, that One Who . . .*

It was easy to get back into contemplation; like falling off a log. Sister Mary Serene was an old hand in the contemplation game by now, having renounced the world, the flesh, the devil and an efficiency apartment in Jackson Heights some thirty-four years ago, entering this convent as a troubled and uncertain young woman and finding at once within its portals, by golly, that peace that *does* surpass understanding. *If only everybody could be a cloistered nun,* she frequently thought, *what a nice and peaceful world this would be. Still to be renounced, of course, but nevertheless nice. Though not to be compared with Heaven, with the Afterlife, the abode of that One Who . . .*

And so on.

Here in the silent chapel of the Convent of St. Filumena on Vestry Street in downtown Manhattan there were at all times throughout the twenty-four hours of the day and night at least three nuns—four at the moment, being sisters Mary Serene, Mary Accord, Mary Vigor and Mary Sodality—on their knees and engaged in the primary task of their order, the contemplation of the Godhead in silence and veneration. The sacristy light above the altar and the sconced candles between the Stations of the Cross along both side walls were very subtly enhanced by indirect electric lighting on a dimmer switch—a contribution by Sister Mary Capable's brother, a New Jersey contractor—giving just enough illumination to show the half-dozen rough wooden pews, the simple altar, the thickly mortared brick walls and the high cathedral ceiling criss-crossed with rough-timbered rafters. In this silent and medieval setting, one's mind quite naturally and without urging turned to thoughts of the Church Militant here below, the Church Triumphant there above, and the Supreme

Being over all, that Essence Whose spiritual effusion . . .

Of course, even for a pro like Sister Mary Serene, contemplation did occasionally pall. Fortunately, at such moments there was always prayer to fall back on, with the usual litany of requests: long life to the Pope, an early depopulation of Purgatory, the conversion of Godless Russia. And recently there was something of even greater urgency for which to pray; namely, the return of Sister Mary Grace:

Dear Lord, if it pleases You to return to us our sister, Sister Mary Grace, from out of the tents of wickedness and the skyscrapers of the deceiver, our little Sisterhood would be eternally grateful. Eternally, Lord. We know it is Sister Mary Grace's ardent wish to return here, to Your dominion, to this life of contemplation and duty. It is our wish also that she return among us, and if it be Your wish and desire—

Klok. Sister Mary Serene turned her head, and on the pew beside her lay a screwdriver, fairly large, with rough black tape around its handle and most of its haft, leaving only the last inch of gleaming metal to reflect the candlelight. Now *here* was a distraction!

Ker-*chunk.* A small canvas bag fell to the pew beside the screwdriver. It was gray and grimy, but neatly tied closed with a pair of canvas strings. Sister Mary Serene picked up this object, untied the strings, and opened out a kind of small toolkit with many pockets containing a number of well-oiled metal objects, some flat, some curved, one spiralled like a corkscrew. Here were tiny needle-nose pliers, here was an oblong of soft springy aluminum, here was a double-pronged electric line tester, here was a pair of wires ending in small alligator clips.

Here, in fact, was a rather good set of burglar tools.

Sister Mary Serene might be unworldly, but she wasn't stupid. It didn't take much to figure out the purpose for all this equipment. She raised her eyes and looked upward, and there was the burglar himself, high above, clinging to the rafters. *Thank you, Lord,* she thought. *Our prayers are answered.*

3

Dortmunder looked down at a lot of nuns. His ankle gave another twinge, and his grip on this rough-timbered rafter became less sure by the second, but what mostly bothered him was *nuns*. He had many reasons to be depressed by the sight of them all, scurrying back and forth down there twenty or thirty feet below, occasionally looking up in his direction, gesturing at one another, running in and out of this church or chapel or whatever it was, many reasons he had to be depressed, and all of them good.

Nuns, for instance. Well, just to leave it at that; *nuns*. Was that crowd likely not to call the law when some clown loaded with burglar tools comes through their roof? Not a chance. So, because it was nuns he'd fallen among—oops; *almost* fallen among, keep holding tight—it meant that among the choices he'd enumerated for himself up there on the roof he'd won the daily double: a broken ankle *and* prison for life.

Also, for a second reason to be depressed, *nuns*. Born in Dead Indian, Illinois, and abandoned at three minutes of age, John Dortmunder had been raised in an orphanage run by the Bleeding Heart Sisters of Eternal Misery, and when you mentioned nuns to *him* no sweet images grew in his mind of kindly penguins feeding the homeless and housing the hungry. No, what Dortmunder visualized when he heard the word *nun* was a large, bad-tempered, heavy-shouldered woman with a very rough and calloused right hand, usually swinging. Or wielding a ruler: "You've been quite bad, John. Put out your hand." Ooo; a smack across the palm with a wooden ruler can create quite an impression. Just looking down at those black-and-whites—still in the traditional uniform, he noticed, not updated with the rest of the Church—just looking at them, even after all these years, could make his palm sting.

Like his ankle. Having decided *not* to drop onto that lower roof, having started to climb back up, he'd been in the wrong posture when his hands had slipped and he'd fallen any which way, landing heavily on an angled roof, bouncing, hitting various portions of himself, and rolling at last down into a trough, his head dangling over the edge, staring down maybe thirty-five feet at extremely hard sidewalk.

Had he yelled when falling, or when he'd hit? He didn't know. He did know he had a whole lot of new aches and bruises and pains and stings all over his body, but he also knew that the sharp fiery twinges in his ankle made all the other pains pale in comparison. "Just like I figured," he muttered, rolled over, managed not to slide off the edge of the roof, and looked back up at the dark mass of the building he'd just left. No cop yet, no flashlight yet, but there sure would be.

Scrambling up the steep slope on all threes—his left ankle hurt by now most of the way to the hip—he came to a small dormer, with a square wooden louvered shutter instead of a window on its front. This shutter was merely held in place by four small metal wings which could be turned aside, so Dortmunder turned them, crawled through into a small dusty black space and pulled the shutter closed behind himself. It kept wanting to fall away from the window, so he reached a narrow screwdriver through the louvers and put two of the little retaining wings back in place.

The space in which he found himself was absolutely black, and apparently quite small; not an attic, not a useful area, but merely a bit of waste between the outer and inner designs. Turning this way and that, trying not to hit his ankle against too many hard unyielding surfaces, Dortmunder blundered across the trapdoor, opened it, and found just below him the wide rafter far above the chapel. Having no choice, out he went.

At first, it had seemed as though he could crawl across this rafter to a pillar on the far side, then shimmy down the pillar (somehow), and thus make good his getaway, but this goddam rough-hewn timber was a little *too* rough-hewn; every time he touched it he got three more splinters. Trying to protect his hands and his ankle and everything else, he'd struggled along to just about the middle of the timber before he'd lost his grip and almost fallen. That's when his coat fell open, and tools began to drop. And now here he was, stuck, above a sea of nuns.

Silent nuns. Even in his present difficulty, Dortmunder noticed that strangeness. The first little group of nuns, having spotted him up here, had run off to get more nuns, all of them seeming very excited, pointing at him, gesturing at one another, waving at him to remain calm, running back and forth, but never saying a word, not to one another and not to him. Robes *whiffed* down there, soft-soled shoes went *pid-pid*, beads and crucifixes *klacked*, but not a word did they speak.

Deaf mutes? Unable to use the telephone? Hope hesitantly lifted its battered head in Dortmunder's breast.

And here came yet more nuns, with a ladder. Apparently, having a man in the rafters was quite an exciting event to this crowd, so they all wanted to participate, which meant there were so many nuns helping to carry the ladder that it probably

14

assayed out to about one nun per rung. This labor-intensive method caused a lot of delay in transferring the ladder from the horizontal to the vertical—thirty or forty of the nuns didn't want to let go—which made for a great *flurry* of hand-waving and head-shaking and finger-pointing before at last it was raised and opened to its tall aluminum A, and pushed over to where its top could poke Dortmunder's dangling knee.

"Okay," Dortmunder called. "Okay, thanks, I got it." Hundreds of nuns held the feet of the ladder and gazed up at him. "I got it now," he called to them.

Oh, yeah? Here he was on a rafter, and there next to him was the ladder, and the physical impossibility of transferring himself from the former rafter to the latter ladder gradually made itself manifest. There was absolutely no way to let go of anything over here, and equally no way to attach himself to anything over there. Dortmunder dithered, unmoving, and time went by.

Vibration in the ladder. Dortmunder looked down, and here came a nun, lickety-split, zipping up to his level. She was small and scrawny, ageless inside that habit, her sharp-nosed ferretlike face peering out of the oval opening of the wimple like somebody looking out of the porthole of a passing ship.

And not much liking what she saw, either. With one brief unsympathetic look at Dortmunder, she pointed briskly at his left leg and then at the first step of the ladder below the top. Nothing goody-

goody about *this* one; she'd fit right in back at the orphanage. Feeling almost at home, Dortmunder said, "I'm sorry, Sister, I can't do that. I think I broke my ankle, or sprained it, or something. Or something."

She raised her eyes heavenward, and shook her head: *Men; they're all babies.* It was as efficient as speech.

"No, honest, Sister, I did." Old habits die hard; seeing the old habit of the nunnery, Dortmunder immediately started making excuses. "It's all swole already," he said, and shifted around precariously to give her a better look. "See?"

She frowned at him. Braced on the fourth step of the ladder, she raised the dangling end of her wooden-beaded sash and pointed at the crucifix on the end of it while raising her eyebrows in his direction: *Are you Catholic?*

"Well, uh, Sister," he said, "I'm kind of, uh, fallen away." He lowered his gaze, abashed, and looked at that stone floor way down there. "In a manner of speaking," he said.

Again she shook her head, and let the crucifix drop. Coming up two rungs, she reached out and grabbed his right wrist—*God,* her hand was bony! —and gave it a yank. "Holy shit!" Dortmunder said, and she stared at him in wide-eyed disapproval. "I mean," he said, "I mean, uh, what I meant—"

An eyes-closed brisk headshake: *Oh, forget that.* Another tug on his wrist: *Let's move it, fella.*

"Well, okay," Dortmunder said. "I hope you know what we're doing."

She did. She treated him like a collie bringing home a particularly stupid sheep at the end of the day, as limb by limb she transferred him off the beam and onto the ladder, where he clung a moment, half-relieved and half-terrified, covered with sweat. More vibration meant that his short-tempered benefactress was hurrying back down the ladder, so it was time to follow, which he did.

Awkwardly. His left ankle absolutely refused to support any weight at all, so Dortmunder hopped his way to the ground, holding on to the sides of the aluminum ladder with fingers so tense they left creases. Left leg stuck out and back at an awkward angle that made him look as though he were imitating some obscure wading bird from the Everglades, he went bounce-bounce-bounce all the way down on his right foot, and when he finally got to the bottom a whole lot of nuns reached over one another's shoulders to push him backwards into a wheelchair they'd just brought in for the purpose.

Dortmunder's fierce friend from the top of the ladder stood in front of him, gazing severely down at him, while all the other nuns hovered around, watching with a great deal of interest. This one must be the Chief Sister or Mother Superior or whatever they called it. She pointed at Dortmunder, then pointed at herself, then pointed to her mouth. Dortmunder nodded: "I get it. You're all of you, uh, whatever. You can't talk."

Headshake. Hand waggled negatively back and forth. Disapproving scowl. Dortmunder said, "You can talk?"

Nods, lots of nods, all around. Dortmunder nodded back, but he didn't get it. "You *can* talk, but you *won't* talk. If you say so."

The wiry little boss nun clutched her earlobe, then suddenly did a vicious right-hand punch in midair, a really solid right hook. She looked at Dortmunder, who looked back. She sighed in exasperation, shook her head, and went through it all over again: tug on right earlobe and punch the air, this punch even stronger than the first; Dortmunder believed he could feel its breeze on his face. As he sat there in the metal-armed wheelchair, frowning, wondering what in *hell* this old vulture was up to, she glowered at him and tugged her earlobe so hard it looked as though she'd pull it right off.

Parties. Dortmunder's head lifted as a memory came to him. Party games, he'd seen people do— He said, "Cha-*rades?*"

A great heaving relieved nod flooded the room; the nuns all smiled at him. The head nun did one last earlobe tug and punched the air one more time, and then stood there with her hands on her hips, staring at him, waiting.

"Sounds," Dortmunder said, the rules of the game vaguely floating in his head. "Sounds like. Sounds like punch? Like lunch, you mean."

They all shook their heads.

"Not lunch? Munch, maybe." (The lost caviar was influencing him.)

Everybody *vehemently* shook their heads. The boss did the charade all over again, more irritably and violently than ever, this time punching her right fist smack into her left palm with all her might. Then she stood there, shaking her left hand, and waited.

"Not punch at all," Dortmunder decided. "Sock?" No. Well, that was just as well. "Hit? Bang? Crash? Pow? Thud?"

No, no, they all semaphored, waving their arms. *Go back one.*

"Pow?"

Many many nods. Several of the nuns did quick charades with one another and silently laughed; talking about him.

"Sounds like pow." Dortmunder thought it over, and saw only one way to handle the situation. He said, "Bow? Cow? Dow? Fow?" The look they gave him when he said *fow* made him skip *gow*. "How?"

Several of the nuns were pointing at the floor or stooping down. Dortmunder said, "Start at the other end of the alphabet?" and they smiled in agreement and relief, and he said, "Zow? Yow? Wow? Vow?"

That was it! Thousands of fingers pointed at him in triumph. "Vow," Dortmunder repeated.

The head nun smiled, and spread her hands: *There. That's the story.*

"I don't get it," Dortmunder said.

A collective sigh went up, the first sound he'd heard from this crowd. While the rest of the nuns all raised their eyebrows at one another, the boss put her finger to her lips, then cupped her hand around her ear and leaned forward to make a big dumb-show of listening.

"Sure," Dortmunder agreed. "It's real quiet. When you've got nobody talking, that's how it gets."

The nun shook her head, did the dumb-show again, and spread her hands: *Get it, idiot?*

"Oh, it's a clue." Dortmunder leaned forward, holding the wheelchair arms. "What is it, like, sounds like quiet? Riot. Diet. No? Oh, you mean *quiet*. Something *like* quiet. A different word like quiet. Well, I mean, when it's real quiet, it's like, you know, it's quiet, you can't hear anything, you like it when it's quiet at night, things get very quiet, you want some other word like quiet, when it's quiet, when there's no horns or anything, it's real quiet and—I'm *thinking!* I'm doing my *best!*"

Still they glowered at him, hands on hips. "Gee whiz," Dortmunder said, "I'm new to this, you people do it all the time. And I just had a bad fall, and— All right, all right, I'm thinking."

Hunched in the wheelchair, not speaking, he thought and thought and *thought*. "Well, there's always silence," he said, "but beyond that I can't— Oh! It's *silence!*"

Yes! They all pretended to applaud, nearly clapping their hands together. Then more and more of

20

them switched over to a pointing thing. Point *here,* then point *there.* Point *here,* then point *there.*

Dortmunder was getting into the swing of it now, gaining confidence from his successes. "I get it," he said. "Put the two things together. Vow. Silence. Vow. Silence." He nodded, and then he *did* get it, and loudly he said, "A vow of silence! You got a—One of those religious things, a vow of silence!"

Yes! They were delighted with his accomplishment, if he'd been a Maypole they'd have danced around him. A vow of silence!

Dortmunder spread his hands. "Why didn't you just write that, on a piece of paper?"

They all stopped their silent congratulations, and looked briefly puzzled. A few of them plucked at their skirts or sleeves to call attention to their habits, suggesting it was just habit, but the chief nun stared at Dortmunder, then reached into her garments and came out with a three-by-five notepad and a ballpoint pen. She wrote briskly, tore off the note, and handed it to Dortmunder.

Can you read?

"Oh, now," Dortmunder said. "No need to insult me."

4

Mother Mary Forcible and Sister Mary Serene wrote notes back and forth with the speed of long practice. Here in the tiny cluttered office of the convent, with its barred window viewing Vestry Street, they sat on opposite sides of Mother Mary Forcible's large desk, shoving their notes at each other with increasing vehemence.

We want Sister Mary Grace back!

God will show us the way.

He showed us last night, in the chapel!

We shall not consort with robbers and thieves.

Our Lord and Savior did!

Get thee behind me, Satan!

It went on like that, the torn-off pieces of notepad piling up on both sides of the desk, until Sister Mary Capable stuck her head in the office door and rested her cheek on her pressed-together hands, eyes closed: *Our guest is still asleep.*

Mother Mary Forcible looked at the old Regulator clock on the wall; nearly seven. The sun was long since up, breakfast finished, Mass attended, floors scrubbed. Shaking her head, she looked at Sister Mary Capable and snapped her fingers forcefully: *Get the lazy lout up.* Sister Mary Capable smiled and nodded and left.

Meantime, Sister Mary Serene had clearly decided on a new tactic. Scrabbling through the scumble of used notes, she smoothed out one of her very first and pushed it across at Mother Mary Forcible:

We want Sister Mary Grace back!

Mother Mary Forcible wrote: *Of course we do. Prayer and contemplation will lead us to the way.*

Instead of writing further, however, Sister Mary

Serene merely pushed the first note over again:
We want Sister Mary Grace back!
  I never denied that!
We want Sister Mary Grace back!
  Please don't be boring, Sister Mary Serene.
We want Sister Mary Grace back!
  Do you wish to encourage crime?
We want Sister Mary Grace back!
  You're as bad as I am!

Sister Mary Serene looked so cherubic and round-cheeked when she smiled. Nodding, she pointed yet again at that same unrelenting message. Mother Mary Forcible sat back, bony fingertips absentmindedly patting the surface of her desk, and brooded.

It was true the entire convent, every member of the Silent Sisterhood of St. Filumena, had been praying night and day for guidance and aid with this Sister Mary Grace problem, and it was equally true the convent had never before in its history had a burglar in the chapel rafters; but could the one actually have much to do with the other? Sister Mary Serene, having been the first to discover the fellow and therefore having an understandable feeling of proprietorship toward him, quite naturally argued that here at last was God's instrument, but Mother Mary Forcible remained a skeptic. While certainly many of God's messengers and instrumentalities over the ages had been unlikely sorts, it was even more certain that most crooks were merely crooks, without much of good or God about them.

On the other hand, the customs of a lifetime are hard to resist. Through almost her entire adult life, Mother Mary Forcible had kept her back firmly turned toward the outer world, had limited her temporal existence to this building, this group of women and this rule of silence, which the sisters were permitted to break only for two hours every Thursday. Her attention and desires had been exclusively directed Upward, relying upon the efficacy of prayer and the mercy of the Creator to answer every need. But with a problem as worldly as that posed by Sister Mary Grace, was it possible that a solution equally worldly was the answer?

Movement in the doorway distracted Mother Mary Forcible from her thoughts and, speak of the devil, here was the miscreant himself, left foot swathed in white bandages, Sister Mary Chaste's cane in his left hand and a mug of Sister Mary Lucid's coffee in his right. His hangdog expression was as it had been, and being unshaven had not at all increased the aspect of reliability in his countenance. "I'm supposed to come to the office," he muttered, exactly like some Peck's bad boy caught smoking in the lavatory.

If Mother Mary Forcible had wanted to teach grammar school, there were plenty of orders she could have joined. With an exasperated look at Sister Mary Serene, who was beaming at the fellow as proudly as though she'd invented him, she gestured briskly for him to sit in the chair to the left of the desk, which he did, putting one dirty-nailed hand on the desktop as he made a kind of Humphrey Bogart twitch around the mouth and said, "I can explain, uh, about last night."

Mother Mary Forcible was already dashing off her first note, and pushing it across to him: *You're a burglar.*

He looked pained. "Oh, now," he said, but the second note was already well under way. He smiled back tentatively at Sister Mary Serene, then read note number two:

We didn't turn you in to the police at the other end of the block last night. We could have.

"Oh," he said. "Police at the other end of the block, uh huh. You figure I, uh . . ."

Mother Mary Forcible looked at him.

"Well," he said, and shrugged, and sighed, and thought it over. "Uh, thanks," he said.

Mother Mary Forcible had the next note all ready; she slid it across the desk.

Possibly you can help us in return.

He frowned, studied the note, turned it over to read the blank back, shook his head. Then he stared around the office, looking for something, saying, "What, you got a safe you can't open or something?"

Too bad this wasn't Thursday; it took an awfully long time to explain the situation.

5

Andy Kelp let himself into the apartment with a credit card, looked into the living room at Dortmunder and May, and said, "It's just me. Don't get up." Then he went on to the kitchen and got a beer. A wiry, bright-eyed, sharp-nosed man, he looked around the kitchen with the quick interested manner of a bird landing on a berry bush. An assortment of gourmet crackers were arranged on a plate on the kitchen table. Kelp took one with sesame seeds, washed it down with beer, and went back to the living room, where May was lighting a fresh cigarette from the tiny ember of the previous butt and Dortmunder was sitting with his bandaged foot on the coffee table. "How you doing?" he said.

"Terrific," Dortmunder told him, but it sounded like irony.

May dropped the sputtering ember in the ashtray and talked through fresh smoke: "I wish you'd ring the doorbell like everybody else, Andy," she said. "What if we'd been in a tender moment?"

"Huh," Kelp said. "That didn't even occur to me."

"Thanks a lot," Dortmunder said. He didn't seem to be in the best of moods.

Kelp explained to May, "On the phone, John said he hurt his foot, and I didn't know if you were home, so I figured I'd save him walking to the door." To Dortmunder, he said, "What did happen to your foot?"

"He fell off a roof," May said.

"Jumped off," Dortmunder corrected.

"Sorry I couldn't come along last night," Kelp told him. "Did O'Hara work out?"

"Up to a point."

"What point?"

"The point where he was arrested."

"Whoops," Kelp said. "And he just got out of the slammer, too."

"Maybe he can get his old room back."

Kelp drank beer and pondered briefly on the accidents of fate that had led to his place being taken last night by Jim O'Hara. There but for the grace of God, and all that. He said, "Where were you while O'Hara was being arrested?"

"Jumping off the roof."

"Falling off," May corrected.

Dortmunder ignored that. "I spent the night in a convent," he said.

Kelp didn't quite get the joke, but he smiled anyway. "Okay," he said.

"The nuns bandaged his foot," May said, "and loaned him a cane."

"They got this vow of silence," Dortmunder explained, "so there's no phone, so I couldn't call May and tell her not to worry."

"So naturally, I worried," May said.

Kelp said, "Wait a minute. You spent the night in a *convent?*"

"I already told you that," Dortmunder said.

27

"Yeah, but— You mean, you *did?* You spent the night in a convent?"

"It was the convent roof he sprained his ankle on," May said, "when he fell off the other roof."

"Jumped off."

"So— I mean—" Kelp, stymied for words, gestured with the beer can, but that didn't fully express his thoughts either. "What I mean is," he said, "what did you *tell* them? I mean, there you are on their roof."

"Well, they doped it out," Dortmunder said. "The other end of the block was all police cars, and there was a burglar alarm going off down there, and all like that. So they kind of put two and two together."

"These nuns."

"The nuns, right."

"Well—" Kelp was still having trouble phrasing himself. "What did they *say?*"

"Nothing. I told you, they have this vow of silence. They wrote a lot of notes, though."

"Notes," Kelp said, nodding, catching up. "Fine. What did the *notes* say?"

For some reason, Dortmunder looked uncomfortable. Also for some reason, possibly the same reason, May looked kind of steely and determined and grim around the jaw. Dortmunder said, "They offered me a deal."

Kelp squinted at his old partner. "A deal?" he asked. "Nuns? What do you mean, a deal?"

"They wanted his help," May explained. "They

28

have a problem, and they were praying for help, and here comes John, falling onto their roof—"

"Jumping."

"—and they decided he was sent by God."

Kelp stopped squinting. Instead, he looked very round-eyed at his old partner, saying, *"You?* Sent by *God?"*

"It wasn't my idea," Dortmunder said, sounding sulky. "They dreamed it up themselves."

"Explain it to Andy," May suggested. "Maybe he'll have some good ideas."

"I already have a good idea," Dortmunder said, but then he shrugged and said, "All right. This is the story. It's this bunch of cloistered nuns way downtown with this vow of silence, and last year they got this new nun joined up, the first new one they had in five, six years."

"That I can believe," Kelp said.

"Well, this girl, this new one, she has a very rich father, and he tracks her down, finds out she's in this convent being a nun, and he kidnaps her."

Kelp was astonished at this turn in the story. "Right out of the convent?"

"Right out of the convent."

"How old is this girl?"

"Twenty-three."

Kelp shrugged. "So she's a grown-up, she can do what she wants."

Dortmunder said, "Except her father's treating her like one of those kids goes off with the cults, you know, the Moonies and like that. He's got her

29

locked up, and he's got this deprogrammer in there, doing his number on her."

Kelp said, "He's deprogramming her out of the Catholic Church?"

"That's the idea. She writes all these letters to the convent, they showed me some, and this guy's just steady deprogramming, day after day. And what she wants, what she says in the letters is, she wants to go back to the convent."

"And her old man's got her *locked up?* He can't do that, not if she's twenty-three."

"Well, he's doing it," Dortmunder said. "So the nuns went to a lawyer to see what can you do, and the lawyer came back and said this guy is very very rich, he has deep pockets like you wouldn't believe, and if they try anything legal he'll just tie them up in court until the girl's *seventy*-three."

"So she's stuck," Kelp said.

"So that was why they figured I was from God, being a burglar and all," Dortmunder explained. "They figured I could sneak into the rich guy's place and bust her out."

"What kind of place?" Kelp asked.

"Penthouse suite on top of a building up in midtown. Armed guards all over. Access limited to one elevator, where you got to use a key. The guy owns the whole building."

Kelp said, "No way you're going to get into that penthouse."

"Don't I know it," Dortmunder said.

"And if you did get in," Kelp went on, "no

way you're going to carry any twenty-three-year-old girl *out*."

"When you're right, you're right," Dortmunder told him, and sighed.

"So what did you do? Sign something?"

"No. We shook hands on it."

Kelp didn't get it. "So what have they got on you? A confession?"

"No."

"Your name? Home address?"

"Nothing. Just that I made the deal, I said I'd do it."

"Well, you *can't* do it," Kelp said, and grinned, saying, "But that's okay, because you don't have to do it. You're home free."

"Well, maybe not," Dortmunder said.

"I don't see the problem," Kelp told him. "You're away and clean, and they can't find you."

"Ahem," said May.

Kelp glanced over at May, and right now she looked like one of the statues on the Washington Square arch; unblinking, determined and made of stone. "Ah," said Kelp.

"Now you see the problem," Dortmunder said.

6

Hendrickson opened the door, then promptly stepped back and reclosed it, and the plate smashed itself to pieces against the other side. Opening the door again, entering the large, neat, plainly furnished living-cum-dining room, stepping over the burritos and the china shards, Hendrickson said, "Well, Elaine. Still at it, eh?"

The furious girl on the other side of the refectory table held up the sign she'd printed her third day here, on the back of a shirt cardboard, in angry red ink: *Sister Mary Grace.*

Hendrickson nodded pleasantly. "Yes, Elaine, I know. But your father would rather I called you by the name he chose for you, when you were born."

She made an elaborate pantomime of throwing up, suggesting that mere mention of her father made her sick, while Hendrickson crossed to the highbacked wooden chair over by the windows, noticing that the Bible on the side table was closed today. Good. He should probably take the damn book out of here, but that would be too obvious an admission of defeat.

In the first few weeks of this assignment, Hendrickson had plied Elaine Ritter with selected biblical quotations, standard practice for a professional deprogrammer like himself, but it turned out the girl knew the Holy Word better than he did, and would top every quotation of his with one of her own. The Bible was left here all the time for her perusal—there were no other books in this apartment, there was no television or radio—but soon she'd started the practice of leaving it open, some scathing rejoinder circled in red ink, for him to find at the beginning of each session. As a result, in the last few weeks he'd ignored the

Bible, whether open or shut, had refrained from quotation, and she was gradually letting up her counter-campaign in that department.

A small victory, that, but Hendrickson's only one so far, and probably the only one forever. Privately, he didn't expect to win this particular war. Sometime in the future, surely long after Frank Ritter had fired Hendrickson for non-accomplishment, Elaine Ritter would most likely simply go mad from rage and boredom and would thereafter be of no use to anyone, including her father and herself, but in the meantime the pay was excellent, the fringe benefits included a fine apartment in this same building and a chauffeured car always on call and a liberal drawing account, and apart from the occasional flung object the work was not unpleasant. Elaine Ritter was a good-looking girl, particularly since her hair had grown back, and except for Thursdays she was silent as the tomb; not a bad companion, all in all, on these long and drowsy afternoons.

It was almost three months now. "They tell me you're the best in the business," Frank Ritter had said, at their first meeting, when Hendrickson had been hired to save his youngest child from the toils of organized religion.

"They tell *me* I'm the best, too," Hendrickson had replied amiably. A large stout man who dressed casually but not sloppily, Walter Hendrickson was forty-two years old and had been a professional deprogrammer for eleven years. Little surprised or baffled him anymore; but that, of course, was before he'd met Elaine Ritter.

"I hire the best," Frank Ritter had said, "because I can afford it, and because I won't accept anything less. Pour your Drano into my girl's head; I want her unclogged and functioning."

"Consider it done," Hendrickson had said, with an airy assurance he now found amusing to remember. *Consider it done.* Lord, lord. There were times when Hendrickson almost felt like praying.

The fact is, Elaine Ritter was not at all the sort of person he usually contended with. His clients were almost always vague and confused, with very poor self-image and only a scattering of half-remembered education. Generally, they had left their homes and gone off with Swami This or Guru That mostly because they were looking for a parent other than the parents they'd left, feeling some need for a parent who was more strict, or less demanding, or more attentive, or less cloying. *Different,* that was the point. Different parents, a different tribe, the growth of a different self who would be so much more satisfactory than the miserable original. Religion and philosophy had little or nothing to do with those kids' actions and decisions, and Hendrickson's task, really, was not much more than to wake them up to the world around them and hold a mirror to their own potential for selfhood. Easy.

Elaine Ritter was something else. No self-image problem for her, and religion and philosophy had *everything* to do with her decision to renounce the world and join that convent down in Tribeca. On the religious side, she firmly believed in God and the Catholic Church. Philosophically, she just as firmly renounced the world that men like her father had made. *Vocation* was a fabulous beast as far as Hendrickson was concerned, but if the beast ever did live, it was in this girl. She knew her own mind, and she would take no shit from Walter Hendrickson.

Too bad. Shit was all he had for her.

He paused a moment beside the highbacked wooden chair and looked out the window at the towers of midtown Manhattan. Seventy-six stories down crawled the busy street. Up here, the gray towers were the only reality. Hendrickson no longer even saw the few faint scratches on the unbreakable windows where Elaine had beat on them uselessly with chairs and lamp bases the first few days she was here. She too had learned to accept the present impasse; he would not alter her into something her father could use and understand, and she would not in the foreseeable future be leaving this apartment atop the Avalon State Bank Tower on Fifth Avenue.

Hendrickson settled himself in the chair. The idea of the high wooden back, and the idea of placing it in front of the window so that his features would be harder to see, was that it depersonalized him, would tend to make his statements more authoritative. A parliamentary trick, and useless here, but there was also nothing to be gained at this stage by moving. "I understand your father's coming home the end of this week," he said blandly.

She curled her lip and pantomimed spitting on the carpet. She wouldn't actually spit on the carpet, of course, she was too well brought up for that.

Hendrickson said, "What shall we talk about today?"

Elaine gave him an icy smile and pointed ceilingward.

Hendrickson's smile was much warmer than hers. "God?" he asked. "No, I thought the topic I'd like to bring up today is filial piety, the duty each of us owes our parents. And the examples I thought I would dwell upon," he said, as she started the pacing back and forth, glowering at nothing, which was her usual reaction to his sermons and which was beginning to wear a noticeable path in the carpet, "the examples I thought might be of clearest meaning to you, are your six older brothers and sisters, their roles and functions in Templar International, your father's company, and their attitudes toward their privileges and responsibilities."

While Hendrickson's calm and confident voice went on, Elaine continued to pace and to glower, undoubtedly storing up various statements to whack him with this coming Thursday afternoon, when once again the monologue would briefly become a dialogue, with a vengeance.

Oh, well, what the hell, it's a job.

7

Dortmunder stumped along Fifth Avenue with his cane and his bad temper while Andy Kelp jogged along beside, saying, "The problem is, where's the profit in this thing? You try to put together a string, somebody to drive, somebody to lift and carry, somebody to show guns to the guards, these people are gonna want to know what's in it for them. I mean, these are professional people, these are not people who're gonna drive and lift and bust heads and unlock doors for *free*. I mean, *you* got to do this on account of May, and I'll come along because we're old pals and it's kind of interesting, but other than us, I don't see where you've got your manpower. I mean, that's the problem."

"That's the problem, is it?" Dortmunder asked him.

"One of the problems."

And here was another of the problems; the Avalon State Bank Tower itself on Fifth Avenue, just a couple of blocks from St. Patrick's Cathedral. The people who invent places like Tribeca don't ever *go* to places like Tribeca; they come here.

The Avalon State Bank Tower rose up from the cement sidewalk like a cross between a massive old oak tree and a squared-off spaceship. The first four floors were sheathed in alternating rectangles of glass and black marble with little dots and strings of green in it, the rectangles edged with copper. Starting from the fifth floor and going on up, the building's skin was gray stone, unadorned. No cornices, lintels, arches, gables or gargoyles interrupted the flow of stone. From poles jutting out at an angle over the sidewalk at the fourth floor level hung three large flags: the United States, New York State and Templar International, this last being, on a yellow field, a black stylized figure that might have been either a tree or the letter T.

Dortmunder stood by the curb, leaned back on the cane, and peered up as high as he could, his mouth open. The blue spring sky was half-obscured by running little puffy white clouds. Somewhere up there, the building stopped. "She'd have to let her hair down a hell of a distance, wouldn't she?" he said.

Kelp said, "What?"

"Nothing. Let's go in."

The street level of the building was half bank and half garden, both with forty-foot ceilings, the garden being more or less open to the public though enclosed, with a small cafe among the birches and beeches and bamboo. The bank was modern and marble and full of the latest ideas in security. Between bank and garden was the entrance to the lobby and its rows of elevators. Dortmunder and Kelp went in there, and stood staring for a while at the column after column of the directory lining one long wall, like a war memorial.

"Lots of people in business," Kelp commented, looking at all those corporate names.

"Mm hm," Dortmunder said.

"Wonder how many are legit."

"The dentists," Dortmunder said. "Let's go for a ride."

There were elevators marked 5–21, elevators marked 22–35, elevators marked 36–58, and elevators marked 59–74. Kelp said, "I thought you said she was on seventy-six."

"That's what they told me."

So they took one of the 59–74s, and Dortmunder pushed 74. Two messenger boys and a blonde in a red dress and a pair of lawyers discussing a tax deal—"They'll take seven mil and go away, but will they come back?"—shared the long vibrating ride with them in this functional metal closet. A messenger boy got off at sixty. The blonde sprayed her throat with breath freshener and sashayed off on sixty-three. The other messenger boy got off on sixty-eight, and the lawyers—"Just so they don't start talking felony, we're basically in the same ballpark"—got off on seventy-one. Dortmunder and Kelp rode on up to the top.

Except it wasn't the top. The helpful "you-are-here" map next to the elevators showed them where the stairwell was, just around the corner, and when they went there and opened the door the plain broad metal stairs, painted battleship gray, continued on up. However, a locked chainlink gate blocked the stairs in that direction. The stairs going down were clear.

"I figured," Dortmunder said.

Kelp leaned his cheek against the chainlink gate and strained to see upward. "Two more flights," he reported. "At *least* two more."

"Well, it's this," Dortmunder said. "Or it's the special elevator that needs a key, that I don't even know where it is. Or we go up through the ceiling."

"Through two ceilings."

"Let's look around."

They wandered the halls and found they were in the shape of an H, with the elevators in the crossbar. Four companies stretched themselves up here, taking a lot of space. There was a firm of architects, with a golden bridge symbol on their main door. A law partnership simply had a list of names on its entrance, while an engineering company sported on its door a black and gold bee inside the huge capital B of its name. The fourth company, taking up one quarter of the H, had a plain white door with very small raised letters on it reading: MARGRAVE.

For five minutes or so they wandered the halls, looking at doors, most of them marked with arrows pointing toward that firm's entrance. At one point, they watched a young woman, looking worried and carrying a handful of papers, come out of one office, cross the hall, and enter another office, but other than that they were alone. There were no windows anywhere, and the feeling after a while was of being underground rather than nearly a thousand feet up in the air.

"The thing to do," Kelp finally said, "is bring May here, show her the proposition, let her make her own mind up."

"She's made her own mind up. Let's look at one of those elevators."

So they went back to the middle of the H and rang for an elevator, which arrived empty. While Dortmunder propped the door open with his back and stood chicky, Kelp dragged the sand-topped butt can in to stand on, stood on it, opened the trapdoor in the ceiling, shoved it out of the way, and looked.

"Well?" Dortmunder said. The elevator door kept bunking him in the back, wanting to close. His ankle was sore and wanted to be placed in a raised position on something soft for a while, like maybe a month. "What do you see?"

"Machinery."

"How close?"

"Right here."

"The shaft doesn't go up to the top?"

"No," Kelp said, peering and peering. "That might be a door there, so they can get to the motor and all, but that'd just get you into seventy-five. This thing doesn't go to seventy-six."

"Figures," Dortmunder said. "Let's take another look at the stairs."

Kelp put the butt can back, Dortmunder released the now-buzzing elevator, and they went to take another look at the stairs. Dortmunder was brooding at the wall and Kelp was examining the lock on the gate when a man appeared in the hall doorway behind them and said, cheerfully, "Help you, gentlemen?"

Dortmunder leaned more heavily on his cane, in order to look inoffensive. "Trying to find the men's room," he said.

"Oh, I'm sorry," the man said, smiling at them. He was about thirty, large, built like a football player with a neck wider than his head and hands made of balloons. He was neatly dressed in a dark suit and white shirt and slender yellow tie, but there was something bulky under the left side of his jacket. "There are no public restrooms up here," he said. "You'll have to go back down to the lobby, turn left, and go into the garden."

"Okay," Dortmunder said.

"It's just around behind the ficus," the man said helpfully, as they headed for the elevators, their tails between their legs. "You can't miss it."

"Really appreciate it," Kelp said. "Thanks a lot."

"Don't overdo it," Dortmunder told him.

8

There's so much unhappiness in this world. The strong prey upon the weak, injustice is rampant, evil succeeds everywhere and good is trampled in the dust. *Ai, caramba,* it makes you just want to piss!

Enriqueta Tomayo did nothing so crude or vulgar, of course, but contented herself with fiercely

42

banging together the frying pans in the soapy water and glaring around at this antiseptic blond-and-chrome kitchen in the clouds, where she'd been working now for over a year. Back home in Guatemala the rich *ladinos* oppressed the Indians with the help of their armies, both public and private, and up here in Nueva York the rich still oppressed everybody they could get their hands on, even their own flesh and blood. By St. Barbara, this Frank Ritter man even oppresses his own daughter. He even defies God Himself!

Enriqueta whammed a frying pan into the drainboard and looked up to see the poor red-eyed little Sister herself coming into the kitchen, sighing, weary with grief. The little Sister gave Enriqueta a wan smile and crossed to the refrigerator for a glass of skim milk, while Enriqueta dried her hands on her apron and delivered herself, at top speed, of several dozen words in Spanish, the essential translation of which was, "You poor kid!"

The little Sister smiled her gratitude, and drank milk. Enriqueta walked closer to her, lowering her voice and switching to English: "Another letter from the good Sisters."

How the poor child's eyes lit up; it was only these letters from the good Sisters that kept her spirit from breaking entirely. Enriqueta, who knew without doubt she would be fired and probably arrested and certainly beaten and undoubtedly deported if Frank Ritter and his minions ever found out about the correspondence she was smuggling between the convent and the little Sister, also knew it was the finest thing, and therefore the only real thing, she could do with what was left of her life. Her own children were grown now, dead or dispersed. The evils of Guatemala were behind her; please, *Dios*, forever. She had grown old and fat, she was here in this strange cold land working as a cook in a kitchen in the clouds for an evil monster and his poor imprisoned daughter—locked in a tower, just like in the fairy stories!—and she had a sodden husband sprawled in their nice apartment in public housing up on Columbus Avenue. What else could she do but help this poor mistreated child in the best way she could?

If only she could somehow smuggle the little Sister herself out of this tower, she'd often thought, but that was just impossible. Enriqueta was never permitted to ride the golden elevator alone, but was always "escorted" up at eleven in the morning and back down again at nine in the evening by one or more of Frank Ritter's falsely smiling guards, those hard men in civilian clothes who looked so much like the men in army clothes back in Guatemala. All she could do was smuggle the little Sister's letters out and mail them, and use her own address on Columbus Avenue for the convent's replies. But even that little bit helped; it was worth it, to see how the child's eyes lit up.

And *how* they lit up this time! With a great joyous smile on her face, the little Sister extended the letter to Enriqueta, pointing at it with her other hand: *Here, read it yourself.*

Occasionally this happened, the little Sister wanting to share some message from the convent, and though it was a difficult trial Enriqueta always agreed and did her best. She *could* read, though English was more of a strain than Spanish, and it was necessary to hold the piece of paper so close to her face it almost touched her nose. Still, though it took awhile, she did at last manage to make sense of the following:

Dear Sister Mary Grace,

Wonderful news! God has seen fit to put us in the way of being helpful to a man who has *just* the skills needed to effect your rescue. He is a burglar by profession, which means he has studied the art of going in or out of difficult or locked places. (He came to us through our roof!)

Before we cast the first stone, my dear, we should remember St. Dismas, crucified with Our Lord, a common criminal who repented at the very end. "This day you shall be with Me in Paradise," Our Lord promised him. So it was St. Dismas, the thief, who was Our Lord's chosen companion on his first momentous journey back to His Heavenly father after his earthly travail, not one of the Apostles or Disciples, a fact we would do well to remember.

In any event, it is our hope, and our constant prayer to the Almighty, that this association with us and rescue of your own self may be the beginning of the path of reclamation for this latter-day Dismas, whose name is John.

Even now he is studying the best way to reach you and bring you out of your imprisonment. If you happen to have any advice or suggestions you might want us to pass along to John, concerning the physical details of your incarceration, I am sure he would be most pleased.

Praying for your early release, long life to the Pope, forgiveness of the souls in Purgatory and the conversion of Godless Russia, I remain, as ever,

Mother Mary Forcible
Silent Sisterhood of St. Filumena

Enriqueta's immediate instinctive doubt of men named John—or men named anything else, for that matter—she kept carefully to herself. This letter had made the little Sister, at least for this moment, happy; what did it matter if at some later time John turned out to be false or incompetent? Enriqueta enclosed her skepticism in her heart, where it could do no harm. "Say!" she said, returning the little Sister's letter and her elated smile, "that sounds pretty hokay!"

9

When May got home from the library, Dortmunder was in the living room, sitting on the sofa, poking at a lot of Polaroid prints on the coffee table with the end of his cane. He didn't look cheerful. "How's it going?" she asked.

"Could be worse," he said.

Well, that was encouraging. "How?" she asked.

"I could have gone down that fire escape with O'Hara."

"No, I meant saving the girl."

"So did I."

"Well." May dropped her purse and a shopping bag of Xerox copies onto a chair. "You want coffee?"

"No, thanks. When Andy gets here, I'll have a beer."

"Well, *I* need coffee," she said. "That library, there's weirder people there than in the subway." Shaking her head, she went on out to the kitchen.

Today was the fifth day of Dortmunder's research into the girl-rescuing operation, and May's day off from the Bohack, so she'd spent it up at the Mid-Manhattan Public Library, in the periodical rooms, reading about Frank Ritter and Templar International and Margrave Corporation and Avalon State Bank, and dropping dimes into the Xerox machine. Fortunately, Andy Kelp had one time showed her the quiet way to get dimes back out of such machines, so the day wasn't as expensive as it might have been. But it was exhausting, much more so than her normal day standing at the cash register.

Back in the living room, May sat in the most comfortable chair, put her feet up on a puffy hassock, sipped her coffee, and watched Dortmunder poke at the pictures with his cane. "You don't look happy," she told him.

"Good," he said. "If I *looked* happy, it'd be a bad sign. That guy Chepkoff phoned this afternoon."

"Which guy was that?"

"The one sent me for the caviar. He paid three hundred on account, you know."

"On account?"

"On account we wouldn't do the job otherwise. So now he called, he wants his three hundred back. I told him, 'We all take risks in this. You it cost three hundred, me it cost a sprained ankle, O'Hara it's probably gonna cost about eight years.' He argued with me, so I hung up on him. The guy's crazy."

May said, "John, do you want to hear about Frank Ritter?" Without waiting for an answer, she went on, "I just spent all day at the library, with a lot of people in overcoats and asleep and scratching their arms and looking at pictures of naked statues. I was learning all about Frank Ritter. Do you want to *hear* about Frank Ritter?"

Dortmunder looked at her in some surprise. "I'm sorry, May," he said. "You're right, yeah. I want to hear about Frank Ritter."

May didn't like to be short-tempered. Taking a deep breath, she said, "All right."

Dortmunder said, "You aren't smoking."

"I gave it up."

"You *what?*"

"I was thinking about it from time to time," she said. "Remember how, whenever there was a letter in the *New York Times* from somebody with

48

the Tobacco Institute, I always used to clip it out and keep it for a while?"

"Scotch-tape them on the mirror sometimes," Dortmunder agreed. "Freedom of choice and all that."

"Sure. Then did you notice, a while back, how I stopped clipping those letters out?"

"No, I didn't," Dortmunder said. "But it's tough to notice somebody not doing something."

"That's true. Anyway, it occurred to me, *I* don't write letters to the *New York Times* and *you* don't write letters to the *New York Times*."

"Well," Dortmunder said, "we're not in business with the public, like the tobacco people."

"The ketchup people don't all the time write to the *New York Times*," May pointed out. "The beer people don't, the pantyhose people don't. All the people that write to the *New York Times* is South African spokesmen and the Tobacco Institute."

"And people from out of town that lost their wallet in a taxi," Dortmunder reminded her, "and the cabby brought it back to them at the hotel, and they never knew New Yorkers were such nice people."

"Well, *those* letters," May said. "What bothers me about *those* letters is, most cabbies aren't New Yorkers, they're from Pakistan. But the Tobacco Institute letters, what bothers me about those is, why talk so much unless you've got something to hide?"

"That makes sense," Dortmunder said.

"So I kept thinking, maybe I'd give it up for a while," May said, "but I could never seem to get started on it. But I was in the library now, six hours steady in there, and there's No Smoking, and I was so distracted by Frank Ritter and the Xerox machines and the people sticking matches in their ears and reading the encyclopedia cover to cover that I hardly noticed. I came out onto Fifth Avenue and reached for a cigarette, and then I said, 'Wait a minute. I got *six hours* on it.' So I gave it up."

"Well, that's pretty good," Dortmunder said. "Probably a smart idea, too. And I guess that's why you snapped at me before."

"I didn't *snap* at you!"

"Oh, right," Dortmunder said. "Tell me about Frank Ritter."

May took another deep breath. "Well, he's rich," she said, "but you probably figured that."

"I did, yes."

"His grandfather was rich, and his father got richer, and now Frank Ritter's got richer than that. What he owns—" She gestured at the shopping bag of Xeroxes. "—I've got a lot of stuff in there about what he owns, and it's mostly banks. But a lot of other stuff, too. Like, somebody starts a new oilfield somewhere, and then Frank Ritter becomes a partner in that company, and then one of his banks loans them the money to get started, and then they hire his construction company to do the drilling and everything, and they hire his laboratory to do the tests, and they hire his security

50

company for the guards and all, and they lease some planes from his plane-leasing company—"

"I'm beginning to get the picture," Dortmunder said.

"Then there's a couple of South American countries," May went on, "a couple of the little ones."

"What about them?"

"Well, I'm not sure exactly how it works," May said, "but I think Frank Ritter owns them."

"Owns *countries?* You can't own countries."

May shook her head and reached for a cigarette, but there wasn't one there, so she pretended she was just scratching. "What happened was," she said, "one of his banks loaned these countries a lot of money. Then the countries went bankrupt and couldn't pay the money back, so some people from the bank and the engineering company and the security company all went down there—"

"In a plane from the plane-leasing company, I suppose," Dortmunder said.

"I guess. Anyway, they all went down there to help the countries reorganize their priorities, and they're all still down there, so I guess Frank Ritter owns those countries."

Dortmunder shook his head. "Now I'm up against a guy owns countries."

"Somebody put him up to be Secretary of the Treasury down in Washington a few years ago," May said, "but the Congress turned him down. One Congressman, they quoted him in *Newsweek,* he said, 'Conflict-of-interest is Frank Ritter's middle name.' "

Dortmunder sighed. "This is some fella," he said. "He's rich, he's powerful, he owns countries, he has his own army and air force. If this guy wants to ground his daughter, I guess he figures he might as well just go ahead and do it."

"She's the youngest of seven children," May told him. "Elaine Gwen Ritter is her real name. She's got three brothers and three sisters, and they all work for the father. The oldest brother runs the Avalon State Bank here in the city, and one of the sisters with her husband runs the magazine company, and like that."

"He's got a magazine company, too?"

"He's got all *kinds* of companies, John," May told him. "I guess the daughter Elaine was supposed to grow up and marry a guy who'd fit in with everybody else, and then go to work for her father. Frank Ritter owns so many things, spread out so much, he likes to have relatives running the different parts. So I guess from his point of view, here's a daughter that isn't pulling her weight."

Dortmunder shook his head. "I don't know, May," he said. "The more I hear— I know, I go along with you, I owe these nuns a little something—"

"Every day you're not in prison the rest of your life, that's what you owe them."

"Yeah, I know that, I know that. But look at this place." He poked at those Polaroids with the rubber-tipped cane, aggressively, the pictures sliding around on the coffee table. "I can't even find the *elevator*."

"You can't?"

"It'll look like something else, right? The special elevator, goes just to the top floor." Dortmunder gave the photos a dirty look. "There's the lobby, every bit of the lobby. There's the garden, with all the skinny trees. I don't know what anybody looks like that goes up to that top floor, so I don't have anybody I can follow and see where they go that doesn't look like an elevator but is an elevator. But even if I find the goddamn thing, May, what then?"

May nodded. "If you just ride it up to the top, that won't help."

"Not much. And it's just me, with maybe Andy Kelp. I can't put together a string on this because what's in it for anybody?"

May watched Dortmunder brood at the pictures of the lobby and the garden and the exterior of the building and the top several floors as seen from a high floor in a nearby skyscraper. "It's very difficult, isn't it, John?" she said.

"That's a terrific description," he agreed, and poked a couple more pictures toward her, saying, "Here's another thing. On the directory here. You know how companies of the same kind always hang out together in this city? All the garment makers in one place, all the diamond merchants in one place, like that. Well, what we've got in this building is a lot of importers and wholesalers from Asia, tons of them all over the building, people that deal in jewelry and ivory and jade and all this very valuable stuff, that they've got right there with them. Maybe almost ten percent of the tenants are like that, in with all the regular doctors and lawyers and accountants. So besides the Frank Ritter private army up on the top, we've got the whole *building* is security conscious."

May sighed. "John," she said, "you've been very conscientious about this."

"Well, I said I'd do it."

"You told *me* you'd do it," May reminded him. "I know that's the only reason you're even trying, and I know you're giving it every bit of your attention, but I guess I'm willing to go along if you say it can't be done."

Instead of smiling with relief, as she'd half-expected, he frowned more deeply than ever, glaring at those photographs. "I don't know, May," he said. "I hate to admit defeat, you know what I mean?"

"It's been five days, John, and you aren't getting anywhere."

"I don't like to believe," Dortmunder said, "there's a place I can't get in and back out again."

"John," May said, "if you decide it can't be done, all I ask is you go back and tell those nuns about it, so they don't go on hoping."

Dortmunder sighed. "Well, I've got to give them back this cane anyway," he said. "I don't really need it anymore. But I still don't want to have to walk away from this thing, not unless I absolutely have to."

"It's your decision," May assured him. "I won't push at all."

54

"I tell you what," Dortmunder said. "Andy's up there now looking into the question of burglar alarms, electronic responses, all that. If there's a way to cut the building out from city services for a while, maybe, I don't know, maybe I could figure something."

May smiled at him in admiration. "You mean, take over the entire building," she said.

"Yeah, for a while. Late at night."

"I like it when you think big, John," she said.

"Well, let's just see—" Dortmunder started, and the doorbell rang.

"I'll get it," May said, but as she got to her feet Andy Kelp appeared in the doorway, saying, "It's only me, don't get up." He was in blue Consolidated Edison coveralls and white hardhat, with the words WILLIS, ENG DEPT stencilled on the hat and the very realistic laminated photo ID pinned to the left breast pocket. He said, "Beer, anybody?"

"Yes," Dortmunder said.

"I have coffee," May said, so Kelp went away and came back with two beers and May said, "Andy? You let yourself in again, and then you rang the bell?"

"Sure," Kelp said. "On account of, you know, that tender moment you were talking about."

May took a deep breath. She reached for a cigarette, scratched, and said, "Thank you, Andy."

Dortmunder said, "What's the story up there?"

Kelp took his hardhat off. "I take my hat off to those people," he said, and sat down, and drank beer.

Dortmunder looked at him. "Which people?"

"The people who set up security in that building, some outfit called Global Security Systems."

"That's Frank Ritter's company," May said.

"Well, they know their onions," Kelp said. "The entire building is wired for anything you could possibly want. Simple burglar alarms, closed-circuit TV, silent alarms that trigger in the building security offices in the basement *and* over at the police precinct four blocks away. Automatic time locks, heat sensors, sound-activated videotape machines. You name it, they got it."

Dortmunder stared at him in angry disbelief. "The *ad agencies* have this? The *travel agents?*"

"No no no," Kelp said, "what you've got is, the building is wired through the main stairwell to every floor. Every tenant taps in and rents as much or as little security as he wants."

"Oh, fine," Dortmunder said. "So maybe on such-and-such a floor there's nothing at all, but maybe there's everything in the world."

"You got it," Kelp told him.

"And no way to tell which."

"Exactly. Also, they got their own back-up generator, so don't think about knocking out the power."

"Oh, I wouldn't," Dortmunder said.

"The heart of it all is down in the basement and the sub-basement," Kelp said, "and believe me it is *very* well guarded."

"I believe you," Dortmunder said.

"Good. You should believe me." Kelp turned

56

to May. "I don't want to sound a sour note here, May," he said, "but I wouldn't send *my* boyfriend into that place, if I had one, if I wanted him back."

May put two fingers to her mouth and drew on a non-existent cigarette. She could smell the nicotine on her fingers. "John," she said, "Andy's right."

"I don't know enough about the place," Dortmunder complained. "That's the problem. Every place in the world has little gaps, little corners not as strong as everywhere else, but I don't know where they are in this place, and there's no way to find out."

"You did your best," May assured him. "Tomorrow's Thursday, isn't that the day the nuns can talk?"

"Yeah."

"I'll go with you," May offered. "I'll explain you did your best."

"My best," Dortmunder said. He drank beer and slapped the Polaroid pictures with his cane.

10

You could hear her from the elevator. *Welcome home*, Frank Ritter thought, and clenched his teeth as he faced the bronze door, waiting for it to open and the onslaught to begin.

Bronze does not make the best mirror. The lone figure reflected in the four bronze walls of this small private elevator appeared to be soft, rounded and apish, none of which was true about the actual Frank Ritter. Sixty-four years old, six feet two inches tall, Ritter kept his body in fine trim with a combination of careful diet, professionally monitored exercise and occasional plastic surgery. In certain lights, he could look younger than his oldest son, Charles, who was just forty.

"In order to *be* vital, you must *look* vital."

"Nobody wants to shake a shaking hand."

"Think about tomorrow and today will take care of itself."

"Work in the twentieth century; rest in the twenty-first."

These were among the self-generated aphorisms included in the commonplace book which Frank Ritter carried with him always, in his left inside jacket pocket, over his heart. With a binding of hand-tooled leather over sheets of thin steel, the commonplace book also served as protection against a well-aimed assassin's bullet; ineptly aimed assassins' bullets Ritter had overcome in the past and was ready to overcome in the future. Most attempted assassins, working out of emotion rather than reason, were likely to be inept, but one might as well prepare for every eventuality.

"In a tough world, be tougher."

Here's how tough Frank Ritter was: One of the printed memo pads on his desk, in addition to *From the desk of Frank Ritter* and *For your immediate attention from Frank Ritter*, was one printed simply *You'll never work in this town again*, with room above for the recipient's name and address and room below for Ritter's small tight signature. Frank Ritter (A) was not given to empty threats, and (B) was on his second hundred-sheet *You'll never . . .* pad.

In all the world, it seemed, full of animate and inanimate objects, the only object he could neither buy nor destroy was his own youngest daughter, Elaine. "The sharpest thorns are in your own roses," read another aphorism in that common-place book, and he did mean Elaine. Now, as the elevator slid smoothly to a stop and the doors prepared to open, Ritter's face became even harder and stonier and more unforgiving than usual, and his sphincter automatically clenched. The doors slid open; here it came.

She was in full cry, striding back and forth in front of the fat deprogrammer, Hendrickson, who merely stood there with hands folded, an amiable smile on his face like a father indulgently watching his small child sing "On the Good Ship Lollipop." Ritter's eyelids half-closed, as though his daughter were playing a bright light on him instead of a piercing voice.

It would be easy, of course, simply to avoid the damn girl for the two hours every Thursday after-noon when her so-called vow of silence permitted her to speak, and in his weakest moments—which weren't very weak—Ritter wished it were possible to take that easy path. But to avoid her during those brief intervals when she would permit her-self to give voice would be to imply that she was a prisoner, that she was being merely *stored* here, which was definitely not the case.

As Ritter himself had told the recalcitrant wretch a million times, she was being *saved* here, *rescued* from childish folly and misguided emotion. She was here because he *loved* her, God damn her to hell and back, and that's why, whenever he was anywhere near New York City on a Thursday afternoon, he made it a point to come up here and listen to the stupid, inane, ungrateful, infuriating little sweetheart. If she weren't his daughter and he didn't love her like his own flesh and blood—well, she was, of course—if his feelings toward her weren't so basically paternal and tender he'd have the goddamn girl blacklisted on the planet Earth.

She was in mid-sentence directed at Hendrickson—something about soft being the way of the transgressor until God got His Hands on you, and then, oh, boy—when she became aware of this new target for her venom and spleen—not very saintly, eh?—and she swung about, yelling, *"There's* the defier now! In the Middle Ages the barons thought *they* could defy God, they thought *their* puny temporal power made them God's equals, God's *superiors,* so they could beat and kick and torture God's emissaries here below, and where are they *now?"*

"They'd be dead anyway, Elaine."

"They're in *Hell!* Burning and roasting endlessly in Hell! Their eyes boiling in their skulls, the charred flesh peeling back ever and ever from their melting bones, the flames clutching and

60

clutching at their screaming tongues, breaths of fire drawn into their suppurating lungs—"

Ugh; whenever the girl got into one of her gloating descriptions of Hell it just made Ritter's stomach churn. Well, that's what the Tums in his pocket were for. Reaching for one, tuning the girl's shrill voice out, he said beneath her diatribe, "Hendrickson, Hendrickson, when is this going to end?"

"Lord knows, Mr. Ritter."

That redirected her fire at Hendrickson: "You dare call upon the God you defile with your every . . ." And so on. Sighing, sucking a Tum, Ritter said to Hendrickson, "Just how much progress do you think you've made so far?"

"Absolutely none, to be bluntly honest," Hendrickson said, without embarrassment.

"You're supposed to be the best."

"Since there are none better at what I do, I *am* the best. If you'd like to try *some* people I can think of, Mr. Ritter, who'd take your money and sneak around behind your back and rape your daughter and claim it was sex therapy—"

"No no no no no," Ritter said, shaking his head and both hands. "I just want to see some sign we're getting somewhere."

"This is, as I've told you before," Hendrickson said, "by far the toughest case I've ever had."

Elaine stood in front of her father, hands on hips, bent forward at the waist, thrusting her agitated face into his, screaming, *"When* are you going to give this up?"

"Never!"

"*When* are you going to let me live my own *life?*"

Ritter was astonished. "That's what I'm *trying* for," he said, in absolute sincerity. "That isn't *your* life, down there with those scruffy nuns! *Your* life is fur coats in the summer! *Your* life is Gstaad and Palm Beach! *Your* life is as wife to a powerful, well-educated man and mother to his children!"

"Like *my* mother?" she demanded. "Is *that* supposed to be my life?"

"Be careful," Ritter told her, raising a finger. "Never say a word against your mother."

"You destroyed her!"

"She is not destroyed. She is an active and productive member of society, which is better than we can say for you. If you took any interest in *this* world, you would have seen a photo of your mother in the *New York Times* just last Monday, in connection with one of her innumerable charity functions, functions which I may say are a much more *realistic* use of finer instincts than this self-centered egotistic withdrawal and cowering away from the world which you claim—"

"My mother's a *drunk!*"

Ritter raised that finger again, but his manner was calm and his voice almost remorseful: "And *that* was a sin against the fourth commandment, as well as against the ideal of charity. Your mother's ailments are not to be bandied about as though she didn't deserve our understanding."

The fact is, Elaine's mother Gwen *was* a drunk.

Ritter's second wife, she was like the first, tall and slender and ash blonde, the both of them having been chosen from that same northeastern mating pool which has furnished hostesses and helpmeets for so many of our better politicians and captains of industry. If there was one flaw with the type— it might have something to do, Ritter thought, with too close inbreeding—it was a tendency toward alcoholism. Generally, they remained for twenty or more years decorative and useful before this tendency made it necessary to replace them, and even afterward most of them remained tractable. One mustn't blame the poor creatures, as Elaine seemed to be doing. It was just something in the blood; alcohol, usually.

Now, having successfully accused Elaine of sin— the girl's stricken look told him his statement had struck home—Ritter pressed his advantage, or his luck, saying sadly, "The sharpest thorns are in your own roses."

She gave him a look of scorn. "The rose grows from a dungheap," she said.

If there was one thing this troubling child had inherited from her father it was a knack for aphorism, and yet somehow she had never yet come up with one he felt worthy of memorialization in his commonplace book. "Elaine," he said.

"SISTER MARY GRACE!"

"ELAINE! *When are you going to give up this nonsense?*"

"*Never!*"

"Then you'll never leave this apartment," he said, calmer.

She was calmer, too. "Oh, yes, I will," she said.

Her assurance was so total that he had to smile at her, and say, "Do you expect God Himself to come down from Heaven and *escort* you back to that miserable primitive convent down there?"

"In a way," she said.

"He's taking His own sweet time at it, isn't He?"

She folded her arms. Her look was defiant, smug, infuriating; not at all what Frank Ritter would call holy. "We'll see," she said.

11

"You didn't tell me they kept birds," May said.

Dortmunder listened to the twittering from within the low stone convent building. "I didn't see them last time."

"Well, that must be nice for them," May said. "Birds make a nice pet."

Dortmunder pulled the thick old rope hanging beside the heavy wooden door and from far inside came a deep *bong-bong*. At once, the twittering stopped, then started again, redoubled. A moment went by, and then the door was drawn open by a buxom smiling older nun in full fig; not one of the ones Dortmunder had met his earlier time here. "Uh," he said, "I'm—"

"Oh!" the nun said, delighted, and clapped her

64

hands together. "You're John! Yes, of course, I remember you in the chapel, you might remember I helped to hold the ladder, I'm Sister Mary Amity, I was almost the second person to see you, just after Sister Mary Serene, we were both in the chapel in contemplation, and she looked up, and then *I* looked up, and oh, I suppose this is your wife, do come in both of you, we're just delighted to have visitors, it doesn't happen very often, isn't it lucky it's just when we're permitted to speak, be careful of the stone floor, it *is* uneven, I'll go get Mother Mary Forcible, what *was* it I wanted to say? Never mind, it will come to me. Don't go 'way now."

"We won't," Dortmunder promised, and Sister Mary Amity bustled away down the long colonnade.

"Well!" May said.

"It's their talk time," Dortmunder said.

"I guess so."

The twittering, now that they were inside the wall, wasn't birds after all but conversation, lots and lots of conversation, much of it taking place in the open courtyard just to their left. The building itself was L-shaped, built away from the street corner, with the open section partly slate-floored and partly turned into flower beds, at the moment bursting with spring blooms. High stone walls separated this yard from the two street sides, while arched walkways or colonnades (or cloisters, actually) ran along the two building facades. Dortmunder and May stood under this walkway, just inside the main front door, and looked out through the stone arch at the chattering nuns, many of whom peeked back while maintaining their conversations with one another, pretending they weren't dying of curiosity.

"Here she comes," Dortmunder said, as Mother Mary Forcible came pattering down the walkway, elbows working as she hustled along. Sister Mary Amity, who'd let them in, jogged in her wake until, just before reaching Dortmunder and May, Mother Mary Forcible turned and said, "Thank you, Sister. I'll take over now."

"Oh," said the sister. "Yes, of course, Mother." She waved as she reluctantly receded, calling, "Nice to see you. Chat again sometime."

"Sure," Dortmunder said. Then he introduced May and Mother Mary Forcible, and extended the cane, saying, "I brought this back. Thanks for the loan."

"Oh, Sister Mary Chaste will be very happy," Mother Mary Forcible said, taking the cane. "She's been using a hoe, not really satisfactory."

"And I wanted to say . . ." Dortmunder said, hesitating.

"Yes, of course. Come along to the office, we'll be comfortable there." She chugged off, and as they followed her down the walkway she said, "Would you care for coffee? Tea?"

"Not for me, thanks," May said.

"I'm just fine, Sister," Dortmunder said.

"We make good coffee, as you know."

"Oh, yeah, I know that, Sister," Dortmunder

said. What he didn't say was, he didn't feel right taking their coffee when he was just here to tell them the deal was off.

The whitewashed walls and scrubbed wooden floors and heavy-beamed ceilings led them to Mother Mary Forcible's tiny crammed office, where she ushered them in, shut the door, put the cane in a corner, and said, "Now."

"See, the problem is," Dortmunder said, while Mother Mary Forcible walked briskly around him to her desk, picked up two thick looseleaf books with black covers, and turned with them.

"John *has* been trying," May said.

"Before we go any further," Mother Mary Forcible said, "I want to give you these." And she extended the two looseleaf books.

Having no choice, Dortmunder took them and stood cradling them in his hands. They were large and bulky and fairly heavy. He said, "What's this?"

"I think I told you," Mother Mary Forcible said, "that Sister Mary Grace is enabled to send us notes from time to time, and we mail messages to her by the same route. We told her you would be coming to rescue her—"

"Oh, well, that was—"

"John did do his best," May said.

"And so," Mother Mary Forcible went on, "she arranged to have these two volumes smuggled out."

Dortmunder looked at the looseleaf books in his hands. "Smuggled out? From *there?*"

May took one of the books from his hands and

opened it. "John," she said. "This is a list of all the tenants, and which security measures they've leased. And here's wiring diagrams. John? Here's the access code for the computer that runs the security!"

Dortmunder was turning the pages of the other book. Floor plans. Staff assignments. Names of vendors and scheduled days of delivery. It went on and on.

"Sister Mary Grace is such an unworldly little thing," Mother Mary Forcible was saying. "She wasn't sure if you'd want any of this, or if it would help at all, but she sent it along just in case, which I thought was very enterprising of her. *Are* they useful?"

Dortmunder looked up. His eyes were shining. "Let us prey," he said.

NUMBERS

12

Tiny Bulcher picked up the Honda Civic and put it on the back of the flatbed truck. He had to climb up, and push and tug the car a bit, to nestle it in next to the Mustang, but when he was done there was just about enough room left for one more small car; a VW Beetle, maybe, or a Mazda. Tiny got down onto the sidewalk and slogged up to the cab, where he opened the door and said to the stocky red-haired driver, "Okay, Stan."

"Hey!" said somebody.

Tiny started to heave his bulk up onto the passenger seat of the cab.

"Hey! Hey, *you!*"

Stan Murch said, "I think that guy's calling you, Tiny."

"Oh, yeah?" Tiny put both feet back on the curb and turned to see what the guy wanted. "You yellin at me, fella?"

"That's my car!" the guy said, sounding very upset, pointing at the Honda Civic. He was tall and slender and had thinning brown hair and a polo shirt that was a little too loose.

Tiny didn't bother to look at the car; he'd seen it already. "Yeah?" he said.

"Well— Well— That's my *car!*" The guy seemed stuck at that point, unable to follow his own thought anywhere. Or maybe he was just distracted by now having this clear view of Tiny Bulcher, who was a kind of mastodon in clothes, a sort of lowland Abominable Snowman, a creature made from the parts rejected by Dr. Frankenstein when he was sewing together his monster. When people found themselves being looked at by this gigantic bad-tempered drill press, generally speaking they did tend to forget what it was they'd been going to say.

After a sufficient silence had gone by, "Okay," Tiny said, with a voice like two boulders being rubbed together, and he turned back to climb into the cab.

"But—" said the Honda owner. "But, wait a minute."

Impatience exuded from Tiny like a heavy fog, probably toxic. "What now?" he asked.

"Well—" The Honda owner gestured helplessly, and looked up and down this quiet sunlit cross-street in the seventies on Manhattan's West Side. "It's," he said, "it's *legal.*"

"Good," Tiny said, and turned away again.

"I mean, it's legal where I'm *parked!*"

"So?" Tiny said. When his brow furrowed, it looked like a set of shelves in the basement.

"So I'm legal! Am I by a hydrant? What hydrant am I by?"

Tiny considered, then lifted a hand like a beachball with fingers and pointed at a fire hydrant way down at the other end of the block.

"What?" The Honda owner was as outraged as anybody ever gets with Tiny Bulcher. "I'm more than twelve feet from that! You want me to call the Traffic Department?"

"Sure," Tiny said, and this time he did climb up into the truck cab, while the guy spluttered behind him. Shutting the cab door, he looked down through the open window and said, "What else?"

"I'm getting a tape measure," the guy announced. Seeing less of Tiny had made him more aggressive.

"Go ahead," Tiny said.

"You'll see," the guy said, pointing at Tiny. "And you'll owe me an apology, too." And he went trotting off.

"You done?" Stan Murch asked.

"Pests," Tiny said. "I hate dealing with the public."

Stan put the truck in gear, and they drove away from there. They turned right at the corner and went up three and over one and stopped next to a Renault Le Car. Tiny got out and picked it up by the front wheelwells and was putting it in place on the truckbed when a horn sounded. "More aggravation," he said. The horn sounded again. "Maybe somebody's gonna eat their horn," Tiny grumbled, and put the Renault down any which way and went around to see a cab stopped next to the

73

truck on the driver's side. He went up to discuss the situation, flexing his fingers, but when he got there the cabby was Murch's Mom, a feisty little woman in a cloth cap, this being her cab and that being what she did for a living, insisting on her independence and not wanting to be a burden on her son, Stanley, who made his living by, among other occupations, collecting things with Tiny Bulcher.

Murch's Mom was calling out her other-side window and up to her son, saying, "I'm glad I caught you. See? I told you, it's always a good thing to tell me where you'll be."

There was a passenger in the back of the cab, a stout man in a dark suit and loud tie. And loud voice: "Say, there, driver," he said loudly, "I have an appointment."

"Hi, Mom," Stan was saying. "What's up?"

"Driver, what is this delay?"

Tiny opened the rear door and showed his unsmiling countenance to the passenger. "Shut up," he suggested.

The passenger blinked a lot. He clutched his attaché case with both hands. Tiny shut the door.

Murch's Mom said, "John Dortmunder called, just after you left. He says he's got something."

"Good," said Stan.

"For Tiny, too," Murch's Mom said.

"Naturally," Tiny said. (A disbelieving voice from the backseat of the cab said, "Tiny?" but then shut up when Tiny rolled an eye in that direction.)

"He says," Murch's Mom went on, "would you meet tonight at ten at the OJ."

"Sure thing," said Stan.

Murch's Mom gestured at the three cars on the back of the truck. "You taking those down to your guy in Brooklyn?"

"Yeah. Going right now."

"Well, don't take the Battery Tunnel," she advised him, "there's some kind of congestion there."

"No, I figured I'd go down Ninth to Fourteenth and over to Second Avenue," Stan said, "take the Williamsburg Bridge, and then Rutledge and Bedford."

"That's good," Murch's Mom said. "Or you could also take the Manhattan Bridge, Flatbush and on down Fulton Street."

"Oh, *really*," grumbled the passenger. Tiny looked in at him, and the fellow busily riffled through the papers in his attaché case, looking for something very important.

"I figure I'll just play it by ear," Stan told his mom, "adapt to circumstances on the street."

"That's a good boy."

The cab went away. Tiny tidied the Renault and got back in beside Stan, and they headed downtown. "I wonder what Dortmunder's got," Stan said. "Something rich, I hope."

"Dortmunder's an amusing fella," Tiny said. His tree-trunk head nodded. "He makes me laugh," he said.

Stan glanced at him. "Sure," he said.

13

When Dortmunder walked into the OJ Bar & Grill on Amsterdam Avenue at ten that night a few of the regulars were draped against the bar discussing the weather or something. "It's 'Red star at night, Sailor take fright,' " one of them was saying.

"Will you listen to *this* crap," a second regular said. "Will you just listen?"

"I listened," a third regular assured him.

"Who asked *you?*" the second regular wanted to know.

"It's a free country," the third regular told him, "and I listened, and *you,*" he told the first regular, "are wrong."

"Well, yes," the second regular said. "I didn't know you were gonna be on my side."

"It's 'Red star in the *morning,*' " the third regular said.

"*Another* idiot," said the second regular.

The first regular looked dazzled with disbelief at the wrong-headedness all around him. "How does *that* rhyme?" he demanded. " 'Red star in the morning, Sailor take fright'?"

"It isn't *star,*" the second regular announced, slapping his palm against the bar. "It's red *sky*. All this red star crap, it's like you're talking about the Russian army."

"Well, I'm not talking about the Russian army," the first regular told him. "It happened I was in the Navy. I was on P-U boats."

This stopped all the regulars cold for a second. Then the second regular, treading cautiously, said, "Whose Navy?"

Dortmunder, down at the end of the bar, raised a hand and got the attention of Rollo the bartender, who'd been standing there with his heavy arms folded over his dirty apron, a faraway look in his eyes as the regulars' conversation washed over him. Now, he nodded at Dortmunder and rolled smoothly down the bar to talk to him, planting his feet solidly on the duckboards, while behind him the Navy man was saying, "*The* Navy! How many navies are there?"

Rollo put meaty elbows on the bar in front of Dortmunder, leaned forward, and said, "Between you and me, I was in the Marines."

"Oh, yeah?"

"We want a few good men," Rollo assured him, then straightened up and said, "Your friends didn't show yet. You want the usual?"

"Yeah."

"And the other bourbon's gonna be with you?"

"Right."

Rollo nodded and went back down the bar to get out a tray and two glasses and a murky bottle with a label reading *Amsterdam Liquor Store Bourbon*—"Our Own Brand." Meantime, a discussion of the world's navies had started up, with references to Admiral Nelson and Lord Byrd, when, in a pause in the flow of things, a fourth regular, who hadn't spoken before this, said, "I think, I *think*, I'm not sure about this, but I *think* it's 'Red ring around the moon, Means rain pretty soon.' Something like that."

The second regular, the Russian army man, banged his beer glass on the bar and said, "It's red *sky*. *You* got a ring around the *brain*, that's what you got."

"Easy, boys," Rollo said. "The war's over."

Everybody looked startled at this news. Rollo picked up the tray with the bottle and glasses on it and brought it back to Dortmunder, saying, "And who else is coming?"

"The beer and salt."

"Oh, yeah, the big spender," Rollo said, nodding.

"And the vodka and red wine."

"The monster. I remember him."

"Most people do," Dortmunder agreed. He picked up the tray and carried it past the regulars, who were still talking about the weather or something. "The groundhog *saw* his shadow," the Navy man was saying.

"Right," the third regular said. "Six weeks ago yesterday, so that was six weeks more winter, so yesterday he come out *again*, you follow me so far?"

"It's your story."

"So it was sunny yesterday," the third regular said, "so he saw his shadow again, so that's *another* six weeks of winter."

There was a pause while people worked out

what they thought about that. Then the fourth regular said, "I still think it's 'Red ring around the moon.' "

Dortmunder continued on back past the bar and past the two doors marked with dog silhouettes labeled POINTERS and SETTERS and past the phone booth with the string dangling from the quarter slot and through the green door at the back and into a small square room with a concrete floor. None of the walls could be seen, because the room was filled all the way around, floor to ceiling, with beer and liquor cases, leaving only a small bare space in the middle, containing a battered old table with a stained green felt top and half a dozen chairs. The only illumination was from one bare bulb with a round tin reflector hanging low over the table on a long black wire.

Dortmunder liked being first, because whoever was first got to sit facing the door. He sat there, put the tray to his right, poured some brown stuff into one of the glasses, and was raising it when the door opened and Stan Murch came in, carrying a glass of beer in one hand and a salt shaker in the other. "The damnedest thing," he said, closing the door behind himself, "I took the road through Prospect Park, you know, on account of the Prospect Expressway construction, and when I came out on Grand Army Plaza they were digging up *Flatbush Avenue*, if you'll believe it, so I ran down Union Street to the BQE and here I am."

"Hiya, Stan," Dortmunder said. "How you doin?"

"Turning a dollar," Stan said, and sat down with his beer and his salt as the door opened again and Tiny Bulcher came in, turning sideways to squeeze through the doorway. Somewhere down inside his left fist was a glass containing something that looked like, but was not, cherry soda. "Some clown out there wants to know was I in the Navy," Tiny said, "so I decked him." He shut the door and came over and sat facing Dortmunder; Tiny didn't mind if his back was to the door. "Hello, Dortmunder," he said.

"Hello, Tiny."

Tiny looked around, heavy head moving like a wrecker's ball. "Am I waiting for somebody?"

"Andy Kelp."

"Am I early, or is he late?"

"Here he is now," Dortmunder said, as Kelp came in, looking chipper but confused. Dortmunder motioned to him, saying, "Come sit down, Andy."

"You know what there is out there," Kelp said, shutting the door. "There's a guy laying on the bar, had some sort of accident—"

"He asked Tiny a question," Dortmunder said.

"He got personal with me," Tiny said.

Kelp looked at Tiny, and his smile flickered like faraway summer lightning. "Whadaya say, Tiny?"

"I say siddown," Tiny said, "and let's get to it."

"Oh, sure." Coming around the table to sit at Dortmunder's right and pour himself a glass of

Amsterdam Liquor Store Bourbon, Kelp said, "Anyway, the other guys out there are trying to decide, is it a service-connected disability?"

"It's a brain-connected disability," Tiny said. "What have you got, Dortmunder?"

"Well," Dortmunder said, "I have a building."

Tiny nodded. "And a way in?"

"A way in."

"And what is in this building?"

"A bank. Forty-one importers and wholesalers of jade and ivory and jewels and other precious items. A dealer in antique silver. Two stamp dealers."

"And a partridge in a pear tree," Kelp finished, grinning happily at everybody.

"Holy Toledo," Stan Murch said.

Tiny frowned. "Dortmunder," he said, "in my experience, you don't tell jokes. At least, you don't tell *me* jokes."

"That's right," Dortmunder said.

"This isn't a building you're talking about," Tiny said. "This is the big rock candy mountain."

"And it's all ours," Dortmunder said.

"How? You won the lottery?"

Dortmunder shook his head. "I got somebody on the inside," he said. "I got the specs on every bit of security in the building. I got two great big looseleaf books this thick, all about the building. I got more information than I can *use*."

Stan said, "How secure is this information? How sure are you of the inside guy?"

81

"One hundred percent," Dortmunder said. "This person does not tell lies."

"What is it, a disgruntled employee?"

"Not exactly."

Tiny said, "I would need to talk to this person myself."

"I definitely plan to arrange that," Dortmunder told him.

Stan said, "So what's the idea? We back up a truck, go in, empty everything we can, drive away?"

"No," Dortmunder said. "In the first place, somebody on the street is gonna notice something like that."

"There's always nosy Parkers," Tiny agreed. "One time, a guy annoyed me and annoyed me, so I made his nose go the other way."

"In this building," Dortmunder said, "there are also seventeen mail-order places, different kinds of catalogue outfits and like that. I'm checking, I'm looking around, I'm being very careful, and what I want to find is one of these mail-order people we can make a deal with."

Kelp said to Stan and Tiny, "I love this part. This is why John Dortmunder is a genius."

"You're interrupting the genius," Tiny pointed out.

"Oh. Sorry."

"The deal is," Dortmunder said, "we'd go into the building on a Saturday night and we wouldn't leave till Monday morning. We'd take everything we could get and carry it all to the mail-order place and put it all in packages and mail it out of the building Monday morning with their regular routine."

Tiny thoughtfully nodded his head. "So we don't carry the stuff out," he said. "We go in clean, we come out clean."

"That's right."

"I just love it," Kelp said.

Tiny leveled a gaze at Kelp. "Enthusiasm makes me restless," he said.

"Oh. Sorry."

"We'll have to pick and choose," Dortmunder pointed out. "Even if we had a week, we wouldn't be able to take *everything*. And if we took everything, it'd be too much to mail."

Stan said, "You know, John, all my life I wanted to be along on a caper where there was so much stuff you couldn't take it all. Just wallow in it, like Aladdin's Cave. And this is what you're talking about."

"This is what I'm talking about," Dortmunder agreed. "But I'm gonna need help in the setup."

"Ask me," Stan said. "I'll help. I *want* to see this thing happen."

"Two things," Dortmunder told him. "First, the mail-order outfit. It ought to be somebody that's a little bent already, but not so bent the FBI's got a wiretap."

"I can ask around," Stan said. "Discreetly. I know some people here and there."

"I'll also ask," Tiny said. "Some people know *me* here and there."

"Good," Dortmunder said. "The other thing is, a lockman. We need somebody really good, to follow the schematics I got and shut down all the alarms without kicking them on instead."

Tiny said, "What about that little model train nut guy from the pitcha switch? Roger Whatever."

"Chefwick," Dortmunder said.

"He retired," Kelp said.

Tiny looked at him. "In our line of work," he said, "how do you retire?"

"You stop doing what you were doing, and you do something else."

"So Chefwick stopped being a lockman."

"Right," Kelp said. "He went out to California with his wife, and they're running this Chinese railroad out there."

"A Chinese railroad," Tiny said, "in California."

"Sure," Kelp said. "It used to run in China somewhere, but this guy bought it, the locomotive and the Chinese cars and even a little railroad station with the roof, you know, like hats that come out?"

"Like hats that come out," Tiny said.

"Like a pagoda," Kelp said. "Anyway, this guy put down track and made an amusement park and Chefwick's running the train for him. So now he's got his own lifesize model train set, so he isn't being a lockman anymore, so he's retired. Okay?"

Tiny thought about it. "Okay," he said, reluctantly.

Stan said, "What about Wally Whistler? I know he's absentminded and all, but—"

Tiny said, "He's the guy let the lion out at the zoo, isn't he?"

"Just fiddling with the lock on the cage," Stan said. "Absentminded, that's all."

"No good," Kelp said. "Wally's in Brazil, without any extradition."

"Without what?" Dortmunder asked.

"In Brazil?" Tiny asked.

"He was helping some people at Customs down in Brooklyn," Kelp told them. "You know, people that didn't want to tie up the government with a lot of red tape and forms and stuff, so they were just going to get their imports at night and leave it at that, you know the kind of thing."

"You said Brazil," Tiny reminded him.

"Yeah, well, Wally, what Wally's problem is, he's just too good at his line of business." Kelp shook his head. "You show Wally a lock, he just has to caress the thing, and poke at it, and see how it works, and the first thing he knew he went through a door, and then a couple more doors, and like that, and when he tried to go back the ship had sailed."

"The ship," Dortmunder said. It didn't seem to him there'd been a ship in the story up till then.

"That he was on," Kelp said, "that he didn't know it. They were just leaving, and one of those doors he went through was into the ship from the warehouse, and it turned out they had some reasons of their own to leave in the middle of the night, so they didn't want to go back to let him off, so he rode along and now he's in Brazil without extradition."

"*That* was the word," Dortmunder said. "Explain that."

"Well, most places in the world," Kelp explained, "you find yourself broke and you don't speak the language and all, you go confess to a crime in, like, Duluth or St. Louis or somewhere, and then the governments get together and do a lot of legal paper on you and they extradite you and the government pays your air fare and you get to St. Louis or Duluth or wherever it was, and you say, 'Oops, my mistake, I didn't do that after all,' and you're home. Only with Brazil, we got no treaty, they won't extradite, so Wally's stuck. And he says Brazil is so poor, most places don't have locks, so he's going crazy. So he's trying to get to Uruguay."

"For the extradition," Dortmunder guessed.

"You got it."

Stan said, "How about Herman X?"

Tiny, who had been observing Kelp so carefully that Kelp was beginning to fidget, now swiveled his head around to look at Stan. "Herman what?"

"X," Stan said.

"He's a black power radical," Dortmunder explained, "but he's also a good lockman."

"He was with us that time we took the bank," Stan said.

"Now, the problem with Herman," Kelp started, and everybody turned to look at him.

"Don't blame *me*," he said. "I'm just telling you the situation."

"Tell us the situation," Tiny suggested.

"Well," Kelp said, "the problem with Herman is, he's in Africa."

Dortmunder said, "Without extradition?"

"No, Herman doesn't need extradition. He's vice-president of Talabwo."

Tiny said, "Is that a country?"

"For now," Kelp said. "There's a lot of unrest over there."

Dortmunder said, "Talabwo. That's the country wanted the Balabomo Emerald that time."

"That's right," Kelp said. "And you gave Major Iko the paste emerald and he brought it home and when they found out it wasn't real they ate him, I think. Anyway, there was trouble back and forth, and Herman was with his radical friends at the UN to steal some secret documents that proved the drought was a plot by the white people, and they came on this assassination attempt, and Herman helped the guy they were trying to kill, and it turned out he was the next president of Talabwo, which is why they were trying to put him out that window, so when he got home he invited Herman over as a thank you, and that's when Herman found out the *vice*-president was figuring on a coup, so now Herman's vice-president, and he says he enjoys it a lot."

Dortmunder said, "He does, does he?"

"Yeah. Except he isn't Herman X anymore, now he's Herman Makanene Stulu'mbnick."

Tiny said, "I am growing weary."

"Well, that's all I know anyway," Kelp said. He poured himself some more Amsterdam Liquor Store Bourbon.

Tiny said, "I know a guy, for the locks. He's a little unusual."

Dortmunder said, "After *those* stories? *Your* guy is unusual?"

"At least he's in New York," Tiny said. "His name's Wilbur Howey."

"I don't know him," Dortmunder said.

"He just came out of the slammer," Tiny said. "I'll have a word with him."

"Fine," Dortmunder said. He hesitated, and cleared his throat.

"Here it comes now," Tiny said.

Dortmunder gave him an innocent look. "Here comes what, Tiny?"

"The butcher's thumb," Tiny said. "You know what I do with the butcher's thumb?"

"There's nothing *wrong*, Tiny," Dortmunder said. "The deal is exactly as I said it was. Only, there's just one more little element."

"One more little element."

"While we're in the building," Dortmunder said, "take no time at all, we go up to the top floor, handle one extra little piece of business. Nothing to it."

Tiny viewed Dortmunder more in sorrow than in anger. "Tell me about this, Dortmunder," he said. "What is this extra little piece of business?"

"Well," Dortmunder said. He knocked back a

little Amsterdam Liquor Store Bourbon, coughed, and said, "The fact is, uh, Tiny, while we're in there anyway, uh, it seems we have to rescue this nun."

14

"How did it go last night?" May asked.

Dortmunder paused with a spoonful of Wheaties in midair. He nodded thoughtfully, pondering the question, and then said, "Well, there was a chancy minute or two when I mentioned the nun, but then it worked out."

"What was the chancy minute?"

"Tiny. He didn't like it."

May was making herself instant coffee, standing in a dapple of morning sunshine reflected twice before coming in the airshaft window. She said, "What didn't he like about it?"

Dortmunder had taken that load of Wheaties on board. He chewed and chewed and swallowed and said, "Nuns. Tiny says nuns remind him of a movie called *Come to the Stable*, and he's mad at that movie."

"*Come to the Stable?*" May poured hot water over brown dust. "Why would he be mad at a movie?"

"Apparently, he was in an armored car job once, and it got screwed up, and he hid inside the air ducts in a movie house for a week. Late at night he'd come out of the ducts and go down and eat the candy and drink the soda, but he could never leave the building because the cops knew a couple guys in the job were still in the neighborhood somewhere, and they were doing a house-to-house search and maintaining a presence on the street and all that. So it was a revival house, and that week they were showing *Come to the Stable,* with Loretta Young and Celeste Holm as these two nuns that were very good to everybody all the time, and smiled a lot. Tiny saw that movie twenty-seven times that week, and he says he's never felt quite the same about nuns ever since."

The phone rang, in the living room. Dortmunder said, "I'll get it," and went away to the living room to get it. Andy Kelp kept wanting to give him a free extension phone in the kitchen, Kelp having access to a place with telephone equipment, but Dortmunder felt one phone was enough in a person's life and frequently too much. Besides, he needed the exercise.

It was Tiny Bulcher. "Yeah, hi," Dortmunder said. "I was just talking about you."

"You don't want to do that," Tiny said. Even on the phone he sounded large, like an approaching cold front.

"Just with May," Dortmunder told him.

"Okay, then. I got my lockman, I thought we'd come over look at those books you got."

"Sure."

"Half an hour."

"I'll be here," Dortmunder said, and hung up, and the phone rang. "Saves me steps," he commented, and answered, and it was Chepkoff, the caviar man. "Oh, it's you," Dortmunder said.

"About my three hundred bucks," Chepkoff said. On the phone he sounded little and mean, which is also the way he looked in person.

"Don't be stupid," Dortmunder said.

"I'm not letting this go, Dortmunder," Chepkoff said. "I want my three hundred dollars."

"Sue me," Dortmunder said, and hung up, and went back to the kitchen, and told May, "Tiny's coming over pretty soon with a lockman he knows."

May was drinking coffee and scratching herself through her cardigan pocket. She said, "Should I leave? I don't go to work till noon."

"No, no, stick around," Dortmunder said. "Listen, you got an allergy or something?"

"An allergy?" May looked bewildered. "Why?"

"The last few days, you've been scratching a lot."

May looked at the hand in her cardigan pocket as though it belonged to somebody else. "Oh," she said. "No, it's nothing. When is Tiny coming?"

Dortmunder placed himself in front of the Wheaties again. "Half an hour," he said, and half an hour later the doorbell rang, and when Dortmunder went to answer in came Tiny Bulcher with a little shriveled-up wiry old geezer who looked as though somebody had crumpled him and then partly smoothed him out again.

"This is Wilbur Howey," Tiny said.

91

Dortmunder looked at the doorway to see if there was any more to him, but apparently not. "How are ya?" he said.

"Terrific," Wilbur Howey said, and cackled.

Dortmunder led the way to the living room, where May sat reading the latest issue of *Working Woman*. Howey tossed a salute in her direction, winked, and said, "Hi, Toots."

"Hi," May said, putting the magazine down and getting to her feet. "Hi, Tiny. Anybody want coffee? A beer? Anything?"

"Just an hour with you on a doubledecker bus, Toots," Wilbur Howey said, and cackled again.

"Shut up, Wilbur," Tiny said. "They ain't no more double-decker buses."

"How about bunkbeds, huh, Toots?"

"Hey, wait a minute," Dortmunder said.

Tiny took Wilbur Howey by the elbow and shook him a little, but Howey didn't seem to mind. He kept cackling and grinning and winking at May. Tiny said, "Take it easy, Wilbur, that's our host's lady friend."

"Say, what's the dif?" Howey wanted to know, and winked at Dortmunder. "We're all just boys together, you know what I mean?"

"No," said Dortmunder.

"I told you last night," Tiny explained to Dortmunder, "Wilbur just got out. He was inside kind of a long while."

"Forty-eight years," Howey said, and winked at everybody, grinning and chirruping as though that was quite an accomplishment.

Dortmunder stared at him. "Forty-eight *years?* What did you *do?*"

"Well, it was just a nickel-dime to begin with," Howey said, "for a lumberyard safe. But I kept escaping. That's me, the escape artist."

"He's good with locks," Tiny pointed out. "The problem is, he's not so good with anything else."

Dortmunder said, "Meaning what?"

"Meaning," Tiny said, "he'd bust out of someplace and go maybe half a mile down the road and then he wouldn't know what to do next."

"It's a big world out there," Howey said, and winked.

"Usually," Tiny said, "when they sent the dogs out, they'd find Wilbur knee-deep in water in a culvert under some state highway somewhere."

"That's where I got my arthuritis," Howey said, and tossed another salute at May.

"Then they'd add a couple years on the end of the sentence," Tiny said, "for the escape. Wound up, it took him forty-eight years to serve a ten-year sentence that he should of got out in three."

"But I kept them on their toes," Howey said, and cackled, and clicked his heels together.

"He's not used to the street yet," Tiny said.

"Wimmin," Howey said, and smacked his lips, and rubbed his hands together. "I got a lotta catchin up to do. Know what I mean, Toots?"

"Not with me, you don't," May said. "I'll see you later, John, I'm going to work."

"You can work with me anytime, Toots."

May rolled her eyes for Dortmunder's benefit

and left the living room. On her way by Howey, he gave her a friendly pat on the behind and cackled. She stopped, turned, and pointed a finger at him, saying, "If you do that again, you'll be very sorry."

"Just here to have a good time, Toots," Howey said, and clicked his heels.

"Brother," May commented, and left the room.

Tiny said, "You're embarrassing me, Wilbur. If I didn't need your fingers, I'd put them in your nose. Sit down and be good."

"You bet," Howey said, and settled on the only uncomfortable wooden chair in the room. He sat there, very upright, feet dancing, fingers playing piano arpeggios on his knees, and grinned and winked in various directions.

Tiny said, "I told you he was unusual. You remember that?"

"I remember," Dortmunder said. "I'll go get the books."

In the bedroom, Dortmunder found May being furious and scratching herself. "They let him out too soon," she said.

"No," Dortmunder said, getting the two loose-leaf books out from their hiding place in the closet. "Not too soon, too late. *Way* too late." He went back to the living room, where Howey hadn't moved from the wooden chair but now Tiny was seated on most of the sofa. "Here's the stuff."

"Say, let's have a look at that," Howey said.

Dortmunder gave him the books, and watched dubiously as Howey began to leaf through one of them. "Well, uh," Dortmunder said. "You know all this later stuff, huh?"

Howey gave him a scornful look. "Whadaya think we got in the pen? Thongs?"

"He knows his stuff, Dortmunder," Tiny said. "He maybe oughta live under a rock, but he knows his stuff."

Dortmunder, still dubious, settled himself in his chair to watch. Several minutes of silence went by—punctuated at one point by May's departure from the apartment, shutting the front door a bit more emphatically than necessary—and then Howey shut the second book, evened them both on his lap, and said, "Well, this is the goods, okay. And it's guaranteed up-to-date, huh?"

"Yes," said Dortmunder.

"Well, there's no problem here." Howey cackled, and did a drumroll on the cover of the top book on his lap, and grinned at Tiny, saying, "If I could get ahold of a tomato the way I can get ahold of this building, whoa, boy, look out, Charlie!"

Tiny said, "Well, Dortmunder? What do you think?"

"I think we'll have to keep him away from the nun," Dortmunder said.

Tiny shook his head. "*I'm* gonna keep away from the nun," he said. "So Wilbur can stay with me."

Howey tapped his fingers and danced his feet and grinned at everybody. "It's a nun got you all this stuff, huh?"

"That's right," Dortmunder said.

"How'd she do it?"

"Beats me."

"Huh," Howey said, and bobbed his head, and clicked his tongue, and thought his own thoughts. "Must be a frisky little nun, huh? Huh?"

15

One of the nice things about being quiet most of the time is that after a while you become sort of invisible, too. Sister Mary Grace (née Elaine Gwen Ritter), small and slender, in flat-heeled soft-soled shoes, wafted through her apartment/prison like the ghost of a nun walled up in a medieval castle. Her large eyes saw everything, her delicate ears heard every word, and most of the time people didn't even know she was there.

Take the matter of the locks. The doors leading to the two stairwells were both armed with very sophisticated electronic locks, using not keys but computers, with a small pad like a TouchTone telephone's buttons, built into the wall beside each door. Hendrickson the deprogrammer, who lived down one flight on seventy-five, used one of those doors, and the guards, whose offices were in the Margrave Corporation space two flights down on seventy-four, used the other. Any number of times Sister Mary Grace had observed—while remaining herself unobserved—those doors being used, and she saw that what the guards and Hendrickson did was punch out a four-number code to unlock each door. Unfortunately, she could never get quite close enough to see *which* four numbers they punched out, nor in what sequence; that unobservant they weren't.

The possibilities were mathematically daunting. The ten buttons on the pad contained the numerals 0 through 9. There were one thousand six hundred possible combinations of any four of those numbers. With the dark-suit-and-necktie guards constantly roaming about, day and night, she would never have long enough to try every combination on one of those doors.

Then, one day in the kitchen, about a month after her imprisonment began, she thought of a possible solution to the problem. What if she could at least learn which four numbers were used, regardless of sequence? There are only twenty-four possible combinations of any specific four-number group, and *that* many variants she could easily try. And a little something in the kitchen told her how to find out which were the four numbers.

The little something was a spray can called Pam, containing a hydrogenated vegetable oil to be sprayed into frying pans in lieu of butter or other shortening. If you spray Pam onto a smooth surface and then wipe it off with a cloth, it leaves long skinny streaks behind, visible in the reflected light when you look at the surface at an angle. If you then touch your finger to that surface and lift the finger without sliding it, what you see when you study the surface at a sharp angle is little bubbles of Pam, raised and left behind by your fingertip.

Sister Mary Grace borrowed the Pam and brought along a paper towel, and sprayed the keypad beside Hendrickson's door, wiping off as much as she could, leaving those long streaks. She then suffered in silence another session of Hendrickson's deprogramming—at least this insufferable fat man had long since given up any reference to God, and now limited himself to discussions of her duty toward her insufferable father—and after he had at last departed she studied the buttons and on four of them clearly stood those bubbles: on 3, and 4, and 7, and 8.

3–4–7–8. No.
3–7–4–8. No.
3–7–8–4. No.
3–4–8–7. No.
3–8–4–7. No.
3–8–7–4. No.
4–3–7–8. No.
4–7–3–8. No.
4–7–8–3. No.
4–3–8–7. No.
4–8–3–7. Yes!

The door opened. Propping it slightly ajar with a wad of balled-up Kleenex, just in case it became necessary to get back and the keypad on the other side of the door had a different combination, Sister Mary Grace tiptoed down the broad gray-painted metal stairs to the next floor, and there was the gray metal door to Hendrickson's apartment, with a keypad beside it. She tried 4–8–3–7, but it didn't work, so she went on down the stairs one more flight to the same closed and locked mesh screen gate that Dortmunder and Kelp would be studying two months later. This gate defeated her. She could see the hall door down on the landing, but if she were to shout, and if someone passing by were to hear her out there in the public hall, what were the chances of that someone being connected to the Margrave Corporation?

Excellent.

So she retreated from the mesh gate, as Dortmunder and Kelp would do later, and went back up to her apartment/prison on seventy-six, where she picked up the Pam again. Back down to seventy-five she went, and sprayed the keypad for Hendrickson's apartment door, and just to be a completist she sprayed the keypad on the outside of her own apartment/prison door as well.

By the next evening, she knew her own door was 4–8–3–7 on both sides, and Hendrickson's door used the numbers 2–5–8–9. After long trial, the right combination turned out to be 9–5–8–2, but then Hendrickson's door was *bolted,* from the inside! The only time it wouldn't be bolted was when Hendrickson was upstairs pestering her, when she'd be unable to get away and come down here. If he were in his own apartment, or anywhere out in the world (using the apartment's front door), this door would be bolted, from the inside, and impassable.

The guards' door was in much more frequent

use, which made things trickier, but that was the only other alternative. The Pam trick got her through it, and down the narrow carpeted stairs with the wood-paneled walls, down two flights—there were only bare walls at the landing on seventy-five—to the back entrance to the Margrave Corporation. Pam again, and into Margrave.

Which was never empty. *Never*. Sister Mary Grace sneaked down there over and over, day and night, risking exposure a dozen times, and it was permanently just no good. There were several offices she could prowl through more or less safely at night, but toward the front of the area there were always people on duty. Men sat at consoles and studied closed-circuit television screens. Men talked on phones. Men unlocked gun cabinets and took out guns or put guns away. Beyond all these men, just glimpsed, women staffed a reception area, day and night, facing the only exit to the public hall. It was impossible to get through.

One of the many reasons Sister Mary Grace needed to escape from this tower was that it was so filled with the occasions of sin. During her two verbal hours every Thursday afternoon, she constantly overstepped herself, committing sins of anger and disrespect, and in her head for the rest of the week she was frequently uncharitable, unforgiving and proud. But the worst was when she had finally accepted the fact that all her cleverness with the keypads had come to naught, that she had merely expanded her prison without escaping from it, and that the farther barriers were absolutely impassable; at that point, and for some time after, she was guilty of the deadly sin of despair.

It wasn't that she exactly contemplated suicide, although she did find herself asking God in her prayers why He didn't simplify matters by drawing her *now* to His Bosom. And she was, without noticing it, eating less and less, until poor Enriqueta Tomayo finally made such a fuss one day, carrying on and crying in two and a half languages (some Indian dialect got in there), that Sister Mary Grace gave up anorexia at once.

Giving up despair, however, took a little longer. She was trapped, probably forever, in a high tower, surrounded by people who did not and would not understand her and who were determined to turn her into something she could never be. She was the butterfly, and this was the rack, and they would eventually break her, but to no one's satisfaction.

She had always felt herself to be different, both from her siblings and from the rest of the world she knew. She didn't care about what the others cared about. She didn't want *things*. She didn't know what she did want until, when she was sixteen, she visited a sanatorium operated by nuns where her mother was "resting." Asking about a separate building she'd noticed on the property, she was told that was where the cloistered members of the order lived, those who had renounced the world entirely and devoted themselves exclusively to contemplation of the All-Powerful.

Around Elaine's house, until then, the concept

of all-powerful had meant only the Ritter family, personified by Frank Ritter himself. Her older brothers and sisters, great galumphing things, bowled one another over for the privilege of serving this ideal. But was there a better ideal? Was there a better way to spend one's only transit here on Earth?

She sought counsel and instruction, and bided her time. Six years it had taken to be sure of her vocation, to be sure she believed in God and loved God and wanted to serve Him contemplatively the rest of her life. Six years, in short, to be absolutely sure she wasn't merely running away from her father.

She was twenty-two, legally and allegedly an adult and capable of making her own decisions, when she went back to that sanatorium and applied to enter the cloister. But the order's rules were that service in the community came first; only after so many years would the cloister be open to her. Frank Ritter's daughter was a semi-public figure; if she were to break from the world it would have to be completely and all at once. And that led her to the Little Sisterhood of St. Filumena and the convent on Vestry Street from which, three months ago, on her biweekly turn to go to the neighborhood grocery store, she was kidnapped by her father's goons and locked away in this tower.

Why shouldn't she despair? But she fought against it, as she fought against Hendrickson and her father and every other target she could find, and at last the news had come from Mother Mary Forcible: a man named John would rescue her. Blessed John! Was there anything she could do to help?

Down in the Margrave Corporation, in one of the offices she could prowl at night, were the thick looseleaf books showing the tower's security systems. Would those help? Similar books, though empty, were in a supplies closet. She took the records, left the blank books in their place, and Enriqueta smuggled them out beneath her voluminous skirts. And now Sister Mary Grace waited, despair all gone, for Blessed John to appear.

On the surface, she was silent. But inside, she sang.

16

Dortmunder and Tiny Bulcher walked up Fifth Avenue together, the Avalon State Bank Tower rising up ahead of them, bleak and gray and stern. When they reached the tower, a green-uniformed man was washing the glass entry doors to the lobby. "That means rain," Tiny said. "Never fails."

They went on inside, and over to enter one of the 5-21 elevators, joining two Orientals in expensive black topcoats, holding attaché cases and talking together very earnestly in Japanese. They paused briefly to look at Tiny, and one of them muttered something that sounded like "Godzilla." Then they went back to their conversation.

Tiny pushed the button for the seventh floor and said, "Now, remember. I don't know this bozo myself. Maybe it's no good."

"So what did your friend say?"

"Nothing. Just told me to come see J.C. Taylor and said he'd phone ahead to set me up. But he acted a little funny."

The elevator door closed. The two Japanese kept talking together, secure in their native tongue. Dortmunder said, "What kind of funny?"

Shrugging, Tiny said, "I don't know for sure. Just a feeling I had."

"I don't want to walk into anything stupid."

"No, no," Tiny said. "This guy wouldn't do anything like that. People don't do humorous things to me, they know I don't appreciate it. I just had a little funny feeling, that's all, the way he talked."

The elevator stopped at seven, and they stepped out to the hall. Behind them, the door slid closed and the Japanese gentlemen rode on up.

The office directory facing the elevators listed far more firms than were on the floors higher up. A ramshackle conglomeration of small companies had rented space on this non-prestige lower floor, leaving richer businesses to pay the higher rents that went with a higher address.

"Seven-twelve we want," Tiny said. "Down this way."

The corridor walls were dotted with doors showing obscure names on their doors. The door of room 712 listed three:

Super Star Music Co.
Allied Commissioners' Courses Inc.
Intertherapeutic Research Service

Dortmunder said, "Which one do we want?"

"J.C. Taylor, that's all I know."

Tiny pushed open the door, and they stepped into a small cluttered receptionist's office. All the available wall space was taken up by floor-to-ceiling gray metal shelves, piled high with small brown cardboard cartons. A door in the opposite wall was marked with the one word PRIVATE. The receptionist, typing labels on an old black manual typewriter on a battered gray metal desk, was a hard-looking brunette of about thirty. She was wearing a pale blue blouse and tight black slacks over black boots. She glanced up when Dortmunder and Tiny walked in, looked back down at her work, finished the label she was typing, and swiveled from the typing side of her desk to the side with the telephone and the Rolodex and the clutter of correspondence and pencils and general trivia. "Good morning, gentlemen," she said. She was brisk and efficient and in an apparent hurry to be rid of them, so she could get back to her typing. "What can I do for you?"

Tiny said, "J.C. Taylor, please."

"I'm afraid he isn't in right now. Did you call for an appointment?"

"I don't like phones," Tiny said. "My friend told me just come over."

She lifted an eyebrow. "Your friend?"

"Fella named Murtaugh," Tiny said. "Pete Murtaugh."

"Ah." Her attitude changed, became both more interested and more guarded. "And your name?"

"Mr. Bulcher. My friend said he'd call here, talk to Taylor for me."

"Yes, he did." She glanced quickly at Dortmunder, as though making up her mind about something, then said briskly to Tiny, "One moment, please," and got to her feet.

Tiny nodded toward the door marked PRIVATE, saying, "You mean, maybe Taylor's in after all?"

"It could be," she said, and suddenly grinned, as though at some private joke. The grin eased the hardness out of her features and made her much better looking. "I'll be with you boys in just a minute," she said, and walked around the desk and through the inner door, closing it behind herself.

Tiny glanced at Dortmunder and said, "What do you think?"

Dortmunder said, "Is this the same kind of funny feeling you got from your friend?"

"Yeah, I guess it is," Tiny said. Then he frowned and gestured at the telephone on the desk. "That button just lit up."

"They're making a call," Dortmunder said. "Checking on us with your friend. Did you tell him there'd be a second guy?"

"Not in so many words."

"Then that's what it is."

The light on the telephone remained on a minute longer, during which time Tiny browsed amid the cartons on the metal shelves. "Hey, look at this," he said, and turned toward Dortmunder with a book in his hand. "Some kind of dirty book."

Inside the book's brown paper wrapper was a maroon pebbled cover, with the title in gold lettering: *Scandinavian Marriage Secrets*. The title page explained that the book was an illustrated sex manual intended for the use of psychiatrists, marriage counselors "and other professionals" in the course of their work. It also said the text had been translated from the Danish.

There wasn't much text, but there were a lot of illustrations. Tiny leafed slowly through them, nodding in agreement, then stopped and said, "Hey. Isn't that her?"

"Who?"

"The receptionist. That's her."

Dortmunder looked. The emphasis of the photograph was on other parts of the two bodies, but the girl's face was clear enough to be recognizable. "That's her," Dortmunder agreed.

"Son of a bitch." Tiny studied the picture some more. "Underneath here," he said, "it calls the guy 'the husband' and her 'the wife.' She didn't have any rings on, did she?"

"I didn't notice." Dortmunder looked over at the desk. "They're off the phone," he said.

"Oh." With guilty haste, Tiny closed the book

107

and moved to put it back where he'd found it. He was just bringing his hand back when the inner door opened and the girl came out. She glanced at Tiny's moving hand and guilty face, but kept her own face expressionless. She looked briefly at Dortmunder, and said to them both, "You can come in now."

"Right," Tiny said. He seemed to be finding himself even larger and more awkward than usual; he had trouble getting around the edge of the desk. But then he made it and went on to the inner office, Dortmunder following him and the receptionist holding the door.

The inner office was also small and cluttered. A large scarred wooden desk stood in front of a big dusty window with a venetian blind half-lowered over it. Large cardboard cartons were stacked up everywhere. A library table against one wall contained envelopes, a postage scale and postage meter, a stamp pad and various rubber stamps, and other necessities for a mailing operation. A small upright piano on the opposite wall was crammed between a tall narrow bookcase and a gray metal filing cabinet. A large audio cassette player and speaker stood atop the piano. The bookcase was packed full, mostly with what seemed to be law books, and the filing cabinet featured a complicated rod-and-padlock locking arrangement. There were only three places to sit: an ordinary old swivel chair behind the desk, a tattered brown leather chair with wooden arms in front of the desk, and a metal folding chair open in front of the piano. There was no one in the room.

Tiny and Dortmunder stopped in the middle of the clutter and looked back at the receptionist, who had followed them in and was closing the door behind her. Tiny said, "What's going on? Where's Taylor?"

Dortmunder pointed at the receptionist, who was grinning again, looking almost but not quite like a schoolgirl playing a joke. "You're it," he said.

Tiny said, "What?"

"That's right," the receptionist said, and edged past them to move around behind the desk. "Grab chairs," she invited.

Tiny said, "What's going on?" He was beginning to look as though he wanted to bite somebody.

Dortmunder, gesturing toward the girl now seated behind the desk, said, "That's J.C. Taylor."

She said, "Josephine Carol Taylor, at your service. Sit down, fellows."

Dortmunder turned the folding chair in front of the piano around to face the desk, sat in it, and said, "You called this Murtaugh guy to check on us."

"Naturally. He hadn't said there'd be two." She was just as briskly efficient as before, when she'd been in her receptionist role, but now without the air of disinterested impatience.

Tiny belatedly dropped into the leather chair, which groaned once and sagged in defeat. "Pete should of told me," he said. "I'm going to mention this to him a little later."

"I guess he thought it was a joke," she said. Her smile turned down at the corners, to show she didn't necessarily agree.

Dortmunder said, "How much did Murtaugh tell you?"

"He said there was a fellow named Bulcher coming over, had a proposition for me, using my office for something on the gray side."

"He didn't say what?"

Tiny said, "He didn't know what. I didn't give him any details he didn't need."

"Same thing he did for you," J.C. Taylor pointed out. She sounded amused.

Dortmunder said to her, "So you don't know if it's something you'll go along for."

She shrugged and said, "As long as I don't have to screw anybody or kill anybody, I don't much care what you do."

"All right." Dortmunder glanced at Tiny to see if he'd take it from here, since he was the one who'd made the first contact, but Tiny was still too dazed by J.C. Taylor's changes of pace, from cold receptionist to hot porno star to cool businesswoman. He sat frowning at the girl with great intensity, as though he'd been given till sundown to either figure her out or go before the firing squad.

So Dortmunder explained it himself: "We're going to do a little burglary."

She was surprised, and showed it. "Oh, *that*

110

kind of thing," she said. "I had the idea you were maybe con artists, you needed a store to show the mark, something like that. That's why you two guys surprised me, you just don't look the type."

"We're not," Dortmunder agreed. "We're going to hit some jewelry places upstairs. We need a place—"

"*Some* places?"

Tiny said, "A couple floors' worth." He'd apparently recovered from his befuddlement enough to decide the thing to do with this woman was impress her.

He succeeded. "Well," she said, "you fellows think big."

Dortmunder said, "We need a place to operate out of beforehand, so we can be in the building through the night. And then we need a place to stash the goods after the job. And then we'll want to mail the stuff out with your own regular goods."

"Accessory before," she said, "and accessory after. What are you offering for these services?"

"Ten percent of what we get from the fence."

"Minimum?"

Dortmunder couldn't be sure yet, so he made a low guess: "Ten thousand."

"When?"

"When we get it."

A smile without humor touched her lips and went away again. She said, "How much in front?"

"Nothing."

"No deal."

"If we had money in front," Dortmunder said,

"we wouldn't be in this. Either you trust that guy you called on the phone or you don't. If you trust him and he vouches for Tiny, you know you'll get paid."

She frowned. "Vouched for who?"

"Mr. Bulcher."

"They call me Tiny."

She grinned at Tiny, and looked him slowly up and down. "Now, I wonder why," she said.

"Never mind that," Tiny told her.

J.C. Taylor was one of the very few people Dortmunder had ever seen who didn't just automatically stand in awe of Tiny Bulcher. On the other hand, she didn't look as though she much stood in awe of anybody. She said, to Dortmunder, "What if you people get caught?"

"Then nobody gets paid."

"And I wind up with twenty years in a prison laundry." She shook her head. "My mama didn't raise me to be a dyke."

"You don't have to be here while it's happening," Dortmunder told her. "It can be set up to look like we broke in. Take a week's vacation."

"No chance," she said. "This is a mail-order business, I have to be on top of it all the time."

"Then if push comes to shove, we forced you into it at gunpoint."

She looked dubious. "Maybe," she said.

Dortmunder said, "But now I've got a question."

"Oh? What's that?"

"What's your operation here? All those names on the door; which one is you?"

"All of them." She held up a finger and said, "Super Star Music. You send us your lyrics, we'll find a melody to fit. On the other hand, you send us your melody, we'll produce the lyrics to suit. In either case, find fame and fortune in the booming music industry." A second raised finger: "Allied Commissioners' Courses; be a detective, send for our one-volume correspondence course. No tests, no instructors, no salesman will call. Free handcuffs and badge included as a special bonus if you act now. Endorsed by police chiefs and police commissioners all across the country."

Dortmunder said, "Endorsed?"

"They have trade magazines for police chiefs," she said. "There's some over there in the bookcase. They do obituaries when a chief or a commissioner dies, and that's endorsement enough for me. You go prove a dead man *didn't* give me an endorsement, and then come back and we'll talk."

"Ha," Tiny said. "That's nice, lady, that's really nice."

She gave him a short nod and a brief smile and said, "Thanks."

Dortmunder said, "And the third company."

"Intertherapeutic Research Service. Be a better lay. Get your marriage working right by studying the detailed illustrations in this marital sex manual, endorsed by famous physicians and marriage counselors and sent to you in a plain brown wrapper."

Dortmunder nodded. He said, "Ever have any questions from the law?"

She shrugged. "Post Office people. Back when I used to do blind mailings to bought mailing lists. But not anymore. Now I stick strictly to magazine advertising. It's safe, it's legal, and it brings them in."

"Who backs you?"

"Me," she said, and she sounded a bit annoyed at the question. "I put in my time as meat," she said, "and I saved my money. I started with nothing but the sex book, two magazine ads, and three months' paid-for desk space down on Varick Street. I don't owe a penny to anybody but Uncle Sam, and as long as he gets his twelve percent he doesn't complain."

"All right," Dortmunder said. "So it shouldn't be a problem."

"The problem," she said, "is cash. I promised my mother on her deathbed I'd never put out without the money on the dresser, and I've never had anything happen to make me think she was wrong."

Tiny said, abruptly, "Hell, honey, money's no problem."

Dortmunder said, "It isn't?"

Turning to Dortmunder, Tiny said, "We can get this little lady some cash, can't we?"

Dortmunder looked at Tiny in astonishment. Where was the bad-tempered mammoth, the Sherman tank with a grudge? This was a Tiny transformed. His brow was as clear as such a corrugated surface could get, his expression was agreeable and hardly terrifying at all, and there might actually be something damn near mellow deep down inside those ball-bearing eyes. From grizzly bear to honey bear in one smooth motion; astounding.

And trouble. "Tiny," Dortmunder said, "we don't *have* ten thousand dollars."

The girl said, "Wait a minute, I'm not asking for the whole ten. But I am talking about cash, *some* cash, green paper I can hold in my hand and look at, no matter what happens next."

Tiny, being expansive, his gravel-on-a-conveyor-belt voice practically mellifluous, said, "You want a couple thousand, honey, is that it?"

"That'll do," she agreed.

Tiny shrugged the problem away. Looking at Dortmunder, being sweet and kindly but not in a mood to be argued with, he said, "I'm good for it, Dortmunder. I'll give her a couple Gs now, we'll straighten it out after the job. I'll get my money back out of her ten percent, no vigorish, no nothing." With a gallant gesture, as though sweeping off a Three Musketeers kind of plumed hat, he told the girl, "Just to help out, make things smooth and nice between friends."

"You give me two thousand in cash," she said, "you can stable sheep in here."

"I'll stick to girls," Tiny said, and gave her a big grin.

Which she ignored, pointedly, saying to Dortmunder, "Anything else?"

"Not from me," Dortmunder said, and got to his feet. "Tiny's going to give you the cash. The job'll be sometime in the next few weeks, we'll let you know a couple days ahead."

"Fine." She stood up behind the desk, saying, "I'll show you out."

Tiny said, "You got a home number? I'll call you when I got the cash."

"You can bring it to me here," she said.

She led the way to the outer office, Dortmunder following, the new Tiny shambling in the rear, saying, "We don't have to be *all* business, do we?"

"As a matter of fact, we do," she told him.

Dortmunder could see the new Tiny drowning in a sea of bewilderment, the old Tiny just beginning to snarl his way back to the surface. "I figured . . ." Tiny said.

"I know you did," she told him, and opened the hall door. "I'll be waiting to hear from you, gents."

Tiny wasn't quite ready to let go: "Do you ever eat dinner?" he asked.

She looked at him, "Are you a burglar or a caterer?"

"Come on, Tiny," Dortmunder said, and led the baffled giant out to the corridor. She closed the door behind them.

A few minutes later, out on the sidewalk, the old Tiny, walking flat-footed and angry, said, "I hate that kind of foul-talking woman. It ain't feminine."

116

"The office looks good," Dortmunder said.

"We'd be better off working with a man."

"We're not gonna get a smoother setup than that one," Dortmunder pointed out. "She's a pro, Tiny. If we leave her alone, she won't make us any trouble."

"Two thousand dollars," Tiny said. He sounded bitter.

"Well, Tiny, that was your idea," Dortmunder said cautiously.

"I know that, Dortmunder." Tiny sounded as though he was thinking about blaming somebody for something.

"You've got two thousand dollars?"

"I'll get it." Tiny sounded really bitter. "Don't worry. I'll get it."

17

Andy Kelp sipped his seventh cup of cappuccino and watched three more burly men walk through the grove of trees and board the elevator, crowding in together as they pulled closed behind themselves the brushed-chrome door marked MAINTENANCE. Kelp looked at his watch and wrote on the notepad beside his cup, "2:27 PM / / /," with an arrow pointing upward.

"Another cappuccino, sir?" the waitress asked.

Kelp leaned forward to survey the bottom of his cup, lightly covered with tan bubbles. "Sure."

The waitress looked at him with something like

awe—*eight* cappuccinos!—but made no remark as she took his empty cup away. Kelp went back to his observation of that obscure door across the way.

He was in the ground-floor garden of the Avalon State Bank Tower, surrounded by tall and slender trees, seated on a white wrought-iron chair at a small round white metal table in the garden's little cafe. To his left was Fifth Avenue, seen through a tall wall of glass, busy and self-important in the sun. To his right was an artificial waterfall, a black stone wall twenty feet wide, down which water poured with a gentle plashing sound, so that the noises of the city disappeared, even when the glass doors to the street were opened; except, of course, for horns and sirens, of which Fifth Avenue is *full*. Straight ahead, through steel-sheathed pots of cherry and quince, past copses of ficus and bamboo, stood the brushed-chrome wall separating the garden from the lobby and reflecting vaguely the garden's greenery, as in some medieval tapestry that had been washed far too often. And on that wall, barely noticeable, was the door marked MAINTENANCE, which, according to those incredible looseleaf books the nun had smuggled out, led directly to the private elevator that serviced only the seventy-fifth and seventy-sixth floors.

Today was Friday, eight days after Dortmunder and May had been given those books, six days since Tiny and Stan had been brought aboard, five days since Wilbur Howey had come dancing

118

and winking into their midst, three days since Dortmunder and Tiny had made their deal with the mail-order company in this building—Kelp wondered offhandedly why they were both so reluctant to talk about that outfit—and the seventh day of occasional surveillance of that elevator. (Between eight in the evening and seven in the morning, when the garden was closed and its entrances locked, elevator traffic had to be watched less comfortably and more sporadically from a car parked across the street.) And of all those days and nights of surveillance, today was the busiest, with very few people coming out but a whole *lot* of guys who looked like moving men going in.

Be a real mess if they moved the nun, just when things were almost set to save her.

Whoops; there came two more of them, tall, big-shouldered guys with close-cropped hair and bunchy jaws. Even before they went over to MAINTENANCE, even before they took a hard look left and a hard look right and then unlocked the door and went through, Kelp was already writing, "2:36 PM / /," with the arrow pointing up.

"Your cappuccino, sir," the waitress said, at the same instant that Stan Murch appeared and said, "You got beer?"

"This isn't beer," Kelp told him, and the waitress said, "No, sir. We have coffee, espresso, cappuccino, tea, herb tea, peppermint tea—"

"No beer," Stan summed up.

"No, sir."

Stan sat down to Kelp's right, where he could

look out at the street. He *liked* traffic. "What's that?" he said, pointing at Kelp's cup.

"Cappuccino."

"And?"

The waitress said, "It's coffee, whipped cream and cinnamon."

"Sounds weird," Stan said.

"It's really very good," the waitress assured him. "That's your friend's eighth."

"Oh, yeah?" Stan considered, then nodded. "I'll have one of those," he said. "And bring me some salt, will you?"

The waitress hesitated, decided not to ask, and left. Kelp said, "Stan, what do you want with salt?"

"You know what I do with salt," Stan told him, and pointed to the whipped cream on Kelp's cappuccino. "Look, you're losing the head already."

"That works with *beer*," Kelp said. "You put the salt in, the head comes back. This is whipped cream."

"So?" Brushing that aside, Stan said, "Midtown is impossible, you know? I took the Battery Tunnel because they quit on the construction today, I was fine coming up the FDR Drive, but then how do you get to the middle?"

"Tough," Kelp agreed.

"So I got off at the UN," Stan said, "I went up to Forty-ninth Street, I waited for the bus."

"Smart," Kelp said. "Just leave the car and take the bus."

"I didn't *leave* the car," Stan said, "I *followed*

the bus. Those bus drivers are the most fearless people on the planet Earth, Andy, they don't care what's happening, people, cars, trucks, they just pull out in that huge monster and *go*. They got a schedule, they got to get across town to the Hudson so the dispatcher can check them off on his clipboard. So what I do, I tuck in behind the bus, I just go where he goes. Fastest way across town."

"But then when you get here, what?" Kelp asked him. "Where do you park?"

Gesturing, Stan said, "Right now, I'm in front of a fire hydrant around the corner."

"They'll tow you."

"Well, no," Stan said. "When I'm coming to midtown, I bring along a little bottle of green radiator fluid. There's always a place to park in front of a fire hydrant, so then I pour the radiator fluid on the street under the front of the car, and open the hood, and take away the radiator cap." He took a radiator cap from his jacket pocket, as illustration.

Kelp nodded judiciously. "Might work," he said.

"For maybe an hour," Stan said. "The cops come along to tow, they see all this, they start thinking about liability."

"They figure you're off calling AAA."

"Exactly," Stan said.

The waitress said, "Cappuccino," putting it down in front of Stan, "and salt." The last part wasn't quite a question.

"And a check," Stan told her.

Kelp looked at him in surprise: "You just got here."

"We're both going," Stan told him, while the waitress stood over them, adding numbers. "Dortmunder says we can quit looking the joint over now, because we're going in. Tomorrow."

"Well, good," Kelp said, and looked at the check the waitress gave him. "I would call this expensive," he said.

"That's what it costs," the waitress said. "It says so on the menu."

"Yeah?" Kelp shook his head. "At this price, I should get to keep the cup." He covered the check with a lot of money, which the waitress took away.

Stan, whipped cream on his upper lip, said, "This is coffee." He sounded like somebody who'd been cheated.

"Yeah," Kelp agreed. "That's what we said. Ten cents worth of coffee, two cents worth of whipped cream and a tenth of a cent of cinnamon, for two dollars and seventy-five cents."

"I'll stick to beer," Stan decided, and put the cup down. "You ready?"

"Hold it." Kelp raised his pencil and watched two bruisers cross the garden, looking around, searching for something. One saw MAINTENANCE and poked the other and they both went over. "Last two," Kelp said, making the notation. "There must be an army up there by now. Okay, let's go." But then the pencil kind of jumped out of his hand and fell on the floor.

"What's the matter?" Stan asked him. "You nervous about something?"

"I am kind of jittery," Kelp admitted. "I think it's all that cinnamon."

18

"Now, be sure you phone, John," May said, removing lint from the lapels of Dortmunder's black business jacket.

"When I get a chance," Dortmunder said.

"You'll have plenty of chance," May told him. "You're going to be in that building over the whole weekend."

"I'll call," Dortmunder promised. The bedroom clock said five minutes to eleven; it was Saturday morning, and he wanted to be in the building and safely tucked away in the offices of J.C. Taylor by noon. "I got to go, May," he said.

She walked him to the front door, tugging at the tail of his jacket to make it sit better on his shoulders. Something inside the jacket went *chink.* "Good luck," she said.

"Thanks, May."

"Wait," she said suddenly. "Let me get my key."

Dortmunder looked at her. "May? You're not coming with me."

"I want to look for the mail."

So Dortmunder waited, and they went downstairs together, and Dortmunder waited again by the mailboxes, where May went through the bills and insurance offers and said, "This is for you. From something called Civil Court."

Dortmunder frowned. "Civil Court? There's no such thing."

Handing him the envelope, May said, "Is there something you haven't told me about, John?"

"No," he said, and looked at the official return address. "Civil Court. Hmmm."

"Why don't you open it?"

Because he didn't want to open it, that's why. Still, if he was ever going to get uptown by noon, he'd have to move on from this vestibule first, so he turned the envelope over, slit it open with the side of his thumb, and took out the legal document within. He studied it a long time. After he understood it, he studied it all over again, and he still didn't believe it.

"John? What is it?"

"Well," Dortmunder said, "it's Chepkoff."

"Who?"

"The guy I was getting the caviar for. He said he wanted his three hundred advance payment back, and I told him, 'So sue me,' because that's what you say to a guy in a situation like that, am I right?"

"And?"

"And I better phone him," Dortmunder said, pushing back into the building.

May followed, saying, "John? You don't mean it!"

"Oh, yes, I do," Dortmunder said. "This is a

summons. Chepkoff's taking me to small claims court to get his three hundred back."

"But he gave you that money to commit a crime!"

"I'm going to point that out to him," Dortmunder said, "when I get upstairs."

Which he did, finding Chepkoff at his office on this Saturday morning, but Chepkoff immediately answered, "What I said in my complaint was I gave you three hundred dollars to perform professional services which you didn't perform. If you want to go into court and say those professional services were a felony, that's up to you. All I'm saying is, professional services, and I got the canceled check with your signature on the back, and I want the return of my three hundred."

"People don't do this," Dortmunder complained.

"I do it," Chepkoff said. "I'm a businessman, and I will not be stiffed for three hundred fish."

"Everybody takes chances!"

"I don't."

"Listen," Dortmunder said. "I'm late for an appointment, I'll get back to you, you just don't understand the situation here."

"Yes, I do," Chepkoff said. "You owe me three Cs."

"I *don't!* I can't talk now, I got to go."

"Listen, Dortmunder," Chepkoff said, "be careful out there. Don't wind up in jail. I wouldn't want you to miss our court date."

Dortmunder hung up, and looked at May. "If the scientists," he said, "ever do find life on some other planet, I'm going there. It can't be as weird as this."

LAMENTATIONS

19

Walter Hendrickson sighed. Sooner or later, he would have to speak, but what would he say? For the last five minutes, ever since he'd come into the girl's apartment, he had sat here silently in the highbacked chair against the window, Saturday noon's sunshine on the top of his head, while Elaine Ritter had stood across the room, watching and waiting. At first, her face had been fixed in the glare with which she always greeted him, but as his silence had continued minute after minute, her expression had reluctantly and slowly altered; first to surprise, then to curiosity, and at last to skepticism; she must have decided by now this was merely a new deprogramming technique. Walter Hendrickson opened his mouth, then closed it, then opened it again. He sighed.

Elaine Ritter planted her feet somewhat apart, placed her fists on her waist with elbows akimbo, leaned her head forward, and raised one eyebrow: *Well? What's it all about?* Really fascinating how she managed to communicate so much without words. On the other hand, without words Hendrickson seemed unable to communicate anything at all, other than a vague unease.

But *what* words? What should he say?

I am the best, he reminded himself. But even the best can be tripped up, particularly by emotion. Over these past few months, while Elaine Ritter had persistently, unremittingly, implacably resisted him, and while Hendrickson himself had moved from self-assurance through wonder to a calm and amused acceptance of his inevitable defeat, it seemed he had all unconsciously also been breaking the cardinal rule of the deprogrammer; he had become emotionally involved with the subject. The fact was, damn it to hell and back, the fact was he *liked* Elaine Ritter, liked her spunk, liked her strength, liked the flailing sharpness of her logic on Thursday afternoons. He would miss her.

Elaine put her heels together, displayed her hands palm up, and gazed long-sufferingly at the ceiling: *What's with this yo-yo, God?*

Hendrickson sighed. He knew what was keeping him silent; the only words he had were words he didn't want to use. But the time had come, hadn't it? There was nothing left for him to say to Elaine Ritter but the truth. "Ah, well," he said, and sighed.

She looked alert, ready for him to go on.

"Ah, well, ah, well, ah, well."

Slowly, she shook her head.

"The truth is, Elaine," he said, then shook his

own head and said, "I beg your pardon. The truth is, Sister Mary Grace—"

That *did* make her eyes widen.

"—the truth is, this is our last meeting."

Her eyes narrowed: *What's up?*

"Your father has decided," Hendrickson said, and sighed, and went on, "to try a different tack."

She leaned forward, very intent.

"I'm out, in short," Hendrickson told her. "Well, we both knew it would happen, didn't we?"

She made *come-on-tell* gestures with both hands.

"Yes, you're right," he said. "Very well. There's a new man coming in next week. I'm sorry, I can't pronounce his name, he's I think Hungarian, or Bulgarian, or one of those things." Hendrickson waved a hand loosely toward Eastern Europe. "Before he defected," he went on, "he was apparently an expert in brainwashing."

She stepped back, wide-eyed, one hand to her throat.

"Your father . . ." Hendrickson sighed.

She did her imitation up-chuck.

Hendrickson sighed again. "You're not entirely wrong," he admitted. "Your father is a strong-willed man, and he's getting impatient, and this Rumanian or Ukrainian or whatever he is, he's been known to convince *cardinals* to change their minds about God, so that's the way they'll try next. There will probably be some physical violence involved, which is not something I would ever do, so I'm out. When I last talked to your father, he was full of what's necessary when you make an omelet."

She bunked the heel of her hand against the side of her head.

Hendrickson nodded. "I'm afraid so," he agreed. "You're the egg they're going to break."

She pointed at him, pointed at herself, pointed her thumb at the door.

He smiled sadly and shook his head. "Can't. They never let me leave this area by myself. If you tell your father this I'll deny it, but in fact I *would* help you escape if I could. Unfortunately, it's impossible. I'm sorry, Sister Mary Grace, but nobody can help you. My advice is, try to get used to that idea."

Her lips moved. Hendrickson, peering at her, thought she had mouthed the word *John*. Saint John the Apostle? Her patron saint, perhaps, to whom she prayed when things looked blackest, such as right now. "John," he said, and nodded solidarity with her.

She looked startled, then clamped her lips shut.

"Oh, it's all right," Hendrickson assured her, pushing down on the chair arms, getting to his feet. He felt very weary. "In the days to come," he said, "under this new fellow, I imagine you'll do a lot of talking on days other than Thursday, whether you want to or not."

She folded her arms and looked mulish.

"We all do our best," Hendrickson said, as much to himself as to her. "Do you suppose God actually does notice? 'Matthew, Mark, Luke and

John, Bless this bed of nails that I lie on.' Good luck, Sister Mary Grace." He smiled again. "You came close to deprogramming *me*," he told her, and went away.

20

And what was this, twitching and winking and jittering around in the lobby of the Avalon State Bank Tower? Bless me if it isn't Wilbur Howey, flashing smiles and winks and salutes and tips of the Howey hat to every passing female, plus one kilted Scot and a delivery boy in a white apron. Dortmunder, entering the lobby, saw him there and a heavy weight seemed to settle on his shoulders; nevertheless, he went over and said to Howey, "Now what?"

Howey turned away from leering at two transvestites on their way up to their electrolysis appointment. Little sparkly eyes focused on Dortmunder, and he said, "Say! I know you!"

"I can't deny it," Dortmunder admitted. "What are you hanging around down here for?"

"This is the place!" Howey did a little two-step, seemed about to twirl, didn't twirl, and said, "And here I am!"

"Not in the *lobby*," Dortmunder told him.

"Say, look," Howey said, "here's the story on that. You know that piece of paper, where Tiny wrote everything down?"

"You lost it," Dortmunder said.

"Avalon," Howey said, and snapped his fingers. "That much I got. I used to know a girl named Mabel, you know, gee, a whole bunch of time ago. So they sound alike, and—"

Dortmunder said, "They do?"

"Mabel," Howey said. "Avalon. Get it?"

"Anyway, you're here."

"Johnny on the spot, that's yours truly," Howey said, and grinned, and popped a salute.

"It's seven-twelve," Dortmunder told him. "Come on."

As they went over to the 5–21 elevators, Howey said, "I never knew any girls with numbers instead of names."

What was there to answer to a remark like that? Dortmunder maintained an increasingly grim silence as they entered an elevator already containing two slender young women dressed for success in dark blue long-skirted suits, plain white blouses and colorful bunchy neckties. They were talking about diet chocolate-chip cookies from a marketing point of view. "Our main subject is the assuagement of guilt," one said, and the other said, "Exactly. Of *course* you're as fat as a hippopotamus and your husband can't stand the sight of you, but every time you reach for a diet chocolate-chip cookie it shows you're seriously trying. No more guilt."

The doors slid shut, the elevator started up, and Howey leaned toward the nearest young woman, winking as he said, "Hi, Toots. I *like* a double-breasted suit, you catch my drift?"

The women turned their young serious gazes on Howey, then on Dortmunder, who was facing front, pretending he was on a street corner in Boise, Idaho, waiting for a bus. One of them said to Dortmunder, "Is this with you?"

"We're a team, Toots," Howey said, lifting his hat as though about to break into song. "We could double-date!"

Still speaking to Dortmunder, the first young woman said, "Shouldn't it be on a leash?"

Dortmunder breathed shallowly, looking at the door.

"Be careful," the second young woman told the first. "It may not have had its shots."

"Say, you know what I like about women's lib?" Howey piped up, while Dortmunder closed his eyes. "I *love* to be free with women! Hotcha!"

The shutters remained closed. Down inside his dark head, Dortmunder heard the first young woman say, "Ouch!" and then the sound of the slap, and then Howey, full of beans, saying, "Say, listen, girlie, didn't you ever hear of a senior citizen's pass?"

The elevator bumped to a halt. Dortmunder opened his eyes and saw the doors sliding open, with the seventh floor corridor just beyond. One of the young women was saying, thoughtfully, "You know, Arlene, the Eskimos may have had the right idea after all."

The other young woman said, "Putting the old-sters out to sea on an ice floe? You bet."

The doors were open. The irrepressible Howey,

135

as Dortmunder lugged him away by the elbow, called back, "Bring your friend, Toots! I got a *lotta* catching up to do!"

Then the elevator and the young women were gone and Dortmunder could release the little madman's elbow. As they made their way down the corridor, Howey said, "Too bad we're busy, huh, pal? Those two were ready, willing and Betty Grable."

"The only thing in this world that gives me any pleasure at all," Dortmunder muttered, "is the knowledge that you're about to meet J.C. Taylor."

"Nice fella, huh?"

"In a way," Dortmunder said, and opened the door leading to Super Star Music, Allied Commissioners' Courses and—last but not at all least—Intertherapeutic Research Service.

J.C. Taylor was being the receptionist again, typing labels. Today she was in a plaid shirt open halfway to the waist, and designer blue jeans. Glancing up when the door opened, she said, "Hail, hail, the gang's all here. There's three guys already inside."

"Good," Dortmunder said.

Meanwhile, Wilbur Howey was inhaling. He'd been inhaling steadily ever since he'd set eyes on J.C. Taylor, slowly rising up on his toes as though the volume of air he'd taken aboard was turning him into a balloon. Finally, he released a bit of that air: "Tooootts," he said, half sigh and half croak. His hand moved up to his hat, moving like

136

part of a mechanical figure, and raised it clear of his wisp-covered scalp.

Now she became aware of him. Her fingers slowed and then stopped on the typewriter keys. Her left eyebrow raised, and the corners of her mouth wrinkled in amusement. "Well, look at this," she said, like somebody finding a really good prize in a Crackerjack box.

"My hat's off to you, Babe," Howey said, which was the literal truth. Apparently he'd forgotten he'd doffed his skimmer—as he himself would undoubtedly have put it—and his upraised arm still held it way up there, like a flying saucer observing human mating rituals.

"You're cute," J.C. Taylor told him.

Self-confidence never deserted Wilbur Howey for long. Waggling the hat, he returned it at a jaunty angle to his head, patted its crown, winked, and said, "And anything *you* want to take off for *me*, Toots, is one hundred percent hunky-dory."

"Ignore him," Dortmunder said.

"Why?" she asked, still amused. Slowly she stood, sinuously, moving her hips a lot more than necessary and arching her back and treating Howey pretty much as though he were the back row in the burleycue; she wanted to be sure she reached him. "What's your name, honey?" she asked, in a sugary voice Dortmunder hadn't heard her use before.

Howey was bobbing up and down by now, almost skipping, his big watery eyes blinking.

137

"Say, Babe," he cried, "they call me Wilbur Howey. I'm little, but I'm wiry."

"And ex-*per*-ienced."

"Oh, *say*, you can't see, any flies on me!"

With a little reflective half smile on her lips, Taylor reached out her left hand and touched the tip of her first finger gently to the side of Howey's jaw, just beneath the ear. Eye to eye, leaning just a bit toward him, breathing deeply and regularly, she slowly moved the fingertip and just an edge of fingernail lightly along the line of his jaw. Howey's bobbing grew more spasmodic, he vibrated all over, and by the time her fingertip had reached the middle of his jaw he was just standing there, spent, mouth hanging open. "Very nice," she told him, patted his cheek, and said to Dortmunder, "He'll be all right now for a while." And she sat down, turning back to her typewriter.

Dortmunder looked at Howey, who continued to stand there, unmoving, dazed, while J.C. Taylor began once again to type. "Come on," Dortmunder said. "Before you embarrass me."

A long sigh from Howey suggested the belated return of that long inhale. Once again his eyes had begun to sparkle, once again that cheery oblivious smile was spreading across his face. "*Say*, Toots," he said. "You and me could trip the— After the job, why don't we— Say, couldn't we just see the world with, uh— Me and you and a roadster built for two— Waikiki Mama!"

Meanwhile, Taylor typed, aware of nothing else, alone in the room.

"Howey," Dortmunder said, firmly. "We go through this door here." And he tugged at Howey's arm.

Howey did permit himself to be led away, but he kept looking back at the unresponsive Taylor, and as Dortmunder pulled him through into the inner office he called back, "Keep them fires hot, Baby, I'll be right back to stoke ya!"

"Oh, no, you won't," Dortmunder grumbled, and shut the door.

In a corner of the inner office there now stood a very large masking-tape-swathed cardboard box which had originally held paper towels. On top of all the stuff piled on top of the piano were two shopping bags from Balducci's deli down in the Village. Stan Murch stood at the window, looking down at traffic, while Andy Kelp picked out a one-finger version of "Camptown Races" at the piano. Pausing in that occupation, he nodded hello, saying, "How's it going?"

"It's been a long day already," Dortmunder told him.

Tiny Bulcher was seated at the desk, studying a book. He nodded his heavy head at Dortmunder and said, "I'm learning to be a detective." He showed the front of the book; gilt lettering said it was the textbook of the Allied Commissioners' Courses.

"That's nice," Dortmunder said.

Stan Murch, still looking out the window, said, "I wouldn't want to be making any getaway through *that* mess down there. Just from here, I can see five separate and distinct gridlocks."

"The idea is," Dortmunder reminded him, "we make our getaway completely inside the building. Just to here."

"That's the part I love," Kelp said.

Tiny gave Kelp a look. "You told us," he said.

The door opened and J.C. Taylor came in, shrugging into a short jacket. To Dortmunder, she said, "Is this everybody?"

At the desk, Tiny closed the detective course book and sat with a belligerent defensive look on his face, as though expecting her any second to demand her desk. Stan's concentration remained mostly on the traffic seven stories down, but Kelp abandoned "Camptown Races" at the far turn and looked alert, capable, ready to be of assistance. And Howey blinked at Taylor with undisguised lust, which she ignored.

"Yeah," Dortmunder said. "This is all of us."

"Okay," she said. "There's a couple things we should talk about before I go."

"Sure," Dortmunder said. "Such as."

"Such as do me a favor and don't use the phone. And if it rings, don't answer. And if anybody comes around and knocks on the door, for Christ's sake don't any of you birds say you're J.C. Taylor."

Dortmunder, thinking of Chepkoff, said, "Process servers?"

"There's always a little lawsuit or two in this business," she said. It didn't seem to bother her much. "Just so J.C. Taylor doesn't get served any papers, that's all I ask. Cover your ass is the name of this game."

"Just a foul-talking woman, that's all," Tiny said. He grumbled it in his low voice, like an earthquake over in the next county, but he could be heard very clearly in this room.

Howey, looking shocked, said, "Say, wait a minute there, Tiny!"

Facing Dortmunder, ignoring the others, Taylor said, "We can always call it off now, if you want."

"Everything's just fine," Dortmunder assured her. "We appreciate the place."

She hesitated a second, not looking away from Dortmunder, and he knew that if anybody said anything now, no matter what, she'd balk and the deal would be off. But Tiny had crunched down into something the size and shape of an irritable Volkswagen Beetle, and the others clearly all sensed something in the air—even Stan, who had turned away from the window now with an air of mild curiosity—so everybody just stood and waited.

And then J.C. Taylor let out a held breath, and nodded, and said, "Okay. These keys"—she dropped them both in Dortmunder's palm—"you'll need. The bigger one's for the men's john, down at the end of the hall on the left. The other one's the office door. I don't subscribe to any part of the alarm service—I mean, what have I got to steal, right?—so you can go in and out as much as you want."

"Fine," Dortmunder said.

"I'll be back Monday morning at eight."

"We'll have the goods in this back room here."

"The mailers you wanted," she said, "are on the shelves outside."

"Good," Dortmunder said. "You got paid?"

"Oh, yes." Her smile had just a hint of mockery in it. "Mr. Bulcher was very agreeable," she said.

A low rumble sounded; maybe a subway train going by far below.

J.C. Taylor looked around the room, giving it one last visual check before turning it over to the sub-tenants. "Just try not to bring the cops in here, okay?" she said.

"That's top of our list," Dortmunder promised her.

"Okay. Well, break a law," she said, and left.

Tiny broke the little silence that followed: "That woman," he grumbled, low and gravelly, as he frowned at the door.

"The office," Dortmunder pointed out. "Forget the woman, Tiny, look at the office."

"I can wait," Tiny said. "But that broad is too unrefined. When this is over, she's goin to finishing school."

21

Once upon a time there was a small and mountainous South American nation called Guerrera, run by a small and fat dictator named Pozos, a man who devoted his life to his fellow countrymen; devoted his life to robbing them, torturing them and murdering them. In the capitals of the great world outside, his domestic arrangements mattered not at all. He was welcomed in palaces and parliaments, his Guerrera belonged to alliances and organizations, he received (and pocketed) foreign aid from great powers. What a happy man Pozos was, all in all!

But then, one dark day, he went too far. He annoyed Frank Ritter.

Frank Ritter's second son, Garrett, was a tall and big-shouldered man of thirty-four, already balding on top and already starting those jowls which would someday be his most salient feature. His body was kept in trim by skiing, sailing and scuba diving, but it seemed there was absolutely nothing he could do to keep his face from rushing toward lax and puffy middle age.

For the past three years, Garrett had been in charge of Mergers & Acquisitions for Templar International, a job that had familiarized him with much of the free world's industry, many of its top executives and most of its bases of wealth. It was time, Frank Ritter had decided, for Garrett to be introduced to the Greater Reality. Or, as Ritter had described it aphoristically in his commonplace book:

"The real world is just beyond the visible world."

In his private suite in the Margrave Corporation

on the seventy-fourth floor of the Avalon State Bank Tower, that Saturday afternoon, Ritter shared a drink and some of his thoughts with his son Garrett before going on to greet the freedom fighters assembling in the larger conference room. "The essential point is," Ritter told his son, "the world has changed. The world *always* changes. I would say that most people in this country still retain a nineteenth-century view of the United States as an independent industrial nation with a republican form of government, wouldn't you?"

"Well," Garrett said, his puffy face frowning above his trim body, "that's what it is, isn't it?" Like all of Frank Ritter's children, Garrett walked warily, but had learned that one was always relatively safe to behave as though Dad knew best.

Now, Dad shook his head and said, "Of course it isn't. And when that's what America *was*, in the nineteenth century, people didn't know it. *They* thought the United States was still an agrarian democracy with a government run part-time by farmers and lawyers. Reality is always one jump ahead of the masses, Garrett."

"Okay," Garrett said, and sipped at his vodka-tonic. Dad didn't like people who drank too much. On the other hand, Dad *hated* people who didn't drink at all. A narrow path, but a sure-footed Ritter child could find it.

Frank Ritter said, "Insofar as America is a major industrial nation, no, it is not. What we are today is the premier technological and service nation. Heavy industry is done in Japan and Germany and Poland. Arms manufacture is done in Brazil and Israel. But American technological pre-eminence has meant increasing partnerships with these foreign industries. Any partnership that survives is merely a gentlemanly form of absorption, so now we have the multinational corporation, and *that's* where power lies today. Not in the UN, certainly, and not in national governments."

"Gee, Dad," Garrett said. "No?"

"No. The multinational is in the position of the bank robber in the old West; all he has to do is ride straight and hard to be safe, because the posse can't cross the border. We have taken over the roles that nations recently held; we wage war, collect taxes through debt service, protect our areas of property and the worker/citizens within those areas, and we distribute power as we see fit."

Garrett, along with his brothers and sisters, had grown up believing that his father spouted two things fairly constantly; verbal nonsense and lovely money. Accept the former with obvious pleasure, and the flow of the latter was unending. "That all sounds exciting, Dad," he said. Past his father, across this tastefully anonymous living room, the window showed a pale blue sky with stray clouds. The skiing would be good in Norway now. Oh, to be in Ostersund, now that spring is here!

"It's more than exciting, Garrett," Ritter said. "It's *real*. The truth is, the pendulum has swung all the way back, several hundred years, and we are today entering upon the next great era of feudalism."

Garrett blinked. Feudalism was something that had wafted by once or twice in college days, leaving no residue. Doubtfully, he said, "You mean, King Arthur and like that? The Round Table?"

Ritter laughed, a sound that always had a threat in it. "I don't mean myth," he said. "I mean reality. Feudalism is a system based not on national citizenship but on loyalties and contracts between individuals. Power lies not in the state but in ownership of assets, and all fealty follows the line of power. Very sensible."

"I guess so," Garrett said, blinking slowly.

Ritter said, "Think of it this way. I am the baron. Templar International and Margrave Corporation and Avalon State Bank and so on are the castles I have built in different parts of my territory, for defense and expansion. The subsidiary companies we've bought or merged with owe their allegiance not to America but to *Margrave*. We reward loyalty and punish disloyalty. When necessary, we can protect our most important people from the laws of the state, just as the earlier barons could protect their most important vassal knights from the laws of the Catholic Church. The work force is tied to us by profit-sharing and pension plans. I don't expect national governments to disappear, any more than the British or Dutch royal families have disappeared, but they will become increasingly irrelevant pageants. More and

146

more, actors will play the parts of politicians and statesmen, while the real work goes on elsewhere."

"With us, you mean," Garrett said. His puffy face lit up with excitement. He thought about buying new skis in Scandinavia.

"And in fact," Ritter said, "this is ultimately a benevolent advance for humanity. Of course, some eggs will get broken in the making of this omelet—"

"Happens," said Garrett understandingly.

"Yes," said Ritter, who didn't like his train of thought interrupted. "But once the omelet is made, this will be a happier, more prosperous, far more peaceful Earth. The test-case of Japanese industry shows us that workers whose primary loyalty is to their employer rather than their citizenship or their union are more contented, more productive, less disease-ridden and longer-lived."

Frowning, vaguely remembering something he'd read in a newspaper on a plane, Garrett said, "Don't they commit suicide a lot?"

"Not at all," Ritter said. "Only among the youngest entrants to the work force, a natural weeding-out process. Japs *like* to commit suicide anyway, it's deeply embedded in their culture."

"Mata Hari," Garrett agreed, nodding.

"Hara-*kiri*," his father corrected, in some annoyance. "Mata Hari was shot by the French government as a traitor."

Grinning uncertainly, Garrett said, "I guess that's a level of power we haven't got to yet, is it?"

"Not in America," Ritter agreed. "Though we're

close. Consider this building we're in. Is it in the United States? Or is it within the sphere of Avalon State Bank?"

"Well, both," Garrett said, brow furrowed. It was so easy to be wrong with Dad.

And apparently he was wrong again. Smiling coldly, Ritter said, "Where does government influence show, Garrett? To begin with, we got a tax abatement in return for setting aside a garden downstairs as a public space, which is so public we get to lock it every night at eight. In this building we have technicians of various kinds who are foreign nationals and who technically can't work in the United States without government permission; the infamous green card. But their employer of record is some foreign subsidiary of ours, therefore no green card needed. But what about, let us say, invasion?"

Garrett, who'd been nodding along like a good son, was brought up short. "Invasion? You mean the Russians?"

"Certainly not. The Russians are the greatest false threat to this country since the Yellow Peril. I'm talking about physical attack on any part of this building. Let's say someone was foolish enough to try to rob our bank or one of our tenants, would the police or the FBI be the first line of defense? Absolutely not. A small part of our army is in this building, Garrett, with equipment as up-to-date as any garrison force on Earth. *Our* sentries would repel attack, and *our* insurance subsidiary would make good any unlikely loss that might be suffered in this building."

"So we're the government here," Garrett said.

"Exactly. The great task for you children in the next generation will be the new distribution of power, deciding which of the new barons will become the new kings."

"King Garrett the First," Garrett said, smiling. He saw himself swooping down a Norwegian glacial slope in an ermine robe and gold crown.

Another thin smile from Dad, who said, "The old terms won't come back, Garrett, only the old reality. If you'll always bear in mind that we are now on the threshold of the new feudalism, that today's CEO is every bit as powerful as yesterday's duke or marquis, you'll never be at a loss when business problems arise."

"I really appreciate all this, Dad," Garrett said, sounding hearty and sincere, looking puffy and false.

A shadow of doubt crossed Ritter's face, quickly obliterated. "That's why," he said, "family is so important. With the obsolescence of national patriotism, ultimate loyalty to the barons must reside in family connections, blood and marriage." He sighed. "Which is one of the many truths I can't seem to get across to your sister Elaine."

Garrett perked up a little. He actually liked Elaine, even though he thought she was sort of wimpy and silly. "How is the kid?" he asked. "Get over all that religion business?"

"We're working on it," Ritter said darkly. A

149

flick of cuff, and he looked at his watch. "Our freedom fighters will be assembling. Time for the pep-talk."

"Freedom fighters," Garrett echoed, and couldn't prevent a slight expression of repugnance to curl his lip. Coming through the Margrave offices to this meeting he had seen them lolling about in the various rooms, telling one another hair-raising anecdotes, nearly sixty hard-bitten mercenaries, merciless veterans of uncounted wars in Africa and Asia and Central America, assembled by Frank Ritter to spearhead the "liberation" movement that would repay that upstart South American dictator Pozos for becoming an annoyance. Garrett considered himself manly, God knows, but he was also civilized, and these "freedom fighters" were nothing but timber wolves in human shape. You could *smell* the testosterone. He said, "I just don't understand why you're assembling that bunch of thugs *here*."

"Security," his father told him. "In any of the more usual staging areas, Florida or Texas or wherever, there'd be too much possibility of information leakage. Most of these men are known to the Federal law-enforcement agencies. If they assemble somewhere, it becomes known. But *anybody* can assemble in New York City without being noticed, that's what this town is for. So they come here, and they'll spend the weekend in these offices and the dormitory, they'll study our maps and models of the terrain, and they'll organize their plan of attack. On Monday, two of our buses will take them out to our airfield on Long Island, where our plane will fly them south to Guerrera, refueling along the way at our resort island in the Caribbean."

This part was fun for Garrett, like playing Dungeons & Dragons back in college. "And when they get there?" he said.

"There's an anti-government underground already in place," Ritter said. "Pro-American, oddly enough, but all involved with land reform and that nonsense. With proper financing, they could probably take over on their own, but they're dirt poor. We negotiated with Mr. Avilez, the rebels' man in New York pleading their case at the UN, and we've arranged a trade of mineral rights for financing, but instead of financing we'll send our own army. The rebels will cooperate until Pozos is overthrown, and then you'll fly down and help them decide who runs the next government."

"So it's not another Bay of Pigs," Garrett said.

"Absolutely not," Ritter said. "We have the people, and we'll go on having the people until we *have* the people." He smiled, and looked around this pleasant room, symbol of his empire, and then frowned, staring at a half-closed door across the way.

"Dad? What is it?"

"I'm not sure." Ritter got to his feet and strode across the room to shove that door open and look in at a small book-lined research library, with refectory table and four heavy wooden chairs in the middle of the room. The door in the opposite

151

wall was closed. Ritter shook his head and turned away.

Garrett had followed him, and now said, "What's up?"

"Strangest thing," Ritter said. "For just a second, I thought I saw Elaine standing in this doorway."

Garrett looked past his father at the library. "Elaine? Down here?"

"Ridiculous, I know."

"You think— Do you think she could have heard what we were talking about? The invasion? Would she tell anybody?"

Ritter's mouth formed a mirthless grin. "She doesn't talk, remember? Besides, it was just a trick of the light, she's locked away upstairs. Come along, let's explain to our freedom fighters what they're fighting for."

22

"I think it's bad luck to whistle in an elevator," Dortmunder said.

Kelp said, "John, you think everything's bad luck." But he stopped whistling.

It was still Saturday afternoon, and so still possible to use the elevators without calling attention to oneself, and J.C. Taylor's office had already become confining. Wilbur Howey had gone into several minutes of frozen dazzled silence when he'd first come across the Scandinavian marriage

152

secrets book, but ever since, he'd been going through it with the avidity of a teenager with a book on hotrod customizing, popping and snapping in all directions and piping, "Say!" at intervals like a mantel clock. Meantime, Tiny insisted on reading aloud great long sections of the how-to-be-a-detective book with an attempted sarcastic delivery but stumbling along slowly and mispronouncing all the long words, while Stan over at the window produced running commentary on Saturday afternoon's traffic on Fifth Avenue and the nearby cross-streets, so when Kelp had pointed out that he hadn't yet seen the places they intended to burgle tonight Dortmunder had immediately said, "I'll show you."

"That's okay, John," Kelp had said. "It's the twenty-sixth floor, right? I can find it."

"I'll *show* you," Dortmunder had said.

To go from the seventh floor to the twenty-sixth floor, because of the wonders of modern technology, it was necessary to take two elevators. They were alone in the first elevator, going down to the lobby, during which ride Kelp, his musical side awakened by the piano in the Taylor office, had started whistling something that might have been "Malaguena" if it had all been in the same key. In the vaulted lobby, with a couple of security guards in pale blue uniforms and black gunbelts chatting casually together over by the closed newsstand, they walked around and took a 22–35 elevator, sharing it with an extremely scruffy four-man rock group arguing about the harmonics. "No," one of them kept saying, "it's *duh*-buh-buh, *duh*-buh-buh." Another one was saying, "That's not even in four-four," when the elevator stopped at twenty-six. "You want *duh*-buh, *duh*-buh," Kelp told them, as he and Dortmunder got off. The doors slid shut on the rock group's astounded and revolted faces.

Dortmunder said, "Andy, I don't think they were looking for your help."

"Well, they needed it," Kelp said. "This is it, huh?"

This was it. An office directory faced them from the wall opposite the bank of elevators. They stepped over and studied it:

ASIATIC ANTIQUE JEWELRY, INC.	2605
DEARBORN JADE IMPORTERS	2601
DUNCAN MAGIC	2608
KOBOL & KOBOL	2614
MACARAN IVORY CO.	2610
THREE CONTINENT IMPORT	2602

Dortmunder said, "They're all wholesalers and importers, so I guess they don't need a storefront down on the street."

"Duncan Magic," Kelp said. "I'll want to take a look in there, too."

"I figured you would," Dortmunder said.

They walked down the corridor together. The left wall was a cream-colored blank, but the right side was a series of plate-glass display windows and glass-paned shop doors, just as though these actually were storefronts down on the street. The first outfit they passed was Dearborn Jade Importers, with figurines and jewelry set out on glass shelves in the windows and the phrase "To The Trade Only" painted in gold letters on the glass door. Beyond them, Asiatic Antique Jewelry had similar displays and the identical statement on the door. Both shops were closed for the weekend.

At this end of the hall was the fire door marked EMERGENCY EXIT ONLY. "You open this door after six o'clock," Dortmunder said, pushing on it, "and you set off the alarm down in the basement."

They stepped through, the door automatically closed itself behind them, and on its other side was the concrete stairwell painted gray that they knew from upstairs. Pointing to a large metal plate mounted low on the wall next to the door, Dortmunder said, "That's the alarm system. Everything goes through there, the simple door alarms and the television monitors and everything else. That's what our friend Howey is supposed to neutralize."

"Weird little guy," Kelp said. "But if Tiny says he's good, he's good."

"Let's hope so," Dortmunder said, and went on, "The reason we picked *this* floor is because none of these companies use the closed-circuit television system, so when we do the bypass there won't be anything missing down in Security Control."

"Gee, I like this caper," Kelp said. "Even without the nun, you know?"

Dortmunder glanced up the stairway. "Yeah, well, the nun," he said.

Kelp said, warningly, "John, if you're thinking what I think you're thinking, don't think it. May would turn you into stew."

"I know that," Dortmunder said. "Believe me I do. I wonder how good Howey is at climbing stairs."

"Well, he'll have all night to get there," Kelp said. "Let's go look at the rest of these places. Where's that magic store?"

"Down the other way, past the elevators."

They went through the fire door again and back down the hall. Past the elevators were more display windows, just on the one side, stretching all the way down to the end. Porcelain, jade, unmounted opals, semiprecious stones, ivory. Figurines, chess sets, rings and bracelets and necklaces of beaten gold with inlaid stones. The windows of Duncan Magic, midway along, with their bright red plastic balls and blue intertwined triangles and multi-colored squares of cloth and shiny lacquered boxes, with their top hats and wands in gleaming black and their false faces featuring eyeless grinning red Satans, were a kind of vulgar party-crasher amid all this restrained gaudiness of wealth.

"Very nice," Kelp said. "*Very* nice." But he was standing in front of Duncan Magic when he said it, looking at the bouquets of plastic flowers and the shiny chrome rings. This was the only place on twenty-six open on Saturday afternoon; inside, fathers and sons leaned on the counters to watch the salesman/magicians manipulate the tricks. Kelp looked as though he wanted to join them.

Dortmunder said, "Okay? You seen everything now?"

"Do you suppose these things come with instructions?" Kelp asked. "So you can see how it's done?"

"Probably so," Dortmunder said. "Otherwise, who'd buy it?"

"Yeah, that's right." Kelp nodded at the Satans, who grinned back. "See you later," he said.

When they got back to the elevators, Dortmunder said, "Let's walk down."

"Walk? We'll do enough of that tonight."

"We ought to check the territory," Dortmunder pointed out, "see is there anything along the way might be trouble."

"What's gonna be along the way?" Kelp asked. "That's the fire stairs, by law they got to keep them clear and open."

"Just to see," Dortmunder said.

"You saw this part of it," Kelp reminded him. "That's what it'll all look like."

Dortmunder shook his head. "Andy," he said, "how much of a hurry are you in to get back to that office down there?"

Kelp thought about that. "Maybe we oughta check the stairwell," he said.

"Good thinking," said Dortmunder.

So they walked down eighteen flights of stairs—there was no thirteenth floor, a thing hardheaded

New York City real estate developers do to propi-
tiate some very old gods indeed—and Kelp had
been correct. Every landing looked like every other
landing, the entire stairwell being empty and clear.
In the wall at each floor was another of those low
metal wall panels concealing the security systems.
And, for the last five flights, they were hearing
somebody whistle, "I Want a Girl Just Like the
Girl Who Married Dear Old Dad." Dortmunder
said, "It has to be, you know. It couldn't be
anybody else."

"I know," Kelp said.

And it was. When they reached the seventh-
floor landing, there was Wilbur Howey himself,
seated cross-legged tailor fashion on the floor. He
had removed the metal plate over the security
system wiring and was now poking around in the
green and yellow and red and black spaghetti inside with a screwdriver and a line tester. Various
other tools were spread out around him on the
floor. He was so absorbed in his work that he
didn't notice Dortmunder and Kelp's arrival until
Dortmunder said, "Howey? What if somebody
sees you?"

"Whoop!" cried Howey, and yanked both hands
out of the panel. Blinking up at Dortmunder, he
said, "Say, there, partner, don't sneak up on me
like that! You don't want to startle a fellow when
he's in there with the burglar alarms. What if my
hand slipped? What if I made a little signal downstairs in Security?"

Dortmunder said, "What if somebody comes along and sees you here?"

Howey grinned and winked and snapped off a salute with the line tester. "Howdy, sir!" he piped. "Howdy, ma'am! Just doing the maintenance here, you know, we never sleep, no sirree!"

Kelp said, "John, he has to clear this door before six o'clock, so we can get *into* the stairwell later tonight."

Dortmunder, not wanting to admit he hadn't thought of that, said, "I just wanted to know did he have a cover story, that's all."

"Say, you think I'm green?" Howey demanded.

"No, no," Dortmunder said. Then, vague memories of British Navy movies unreeling in the back of his mind, "Carry on," he said, and reached for the doorknob.

"Whoops!" cried Howey. "Don't touch that! Say, pal, just hold it there, will you, give me a minute here." He poked deep inside the panel with a screwdriver, while Dortmunder gave the top of his head an unfriendly look, then finally said, "Okay, pal, you can open it now."

"Thanks a bunch," Dortmunder said, and he and Kelp went through and down the corridor to Super Star Music, etc. Using the key Taylor had given him, Dortmunder locked the door, which he discovered when he tried to open it. "I guess Howey left it unlocked," he said, clenching his teeth.

"So he could get back in," Kelp suggested.

"That must be it." Dortmunder unlocked the

159

door and they went into the outer office, where the phone on the receptionist's desk reminded him of an obligation. "Taylor said not to use the phone," he said, "but this is just a local call."

"And it's still kind of business hours," Kelp said, "lots of offices still open on Saturday afternoon."

"I promised May I'd call," Dortmunder explained, reaching for the phone. But when he dialed, there wasn't any answer.

23

May stood across the street from the battered old warehouse building. Three stories high, of crumbling brick with the mortar flaking out, it had rows of small-paned windows across the front, all of them black with dust, their wooden frames still showing some remnant of an ancient coat of green paint. No lights showed behind those windows, no plants, no curtains, no movement.

But this was definitely the address, in an old corner of Brooklyn that looked as though civilization had been tried here, had failed, and had moved on, leaving behind hulks that were less interesting than but just as dead as any Aztec ruin in the jungles of Mexico. In the six-block walk from the subway, May had seen more cats than people, and none of them, animal or human, had seemed particularly well fed. And now, in front of the warehouse itself, for just a second, her resolve faltered. What hope could there be inside any building that looked like that?

Still, she'd come this far. Taking a deep breath, May reached into her purse for a cigarette, found none, remembered, made a face, and got annoyed at herself. This annoyance carried her across the potholed street, where she had a choice between a lumpy green door in the middle of the facade or a trash-strewn blacktopped driveway running down the side of the building to a loading dock. She turned toward the door, and found thumbtacked to it a 5×7 card still bearing the faded words in once-red magic marker: TIPTOP A-1 CHOICE FOODS—OFFICE. Going up the two flaking slate steps, she pushed open this door, which contained three visible locks, and stepped inside.

Now she found herself in a small square room with gray linoleum on the floor and paneled walls, each sheet of paneling different, presenting an anthology of poor imitations of various woods; cedar, walnut, oak, and something unidentifiable and silver. There was absolutely no furniture in this space, though a lot of cigarette butts and scraps of paper on the floor suggested occasional occupancy and a three-year-out-of-date calendar on one wall was sort of decorative, showing an illustration of boys at a swimming hole over some other August.

A small window in the opposite wall was covered by a clear plastic panel with round holes in it to permit air or conversation to get through. May went over there and looked through into an even smaller space, crammed with filing cabinets and a

161

small wooden table, at which sat a small wrinkle-faced woman in a black sweater, gold necklace chains and earrings and a bright red wig. She was talking intently on the phone, and when she saw May she made a disgusted face and said, "Hold on, Helen." Shaking her head at May, she called, "Not hiring!"

May put her mouth close to a couple of the airholes and said, slowly and distinctly, "Mr. Chepkoff, please."

This irritated the woman even more. "Who's he?" she yelled. Before May could answer, she said into her phone again, "Hold on, Helen."

"He's the owner here," May said, and took the Civil Court document out of her purse to read aloud what it said: "Otto Chepkoff, Tiptop A-One Choice Foods, two seven three dash one four Scunge Avenue, Brooklyn, one one six six six."

Somehow, the woman's wig managed to get even more red, as she shouted, "You serving papers?"

"No, no," May said, and turned the document around to press it against the plastic so the woman could read it. "*We* were served," she said. "That's what I'm here about."

"Oh, you want to *pay*," the woman said, leaping to another wrong conclusion. Saying into the phone once more, "Hold on, Helen," then switching it to her other hand, she waved largely off toward her left, shouting, "Go round the loading dock!"

"Is Mr. Chepkoff there?"

"Hold on, Helen," the woman said, and waved again. "Just go round there, go round there, he's there, just go round!"

"Thank you," May said. Putting the document away in her bag, she turned toward the door as the woman said into the phone, "Helen, where were we? Helen? Helen?" Glaring at May, she yelled, "She hung up!"

"So would I," May told her, and left the office and walked around the front of the building and down the filthy blacktop drive to where dog-eared concrete steps led up to one end of the loading dock. Beyond it, through a large wide opening, was a dim storage space filled with cardboard cartons in great piles and the sounds of men shouting. May went in there and waited for her eyes to accustom themselves to the gloom.

Most of the space, and most of the yelling, was off to her left. Looking down that way, she saw aisles formed by great stacks of boxes and mounds of sacks, and in one of the aisles two men were loading crates onto a large wooden cart while a man with a clipboard yelled at a man in a knee-length white lab coat, who yelled just as forcefully back.

May walked down there to join the scene, though at first no one noticed her, and even up close she couldn't figure out what the yelling was about. The two chunky men loading the crates, who had been ignoring the argument, ignored May as well, while the arguers only had eyes for each other. The clipboard man was big and burly, with a dead cigar in his teeth and a black wool cap pulled down to his eyebrows and a way of slashing the air with his clipboard that suggested he was on the verge of some truly awesome violence. The man in the long white (very dirty) lab coat was small and narrow and older, with a pinched-in gray face and a russet-colored Kennedy-style wig that was, if possible, even more astonishing than the office woman's red monstrosity. Inside his white coat he was wearing a dark three-piece suit and white shirt and black tie. He was the one who finally noticed May standing there, and his reaction was to point first at the clipboard man and bellow, "SHUT UP!" (astonishingly, the astonished clipboard man shut up) then point at May and bellow, "NOT HIRING!"

"I wouldn't work for you," May told him, "for a million dollars an hour."

The clipboard man gave her a surprised look. "Then you're crazy," he said. "For a million dollars an hour, you could put up with certain things."

"Not rudeness," May said. "I have an aversion to rudeness."

The white-coated man said, "That's why you walk into a private conversation uninvited? That's why you eavesdrop on a business discussion? That's why you trespass on private property?"

May looked at him. "I bet you're Mr. Chepkoff," she said.

"He's out today," the white-coated man said, and the two crate-loaders stopped to give a sardonic laugh. The white-coated man glared at them:

164

"This is a holiday? This is a vacation? Here I am, I'm at the beach, I didn't know it, I didn't bring my suntan lotion?" The crate-loaders gave each other long-suffering looks and went back to their work, and the white-coated man glared at May instead. "So he's out," he said. "So who should I tell him popped in unannounced and without an appointment, to tell us all about her aversion to rudeness?"

Not trusting herself to speak, May took the Civil Court paper from her pocket and extended it toward Chepkoff—for it was indeed he—who recoiled like a vampire seeing a cross. "Get her away!" he shouted. "Get her away!"

"This isn't a summons," May told him, tired of the whole business. "Or, it is, but it isn't for you. It's the one you served on John Dortmunder." She opened it and held it out for him to read. "See?"

He squinted. He took heavy black-rimmed glasses out of his lab coat and put them on and leaned forward and squinted again. "Ah," he said. Stepping back, he put the glasses away and said, "So you'll come into my office."

The clipboard man, bristling, said, "Wait a minute. What about—"

Chepkoff rounded on him: "What *about?*" he yelled, outraged. "What about *what?* Look at your order form! You paid for *shit!* You're *getting* shit!" And he spun around, in a swirl of white coattail, and stomped away, while the clipboard man gaped after him, dead cigar sagging down onto his chin.

Assuming she was to follow, May followed, and Chepkoff led her to an open space in the middle of the warehouse, the hub of all the aisles, where a small glass room had been constructed, containing a cramped but functioning office. Chepkoff yanked open the glass door to this cubicle, gestured impatiently for May to precede him in, followed her, slammed the glass door with a sound one decibel below total destruction, and said, quietly for him, "So you've got my three hundred dollars."

"No, Mr. Chepkoff, I—"

"*No?*" Chepkoff's eyes bulged, as though he were being strangled. "*Noooo???* What are you *doing* here?"

"I thought we could talk about the—"

"Talk? Listen, whoever, Mrs. Dortmunder, whoever you are, there's an expression, I want to know do you know this expression, you'll tell me if you've ever heard an expression along the lines of this expression, I'm gonna tell it to you right now, are you listening?" He stared. "Well?"

"I'm listening," May said.

"Good." Chepkoff opened his mouth wide and enunciated with great elaboration, at the same time writing the letters in the air with the first finger of his right hand. "Mon-ney," he said, and paused, and said, "talks. You got it? You heard this somewhere?"

The clipboard man, having followed, now started pounding on the glass door out there, waving his clipboard and yelling. May said, "Mr. Chep—"

"*You* don't talk," Chepkoff told her. "*I* don't

166

talk. John *Dort*munder doesn't talk. This asshole here"—with a gesture at the furious clipboard man —"doesn't talk. *Money* talks."

"You don't understand the business John's in," May said. "He takes a—"

"I know the business this John is in," Chepkoff said, "but do you know the business *I'm* in?"

"Mr. Chep—"

"Just look, just take a look," Chepkoff invited, waving his arms at the warehouse all around them. "You see what we got out there?"

"Food," May said. "But what I'm—"

"Details," Chepkoff insisted. "Not just food, but *what* food? Let me tell you what I got out there, let me just give you a rundown on this. Let's have a meeting of minds here."

"You don't have to—"

But he was going on, unstoppable: "What I got in this building, lady, whoever you are, let me tell you what I got in my *business*, what with what I make my *living*." While the clipboard man continued to shout and yell and bang on the glass outside, Chepkoff pointed this way and that at the merchandise, saying, "I'll tell you what I got. I got dented canned goods. I got week-old bread. I got frozen foods that thawed in the train, packager overruns, hijacked toilet paper, grade Z vegetables, meat they didn't want at the orphanage, and dairy goods with doctored dates. That's what I *got* here, you follow me?"

"Mr. Chep—"

Leaning closer to May, his eyes as mad as

Raskolnikov's, Chepkoff said, "Lady, I work with a margin narrow enough to slit your wrist. Are you getting the *sense* of this? I do not give three hundred dollars to somebody, he should *maybe* bring me some salable merchandise. I get delivery, or I get—" And abruptly he spun around and screamed through the glass at the clipboard man, *"Shaddap shaddap shaddap!"*

The clipboard man didn't shaddap. He yelled instead something about not accepting delivery, and Chepkoff yelled something back, and May stepped a bit closer to the desk. Examples of various kinds of forms on the desk she put in her purse, then stepped closer to Chepkoff and politely said, "Excuse me."

Chepkoff paid no attention. He and the clipboard man were back at it full-tilt by now, hampered not at all by the sheet of glass between them. "Excuse me," May said again, and when Chepkoff still ignored her she kicked him in the ankle.

He jumped, spun around, stared at her in astonishment, stared at his ankle, stared at her. "You—" he said. He was overcome with horror. "You— You touched my body!"

"I'll wash my shoe later," she assured him. "I'm trying to leave now, you see, and you're blocking the door." She stepped around him—he continued to stare, not believing it—and opened the door. The clipboard man was also silent, trying to figure out what was going on. May stepped through the doorway, looked back at Chepkoff, and said, "I was hoping we could have a civilized discussion, but no. John should never have had dealings with you." To the clipboard man she said, "Neither should you." And she walked away toward the loading dock, leaving a lengthening silence in the background.

As she passed the crate-loaders, one of them grinned and winked and handed her a can of chicken gumbo soup, but the ends of it were a little bulged so when she got to the street she threw it away.

24

Dortmunder smelled mayonnaise. Opening his eyes, he saw the small jar not far from his nose and thought: Why is there a bottle of mayonnaise in bed? "May—" he said, and sat up, and his back gave a terrible twinge of pain as he realized he wasn't in bed after all, he was asleep on a desk under the flat white glare of a fluorescent ceiling fixture. Sleeping on a desk, seated on a chair, slumped forward, next to a bottle of mayonnaise.

J.C. Taylor. Receptionist's desk. Avalon State Bank Tower. Burglary of an entire floor. Rescue of Sister Mary Grace. Got it.

Dortmunder had been sitting here, at J.C. Taylor's receptionist desk, waiting for midnight. He remembered closing his eyes because the light was so strong, and then there was a fuzziness, and then the smell of mayonnaise, and now here he was again, and the small digital clock on J.C. Taylor's desk said 2:11. And where the hell was everybody else? Gone off to pull the caper without him?

No. Across the way, seated on the floor, Coors cap pulled forward over his eyes, asleep with his mouth open in a revolting way, was Wilbur Howey, a copy of *Scandinavian Marriage Secrets* open facedown on his lap. And the sound from the other room that was like a Winnebago's tanks being emptied must be somebody snoring.

2:11. In fact, 2:12 already. Time to get going. Dortmunder stood up, and immediately sat down again, because his back seemed to have fused into some position he'd never known before. "Oh," he said. "Oh, boy." He rocked slowly back and forth, lifting first this shoulder, and then that, and when the clock reached 2:14 he tried again. This time he made it to his feet, though he did keep some fingertips in contact with the desktop just to be on the safe side. "Howey," he said, rasping, then cleared his throat and said, "Howey," and the little man jerked in his sleep like a dog dreaming, moving his legs so that the book fell off his lap onto the floor and closed.

"Where the hell is everybody?" Dortmunder demanded. For answer, Howey closed his mouth and made smacking sounds.

Limping a bit, Dortmunder made his way around the desk and across the office and on into the next room, which looked like the aftermath of a reform school reunion. Tiny Bulcher, the snorer, lay sprawled atop the desk, arms outflung and cheek against the green desk blotter, massive body dwarfing the swivel chair. Andy Kelp slept twisted like a vine through the metal folding chair in front of the piano, while Stan Murch had dragged the old brown leather chair over to the window and was draped unconscious on it like an abandoned set of overalls. Half-sandwiches and empty yogurt containers and soda cans were scattered everywhere.

"Couldn't *anybody* stay awake?" Dortmunder demanded of the room at large, and Andy Kelp shifted on the folding chair, his elbow brushing the piano and producing a quote from *Wozzeck*, which in turn made Tiny rumble and change position, knocking a phone book onto the floor. Stan Murch sat up straight, clutching for a non-existent steering wheel, crying, "I'm awake, I'm awake! Stay in your own lane!" Kelp then jolted up, wide-eyed and glassy-eyed, attempting to stand without disentangling himself from the folding chair, which meant he toppled over into the piano—excerpt from Bartok's *Mikrokosmos*—before tumbling to the floor. All of this racket roused Tiny, who reared up like a walrus, flinging his arms wide, clearing the desk of everything that had been on it, before lunging away in astonishment, causing the swivel chair to over-balance and tip him backwards onto the floor, huge thick legs waving in air. Meantime Stan, desperately trying to make a left turn, hurtled out of the leather chair and into the side of the desk, just under where a

171

lot of staplers and pens and desk calendars and memo pads were falling.

There then followed a brief silence, with dust motes. Dortmunder looked around. "Are you finished now?" he asked.

"Say!" shouted Howey from the other room, followed by a crash that was probably a full rack of metal shelves going over, with several thousand books.

"Hand-picked," Dortmunder commented to himself. He looked at his own right hand with dislike. "Hand-picked," he repeated.

25

Dortmunder hunkered down next to Howey and said, "You're sure you know this stuff."

"I'm sure," Howey said. It was nearly three in the morning, they were all awake now, they'd all visited the men's room, they'd all washed their faces and slicked their hair, the worst of the chaos in Taylor's office had been cleaned up, and now here they were on the landing up on twenty-six, waiting for Howey to make it possible to open the fire door.

Dortmunder said, "It isn't I doubt you or anything."

"Good," Howey said. He had seated himself on the floor in front of the panel concealing the alarm systems, his tools in a magic circle around him as he removed first the top left screw from the panel, and then the bottom right, dropping both into his shirt pocket. Tiny and Stan and Kelp sat on the steps watching, sometimes yawning.

Dortmunder said, "It's just there's a lot more security on this floor than down on seven."

"I know," Howey said. He loosened the bottom left screw but not all the way.

Dortmunder said, "I mean, this is a pretty critical moment right here."

"Sure is," Howey said. Tugging the top left corner of the panel away from the wall, he inserted the orange plastic handle of a screwdriver in the space and slid it down as close to the bottom of the panel as possible, forcing the top left corner to bend farther away from the wall.

Dortmunder said, "This'd be a hell of a time to have something go wrong."

Howey took a deep breath and turned away from his work. "Say, listen, pal," he said. "Don't I hear your mother calling?"

"Huh?" Dortmunder actually listened for a second, before giving Howey a very squinty look. "Meaning what?" he demanded.

Howey gestured a thumb over his shoulder at the rest of the crew, saying, "You know, you ought to be over there with the peanut gallery."

Dortmunder pointed at the orange-handled screwdriver stuck partway behind the panel. "Just as an example," he said, "'Just to make me more easy in my mind, what's *that* for?"

"Well, then, I'll tell you," Howey said, taking a screw out of his shirt pocket. Reaching past the top left corner of the panel, he slipped the screw back into its hole. Tightening it with another screwdriver, he said, "You see, what the story is here, the way this system is set up, according to those diagrams you got, if anybody takes both of these top screws out after six P.M., that automatically all by itself sets off an alarm down in Security. You see what I mean?"

"Oh," Dortmunder said. "So they'll know if somebody's tampering."

"Say, by golly, you do catch on right away," Howey said. "So what I'm doing here . . ." He now finished removing the bottom left screw, loosened the top right screw just barely one turn, and pivoted the whole panel around on that screw till it cleared the space behind it. Then he tightened the top right screw again, and the panel stayed where it was, out of the way. *"That's* what I'm doing," he said.

"That's pretty good," Dortmunder said, admiring it.

Howey grinned and nodded, then said, "Now, listen, I know you're the boss of this outfit and all that, but while I'm down here, you know what I mean? Amscray."

From over on the stairs, Tiny said, "Dortmunder, come over here. I can't see through you what he's doing."

Well, this actually was a very different and more reliable-seeming Howey than they'd been dealing with before. He'd left that marriage secrets book behind without even a murmur, he'd climbed the eighteen flights of stairs without a fuss, and he was getting down to work here with apparent competence and no fooling around. Deciding it would be safe enough at this point to delegate responsibility, Dortmunder said, "Okay, then, you're on your own," and went over to sit with the others and watch Howey go to work.

This clearly was a more complicated setup than the one down on seven. Inside the panel, rows of printed circuits on thick board—soldered road-maps on one side, color-coded spaghetti of wires on the other—were packed in together in vertical lines like a robot's library. Howey's fingers and narrow-nosed tools prowled carefully among it all, touching a wire here, a connection there, a plastic-enclosed chip somewhere else. Poking delicately into the innards, he altered some links, severed others, and made new connections with the help of wire of his own plus a blue-gray sticky stuff that looked like chewing gum or Playdoh. From time to time, he used a line tester, and it always lit up.

It took awhile, even without Dortmunder's help. After ten minutes or so, Howey began to make clucking sounds of annoyance and grunts of frustration every time the line tester was used and again came up positive. "Say, you're a cutey, ain'tcha?" he was heard to mutter at one point. But finally he pushed himself back from the panel, turned to the others, and said, "Another Wilbur Howey special, gents. It's all yours."

Everybody else stood up and stretched, while Dortmunder said, "You're positive."

Still seated on the floor amid his tools, Howey gave Dortmunder an exasperated look, saying, "Say, do stars fall on Alabama? Go ahead and open it."

"Sure," Tiny said, and went over to the fire door, but Dortmunder noticed that Howey kept alertly staring into the alarm system while Tiny pulled it open, and it wasn't till the door was ajar that Howey gave a great big smile of satisfaction— and relief—and busied himself putting his tools away.

First Tiny, then Kelp, then Stan, then Dortmunder, and finally Howey with his full tool kit came through the fire door, Howey letting it close gently behind them. Just on their right were the display windows of Asiatic Antique Jewelry. The lights in there were off, but the corridor lights still burned, and in their illumination the colored jewels gleamed, each clutched in a tiny fist of silver or gold. "I call that beautiful," Tiny said.

They walked to Asiatic Antique's entrance and Howey said, "You want me to open this one?"

"*I'll* take care of that," Tiny said, approaching the door. "Anticipation," he said, biting down on the word as though it were an apple. "It's always been tough for me to wait. When I was very young, all the time, two-three weeks before Christmas, I'd go downtown and shoplift some toys." Lifting his right foot, he kicked the door open.

26

When things first started to go wrong at the nuclear plant in Pennsylvania called Three Mile Island in March of 1979, various dials and gauges reported the fact, but nobody would believe them. Sometimes dials and gauges break down, and then people go through a lot of trouble and difficulty, and at the end it turns out it was just another dial or gauge breaking down. When you come along with your clipboard every day, and the dials and gauges always stay in the same range, then that's what you're used to, and what you expect to see. So when the Three Mile Island dials and gauges began to say that something was wrong, people tapped the glass fronts of the dials and gauges with their fingernails and waited to see what happened, and decided that once again the only thing that was wrong was the dials and gauges. After all, nothing seriously wrong had ever happened before.

When things started to go wrong at the chemical plant in Bhopal, India, in January of 1985, various dials and gauges reported the fact, but nobody would believe them. Sometimes dials and gauges break down, and then people go through a lot of trouble and difficulty, and at the end it turns out it was just another dial or gauge breaking down. When you come along with your clipboard every day, and the dials and gauges always stay in the same range, then that's what you're used to, and what you expect to see. So when the Bhopal chemical plant dials and gauges began to say that something was wrong, people tapped the glass fronts of the dials and gauges with their fingernails and waited to see what happened, and decided that once again the only thing that was wrong was the dials and gauges. After all, nothing seriously wrong had ever happened before.

The Avalon State Bank Tower, in addition to stretching seventy-six stories into the sky, also extended four stories down into the ground, nestling itself into a sliced-out pocket in the bedrock of Manhattan Island. The bottom two floors were all machinery and metal ladders, like the bowels of a great ocean-going passenger liner—which in many ways is what a skyscraper is, massive and self-contained and compartmented, except that the skyscraper is always moored in the same place, and of course it's standing on end, and come to think of it skyscrapers don't float, and maybe they aren't anything like each other at all. Forget the whole thing.

The third story up from bedrock was storage, including fireproof and earthquake-proof and presumably nuclear-destruction-proof warehousing of files and documents and negotiable paper and certain embarrassing videotapes. Also on that floor were firefighting and mob-fighting equipment and three entire rooms of extra desks. And the level just below the street was Security.

Security, in addition to locker and shower rooms, gym, dormitory, several offices and three detention cells, also included a large General Operations Room in which there was a background hum all the time and the walls were lined with closed-circuit TV monitors and banks of red lights (none of them glowing) and all sorts of dials and gauges. Half a dozen men were on duty in GenOps through the night, dressed in the livery of Frank Ritter's service, being light blue uniforms with "Global Security Service" curled around a globe on their shoulder patches. These men sat at long tables covered with more dials and gauges, with telephones and intercoms and radios ready to hand, and at 3:04 on this Sunday morning in spring one of these men frowned down at an indicator on the table in front of him, and said, "Huh?"

It had been quiet for some time in GenOps, so now most of the other men in the room glanced over at the first man, and one of them said, "What's up?"

"I got me a blip," said the first one. He frowned more and more deeply at that indicator, a small square window with a small circular rod within, painted red on one side and green on the other. Always until now, except for two brief periods when the system had been undergoing intensive tests, the green side of that rod had faced up. But now, since twenty-seven flights up a man named Wilbur Howey had just slightly misread a schematic and didn't realize that the removal of *either* top screw from the wallplate over the security feed would trigger a reaction down in Security, that circular rod had just flipped over, like a tiny slot machine, and now showed red.

Nobody else in the room got really what you could call excited; nobody came over to look at this blip. After all, nothing had ever gone really wrong in this building, and all anomalies had eventually had their explanation. One of the guys across the room said, "What kind of blip?"

"Just a—" The man with the blip tapped the glass with his fingernail, but the rod remained red side up. "Just one little indicator here," he said, and looked up at the walls full of indicators. Nothing wrong on any of them. "Something up on twenty-six," he said, where at that moment Wilbur Howey had paused in his work to explain what he was doing to Dortmunder, thus delaying things and keeping that disturbing little indicator red.

One of the other men frowned at all the television monitors. When you have seventy-four floors to think about, you aren't necessarily going to remember every detail of which floors do and which floors do not employ the closed-circuit TV scanning option. "I don't see anything moving," this man said.

Another man said, "You want to call the lobby, send somebody up to look?"

The first man shook his head at the red indicator. Wilbur Howey, finally having been left alone by Dortmunder, reinserted the missing screw as the man reached out and tapped the glass again with the same fingernail, and the rod flipped back

180

to green. "There it is," the security man said. "It's okay now."

"Keep an eye on it," one of the other men suggested. "If it does it again, leave a note for Maintenance on Monday."

The first man tapped the glass. The indicator stayed green, and upstairs Tiny Bulcher kicked open the door to Asiatic Antiques. "No problem now," the security man said. "Everything's fine."

27

On the sixtieth floor, Howey wanted to stop *again*. "We've only got the weekend, you know," Dortmunder told him, disgusted.

Howey looked like a man full of snappy answers, of which he would unburden himself once he caught his breath. Meantime, he sat on the top step at the sixtieth floor landing, fanning his blotchy red-and-white face with his Coors cap, glancing bright-eyed but speechless up at Dortmunder from time to time, and breathing like an obscene phone caller in a hurry. Dortmunder's watch, which was always a few minutes either fast or slow, read around ten minutes to four. It had been his plan to get up to the top of the tower, rescue Sister Mary Grace, and bring her back with him to J.C. Taylor's office by six, before anybody was up and about, but Howey was slowing things considerably. Almost four in the morning, and they still had another fourteen flights ahead of them just to reach the doors Howey was supposed to open so Dortmunder could *begin*. "Any time you're ready," Dortmunder said. Of course, he didn't want the fella to become totally incapacitated, or dead, or anything of a *real* problem nature like that, but on the other hand there was a certain sense of urgency here that wasn't being aided by a member of the string who has to sit down and take it easy every couple minutes.

"Say," Howey said, but that was it; he went back to breathing.

"Write me a note," Dortmunder suggested. "Take a vow of silence."

"By golly," Howey said, and quit again to breathe. Then he slapped his Coors cap on his head, took a *deep* breath, grabbed the railing with both hands preparatory to pulling himself to his feet, and said, "Say . . . you couldn't find a . . . nun . . . in a dungeon, could ya?"

"Tower," Dortmunder said unsympathetically. "That's all I've got."

"Whoosh," said Howey, and heaved his butt up off the metal stair. On his feet, he held the railing and gazed up the endless stairwell, Adam's apple bobbing in a scrawny throat that looked like a beer can somebody had squeezed with his hand. "I never was a mountain climber," he announced. "Wimmin, that's all *I* ever wanted to climb."

"Think how easy it'll be on the way down," Dortmunder told him.

"Sixteen times . . . how many floors? Seven

to seventy-four, but no thirteen, that's, uh, uhhh . . ."

Dortmunder said, "Can you do math and climb stairs at the same time?"

"Maybe," Howey said, and at last started off, trudging up the steps, bony hand gripping the metal rail. Dortmunder hefted Howey's toolbag—Howey couldn't carry it himself, of course—and followed.

Fourteen flights ensued—very, very slowly. Dortmunder kept switching the toolbag from hand to hand. Occasionally, Howey would wheeze out a "Say," or a "Whooey," and once he stopped entirely in the middle of a flight to announce, "One thousand and fifty-six!"

Dortmunder, just changing hands with the toolbag, collided with Howey's back, lost his balance, did not fall down a flight of stairs, and said, "Now what?"

"That's how many steps!" Howey said, turning around, giving Dortmunder a triumphant look, which then faded to a frown as he said, "I think it is, anyway. Let's see . . ."

"Walk," Dortmunder told him.

Howey turned and walked, one step up at a time, planting his feet solidly like a man in magnetic boots crossing a metal ceiling, and without further incident the two travelers corkscrewed on up the unchanging stairwell to the seventy-fourth floor, where Howey gasped, looked at the gate closing off the top two floors, pointed at it, gasped, shook his head in contempt, panted awhile, pointed at the gate again, and said, "Two minutes. Open it right up."

"Fine," Dortmunder said. "And in three minutes you'll have a whole lot of new friends with guns in their hands." He pointed at the usual security panel low beside the hall door. "We go through there."

Howey frowned at the gate. "Why not this way? Straight up the stairs."

Dortmunder put Howey's toolbag down by the security panel and said, "Didn't you look at the specs? From here on up, it's a different security system. You can't touch it at all."

"Is that so, now?" Howey seemed quite pleased by this piece of news. Scratching his grizzled jaw with his knuckles, gazing at the gate with new respect, he said, "They must really like that little nun up there, you think so?"

"They want to keep her anyway," Dortmunder said. His watch said around quarter to five. "Come on, Wilbur," he said.

The use of the first name was apparently just the personal touch that was needed; with no further ado, Howey assumed his cross-legged seated position in front of the security panel, did the maneuver with the screws—

("Goddamn!" said the same fellow down in security in the basement, "there goes another one!" He bunked the glass with a knuckle, and the rod flipped back from red to green. "No, it's okay," he said. "Goddamn things.")

—and poked briefly inside among the wiring

184

and control sheets, whistling, "Daisy, Daisy, Give Me Your Answer, Do," between his teeth. "Hardly a thing up here," he commented at one point. "No security at all."

Dortmunder knew that to be true, from the ledger books Sister Mary Grace had smuggled out. The engineering and architectural firms on this floor used only simple-level alarms on their main entrances, the law firm used a little heat-activated and voice-activated stuff in a couple of rooms, and the Margrave Corporation didn't use any of the building's security at all. There was also, according to the plans, another staircase up to seventy-six from Margrave; that's the way Dortmunder would go, once Howey cleared the way.

It was hard to tell exactly what Margrave itself was, except it was a corporation, it had offices, and it was tied in with other of Frank Ritter's holdings. But whatever it might be, the way Dortmunder had things figured, he wasn't likely to run into anybody doing business inside there at five in the morning, and once within Margrave it shouldn't be impossible to make his way up to where the nun was being held. Generally speaking, Dortmunder thought of himself as a kind of utility infielder in the smash-and-grab line, not a specialist like Wilbur Howey but someone who could go past ordinary locks and security devices without too much trouble. So when Howey sat back on the floor, smiling with the satisfaction of a craftsman at the height of his powers—seventy-fourth floor, after all—and said, "She's all yours,"

Dortmunder said, "That's fine, Wilbur. Close the panel up again so it doesn't look like anybody's come through, then go on back down. I'll take it from here."

Howey said, "Sure you don't want me to do the office door?"

"I've seen the specs," Dortmunder assured him, opening the fire door to the hall (nothing went wrong down in Security's basement). "That Margrave door's a breeze. It'll open all by itself when it sees me coming." Touching his temple in a little half-salute of farewell to Howey, saying, "See you in a little while with Sister Mary Grace," Dortmunder stepped through to the hall, letting the fire door ease itself closed behind him. Almost whistling—like Howey—he went around the corner to Margrave.

Where the office door opened itself for him and a burly man in camouflage gear, holding a Russian AK-47 assault rifle casually in his right hand, looked out at Dortmunder and said, in exasperation, "Another straggler. Come along, fellow."

"Um," said Dortmunder.

"Come on, come on," the burly man said, making shooing motions with the rifle as though it were a broom, sweeping Dortmunder in. "We're late as it is," he said.

"Oh," Dortmunder said. "Uh huh." He walked into Margrave.

28

The trouble with these ruthless-killer types, Virgil Pickens thought as he led the final straggler down the halls of Margrave to the assembly room, is they're not so good on discipline. Here's this fellow wandering around the public corridors when he's supposed to be learning the tools of his trade.

The error, made by The People Upstairs, was that all the political orientation lectures had been done first, and for people like this crowd the politics and the social situations are utterly without interest. All they want to know is, what does our side look like, what does the other side look like, and what do I kill them with? We're to that part now, Virgil Pickens thought, but the boys are already turned off.

Well, it was his job to turn them back on. Walking into the assembly room, a brightly lit small theater with seating for about a hundred in rows of red plush movie-house seats (but no tilt to the floor) all facing a small stage with a movie screen mounted on the rear wall, Pickens saw that less than half the troops were in conversation, in small clusters in the aisles, and those conversations stopped the instant he appeared, the talkers turning hooded, watchful, unfriendly eyes in Pickens' direction, he representing The People Upstairs. The rest of the boys meanwhile sat around singly or in pairs, silent, brooding at the blank movie screen, smoking from cigarettes held cupped in their palms, scratching their old tattoos, and looking mutinous. They were all just recently up and had their breakfasts, and were still sleepy and feeling mean. These, as Pickens well knew, were not folks to bore; these were folks to react to boredom by making a little excitement in the area.

"Grab a pew," Pickens told the straggler—a deceptively mild-looking fellow—and headed for the stage, saying loudly, "Find your seats, gents, we're gonna talk about death and destruction."

A low general growl answered him, probably composed of equal parts appreciation and irritation. Pickens went up the four steps to the stage and over to the card table standing in front of the movie screen. Something lumpy on the table was covered with a red-white-and-blue flag composed of various triangles and stars. Standing behind the table, facing the crowd, Pickens held the AK-47 aloft, gripping it just forward of the magazine—if the screen behind him had been red, he'd have looked *exactly* like a Bolshevik poster of the early twenties—and said, "Some of you know this weapon, do you?"

"Shit, yes," said a lot of voices, while a few others said, "AK," some said, "Rooshen," and one voice called out, "Where's it from?"

"This one," Pickens told the questioner, smiling, because the idea here was to arouse everybody's interest, "this one's from Czechoslovakia. It's a good one."

"That's nice," said the questioner.

It was nice. The odd thing about it, even though the AK-47 was a Russian design—with some help from captured German designers and engineers after the Second World War, the Russians having been very impressed by the Wehrmacht's Maschinenpistole MP44—the examples of it made in the Eastern European factories of the Warsaw Bloc tended to be a lot better than the ones actually made in Russia. Waggling this Czech-made rifle, Pickens grinned at his troops and said, "You've taken more than one of these away from little brown people here and there, haven't you, boys?"

A low chuckle went around the room; they were warming up. The AK-47, particularly the model like this one with the metal folding butt so it can be reduced to a concealable twenty-four inches long, has been in the last thirty years the absolute favorite weapon of guerrillas, terrorists, freedom fighters, mercenaries and other bloodthirsty types all over the world, with only the Israeli Uzi even approaching it in popularity. Pickens smiled warmly at his boys, smiled warmly at the weapon in his hand, and said, "So here it is. And now"—with pause for dramatic effect—"you can forget the goddamn thing!" And he flung it side-arm, straight away from himself and off the stage to his right, where it crashed into the wall and fell on the floor behind the side curtain.

That woke them up. Simple minds, simple pleasures; Pickens knew how to deal with rough boys like this, it was his living. Still smiling, he picked up the flag from the table by two of its corners, and displayed it, saying, "By the way, this is the Guerrera flag. When we get down there, if you see anybody wearing this or waving it or standing next to it, cut him down. That's our meat."

The boys purred, looking at the flag. One of them called out, "What's our side look like?"

"Green armbands, whatever rags and patches they might be wearing." Pickens still held up the flag. "Our friendly forces down there are *very* irregular, boys, stand well back if they decide to fire on something."

That produced the comfortable laugh of the professional thinking about amateurs, which Pickens ended, in his carefully paced presentation, by balling up the Guerreran flag, hurling it off-stage in the same direction as the rifle, and showing another assault rifle lying on the card table. He picked this one up, held it out in front of him, and said, "Gentlemen, the Valmet."

"That's that Finnish fucker!" cried a voice.

"Very good," Pickens told him, grinning as though he didn't at all mind having his surprise spoiled. "That's just what this is, the Finnish M-60 Valmet. Essentially, this is the design of the AK-47 adapted to the needs of Finland. It's *like* an AK-47, but it *isn't* an AK-47, so it isn't as familiar as you might think, and if you don't keep the differences in mind, the head you blow off may be your own."

He had their attention now. Weapons, travel and money were the only things these fellows cared about, probably in that order. Holding the Valmet out, pointing to its features, Pickens said, "In the first place, you'll notice it's all metal, much of it plastic-coated, it doesn't have the AK's wooden stock or handguard. That's fine in a cold country like Finland, but we're going to a hot country, so keep this thing in the shade. The other thing, you'll notice it doesn't have any trigger guard, just this little piece of metal out in front here and nothing down under the trigger at all. The later model, the M-62, they added a skimpy little guard on the bottom, and some of you'll have those, but mostly we've got the original, the M-60. And you see also there's almost no curve to the trigger itself. Now, the reason for all that is, the Finnish troops have to be able to fire this thing with big heavy mittens on, because of the cold you got up there in Finland. And what it means to *you* is, you don't have that guard there where you're used to it, to protect you if your mind wanders. And your finger wanders."

A voice from the auditorium called out, "Why the fuck are we taking some fucking North Pole fucking weapon to the fucking tropics?" A lot of other voices growled agreement with the sentiment.

"Well, now, that's The People Upstairs," Pickens said. "They make the decisions, I just implement them. They didn't want to use Warsaw Bloc weaponry because they don't want anybody saying the revolution's Cuban supplied. And they didn't want to use NATO weapons because they

191

don't want anybody saying we're fronting the CIA. And maybe they got a price on these Valmets, I don't know."

"It's always the same fucking thing," cried a disgusted voice. "They want us to fight the wrong fucking war with the wrong fucking weapons on the wrong fucking terrain at the wrong fucking time of the year."

"You're goddamn right!" several voices cried, with variants. More and more of them got into the thing, some rising in their places to make their points, shaking their fists, yelling out their professional opinions.

It was becoming bedlam out there. Pickens hunched his head down into his shoulders, and waited for the storm to subside.

It wasn't easy, dealing with homicidal maniacs.

29

Dortmunder's mouth was dry. His hands were wet. So far, the seat was dry. He was up here looking for a nun, and all of a sudden he's in this absolute army of killers. Attila would be happy to come back and hang out with these guys; all Dortmunder wanted them to do was disappear.

They were an excitable crowd, too. Almost anything might set them off; disliking the weapon they were supposed to use in their upcoming slaughter, for instance. There was no telling how excited they'd get if they found out there was a noncombatant among them; a sheep, in wolf's clothing.

Dortmunder did his best not to think about any of the various things that might happen to him if they found out the truth. He tried very hard not to visualize himself being torn limb from limb, and then the limbs being gnawed on by a lot of guys with heavy jaws and big teeth. He tried and tried and *tried* not to imagine the burly man leaping off the stage, foaming at the mouth, M-60 Valmet swinging in the air above his head as he came charging up the aisle. He worked hard to avert his mental gaze from images of himself being tromped into a welcome mat under all these tight-laced paratrooper boots. He struggled and strained to keep these triptychs of his own martyrdom absolutely out of his mind. He failed.

The nearest desperado, two seats to Dortmunder's right, was now on his feet, shouting toward the stage and waving an arm decorated with a tattoo of a snake entwined with a woman in what appeared to be an improbable sex act. Suddenly this fellow stopped, glared over at Dortmunder, and yelled, "You *like* that fucking snowman weapon?"

Dortmunder looked around. His seat was on the aisle, three quarters of the way back, and from here he could see he was just about the only person still seated. Everybody else was up and yelling at the stage, or at least arguing with his neighbor. *Don't be conspicuous!* Leaping to his feet, "Heck, no!" Dortmunder told the guy with the snake and the woman. "I mean, *hell*, no! I mean, *shit*, no!"

"Fucking-A well told!" the guy announced, and punched the air. When he made a muscle, the woman and the snake interacted.

Join in, Dortmunder told himself. Waving an arm with no tattoo on it at all, he yelled toward the stage, "Hell, no, we won't go!"

The snake-and-woman man reared back. "What the fuck you mean, we won't fucking go? We don't fucking go, man, we don't get fucking paid!"

"Right," Dortmunder said. Waving his other arm—no tattoo on that one, either—he yelled, "We'll go, but we want a better gun!"

"Weapon," the snake-and-woman man said.

"Weapon!"

The snake-and-woman man took a step closer to Dortmunder, eying him with a certain repelled curiosity. "Listen, fella," he said. "Where do you—?"

Crash.

Everybody stopped, including the snake-and-woman man. Silence fell. Dortmunder blinked, and looked toward the stage, where the burly man, evidently having had enough, had pounded his Valmet assault rifle like a gavel onto the card table, which had done the card table no good at all. It had crumpled, and the burly man had pounded the floor right through the table, making a racket bigger than the racket coming at him. Into the startled silence he'd created, he said, "Goddamnit, boys, I don't like The People Upstairs any more than you do, but they hired us for this thing, and we're taking their goddamn shilling, and that's *it*. This is the hand we've been dealt, and we either fold or play. It happens this is what I do for a living, so I'm gonna stay and play. You gonna fold?"

The raucous and colorful responses he got this time were generally along the lines that everybody intended to blankety-blank stay and play the blankety-blank hand. "I never fold a bad hand!" Dortmunder shouted, getting into the swing of things, and immediately felt the snake-and-woman man's eyes on him again. What did I do wrong *now?*

Fortunately, there was another distraction, because the burly man followed up his challenge by saying, "Any more questions?" and somebody behind Dortmunder and off to the right yelled out, with a voice you could use to scour frying pans, "When do we get our hands on those fucking Finnish nose-ticklers?"

"As a matter of fact," the burly man said, grinning as though he'd been waiting for this question, "how about right now?" Then he called, "You in the back there, open the door and let them in."

A stir of interest, as everybody turned to look, and an extra stir of interest from Dortmunder, who suddenly saw a way out. I'm near the back, he told himself, and I'm on the aisle, and I'm already standing. Quick as anything, he turned and stepped into the aisle, happy to do the burly man's bidding right up to the point where he would step *through* the door he'd opened, and run like hell.

Except not. Somebody from the half dozen rows behind Dortmunder had also moved, and was already reaching for the door handle. Heck. Hell. Shit! Stepping back in from the aisle, pretending to be unaware of the snake-and-woman man's eyes on him, Dortmunder watched that other son of a bitch open the door.

Several building security men came in, neatly pressed and creased in their blue uniforms with their handguns in polished leather holsters on their belts. Never had legitimate authority—even fairly legitimate authority—looked so good to Dortmunder. I'll surrender to those guys, he thought, I'll throw myself on their mercy because they just might have some mercy to throw myself on. But even as he thought that and inhaled the deep breath prior to making a mad dash for capture, he heard the snigger going around the room, among all these suddenly grinning tough guys; the sound of leopards looking at house cats. Forget it; there'd be no safe harbor for Dortmunder there.

The security men sensed the atmosphere, too, and moved stiffly, frozen-faced, maintaining their dignity even though pushing large wheeled luggage carriers down the aisle to the front of the room. Wooden crates, their tops already pried off, were piled on the luggage carriers, and when they reached the front the burly man took a folded sheet of typing paper from his pocket, unfolded it, and said, "Okay, everybody sit down."

Everybody sat down. They *do* obey, Dortmunder thought.

"I'll call off your names now," the burly man said, "and when I do you come up and sign out your weapon, then stand along either side wall."

Call off your names? Dortmunder stared at that piece of paper in the burly man's hand. *His* name wasn't on that paper. No name he'd ever used or could possibly answer to was on that paper.

Talk about slow death. Sixty people were now going to get their names called, one at a time. They were going to get up, one at a time, and walk to the front of the room and sign whatever name had just been called. One at a time they would get their assault rifles, and then they would go stand along the side wall, until every name had been called and every rifle had been given out and every seat had been emptied.

Except one.

Wait a minute. Stand along the side wall? How come? Dortmunder felt a sudden little trace of irritation, tucked away inside his larger and more pervasive sense of doom and destruction. Why did everybody have to stand along the side wall? If they all came back to their seats with their Valmets, at some point Dortmunder would simply pretend he'd already gotten his, and maybe, just maybe, just slightly possibly, he would get away with it. Even with the gimlet eye of the snake-and-woman man so frequently on him. But not if everybody's going to wind up standing along the side wall, holding their guns. Weapons.

Somebody else apparently had the same question, if not the same problem: "How come we stand against the wall?" came the shout.

The burly man shook his head, grinning almost fondly at these ruffians and rowdies. "I don't want you bringing your toys to your seats," he said, "where maybe the guy next to you doesn't have his yet, he's a little impatient, he wants to look at yours. We're all gonna remain calm."

That's what you think, Dortmunder thought.

Was there a way out, any way at all? Could he raise his hand and be excused to go to the bathroom? Not very likely, though, in fact, given his current situation he sort of did have to go to the bathroom. Well, how about this? In the middle of the weapons distribution, could he get to his feet as though responding to his name and then *back* up the aisle to the exit, pretending to walk forward toward the stage? No. Could he wait till most of the names had been called, and then quietly slide under his seat and crawl under the rows of seats to the exit and . . . open the door in full view of everybody? No.

A voice on the other side of the room called, "We get the ammo now?"

That drew a laugh, for some reason. The burly man smiled, and let the laugh work itself out before saying, "No, I don't think so, boys. You'll get cartridge clips on the plane, same time you get your green armbands."

"When do we get to practice with the fucker?" the snake-and-woman man shouted.

"When you land in Guerrera," the burly man told him. "Just shoot at people till you hit one; then you'll know it works."

"Why don't we shoot at these little blue boys here?" somebody asked, and everybody else laughed deep in their throats, and the security men blinked a lot, looking as stern as they knew how and pretending they weren't dressed in blue.

"These are friendlies, boys," the burly man said indulgently, but it was obvious to everybody in the room, including Dortmunder and the security men that the "boys" might just as readily as not rip these friendlies into little pieces just for the fun of it.

But now the burly man cried out, "Let's get on with it, boys," and consulted his list, and called, "Krolikowsky!"

A guy with scars on his face and a missing ear got up and went forward to sign for his Valmet.

"Gruber! Sanchez!"

Maybe somebody didn't show up, Dortmunder thought, slumping in his seat. Why not? It happens. Some guy misses the bus, or forgot to set his alarm. You get any group together, you get somebody calling the roll, there's always some name that gets called and nobody at all says, "Yo," and everybody looks around, and the person calling the roll makes a disgusted mouth and notes something on his clipboard and that missing guy is in trouble.

Well, not trouble. Not real *trouble*. Not like *this* trouble. But the point is, why wouldn't that happen now? (Probably because this group had already been assembled some time ago and everybody knew who was or wasn't here, but let's ignore that possibility.) If it *did* happen, if the burly man called out a name and nobody responded, then just as the burly man was looking around the room, ready to make a disgusted mouth and note something on that piece of paper, Dortmunder would leap to his feet and march forward and sign himself out an assault rifle.

Okay. A plan. Dortmunder sat tensely in his seat and waited for the little man who wasn't there.

"Messerschmidt! Booneholler!"

It wasn't taking long at all, not nearly as long as it should. Dortmunder slumped deeper and deeper into his seat as the army armed itself, trying to think of an alternate plan just in case the first one didn't pan out. Shout *"Fire!"* in a crowded theater? Not this time; somebody would fire . . . a gun.

"Barbaranda! Peabody!"

Peabody? The snake-and-woman man was named *Peabody?* Dortmunder moved his knees out of the way and Peabody marched on down the aisle to get his weapon. The tattoo on his other arm involved a woman and an eagle.

"Mordred! Gollum!"

Fewer and fewer remained in their seats, more and more were lined up along the walls on both sides. They looked meaner standing up. They looked a *lot* meaner with assault rifles in their hands.

Could he pretend to have amnesia? No.

Could he rise at the same instant as somebody else and then claim *he* was Slade or Trask or whoever, and the other guy was the impostor? No; not for more than about eleven seconds.

"Zorkmeister! Fell! Omega!"

And that was it. And this was a party to which everybody had come; there were no no-shows here. There were only the now-empty wooden crates, the half dozen nervous security men, the burly man with his list up on stage, thirty armed barbarians lining each side wall, and Dortmunder. Seated. Alone. In the middle.

The burly man's frown pressed against Dortmunder like a heavy wind, even from this far away. "Say, there, fellow," he called, holding up his piece of paper and rattling it, "how come your name isn't on this list?"

Think of something, Dortmunder ordered himself. "Uhh," he said, and thought of nothing. "Yeah," he said, aware of all those eyes, all those weapons. "Um," he said.

The burly man turned his own Valmet around and pointed it in Dortmunder's direction, saying, "*This* piece of armament, fellow, has a full clip in its belly. Name, rank and serial number, boy, and don't hesitate."

Dortmunder hesitated; he couldn't help it. But he had to say *something*. "Well, uh, my name is Smith."

"Haw," said some of the people on the sides, but the burly man and his Valmet didn't seem amused. Why did I say Smith? Dortmunder asked himself. It's just gonna make them madder.

"On your feet, Mr. Smith," the burly man said. "I am about to display the Valmet's recoil action. Up!"

Dortmunder stood. He was still looking for a plan. Pretend to have a heart attack? Claim to be a policeman, and put them all under arrest? How about . . . how about . . . how about if he said he was from the company sold these people the Valmets, and the check bounced, and he was here to repossess them?

"Out in the aisle, Mr. Smith," the burly man said, and Dortmunder obeyed, and the burly man said, "Now, boys, you'll notice the recoil of this weapon is mainly rearward, with not much barrel rise, so you can place just about as many rounds as you want in a narrow target area without pause. Any last words, Mr. Smith?"

"I can explain," Dortmunder said—my last words are a lie! he thought despairingly—and the lights went out.

Click. Snap. Darkness, pitch-black, just like that. Dortmunder wasted a full hundredth of a second being startled before he turned and ran like a chicken thief in the general direction of the door.

Whack! The door was closed. Dortmunder knocked it open with his forehead, nose, knees, elbows, knuckles and belt buckle, and the hall lights were out, too. Behind him, a whole zoo of noises suddenly erupted, roaring and squawling and braying and barking, and over those noises came a rapid BAP-BAP-BAP-BAP, huge and echoing in the enclosed air of that room. The door shuddered, hit by a couple of rounds, and Dortmunder caromed off it, arms flailing wildly as he reeled into the blackness of the hall, where a small cold hand closed around his wrist.

"YIIIII!!!" Vampires, ghouls, things that go bump in the night. This was even worse than the Valmet!

A second hand groped for his mouth, to shut it, found his nose instead, and squeezed. "Ngggg," Dortmunder said, and the first hand tugged at his wrist while the second hand released his nose, patted his cheek, and departed.

A friend? In this madhouse?

Well, somebody turned off the lights, right?

Dortmunder allowed himself to be drawn away from the yelling and shouting back in the theater, pulled along at a half-trot by this small but strong hand encircling his wrist. They made a turn, the sounds in the background grew fainter, and then a pale light appeared back there, showing behind them at the corridor turn. "They've got the lights on," Dortmunder said, and in the dimness peered at his rescuer.

A girl. Early twenties. Short, slender, in blue jeans and high-necked long-sleeved full-cut black blouse. Grim-faced and fiery-eyed she was, as she glanced back toward the light, then pushed open a door on the left side of the hall. They entered an

203

ordinary office, empty, brightly illuminated by ceiling fluorescents. Slamming the door, leaning against it, taking a deep breath, the girl looked at Dortmunder, held up her right hand with one finger pointing up, tapped two fingers of her right hand to her raised left forearm, held up one finger again, tugged her earlobe, and blew him a kiss.

"Yeah, yeah, I know," Dortmunder told her. "Kiss, sounds like sis, you're Sister Mary Grace."

She nodded and smiled, making an A-OK circle of thumb and forefinger.

"I'm, uh," Dortmunder said, but what the hell, might as well admit it. "I'm John Dortmunder."

She nodded again, patting the air: She too had figured things out.

Dortmunder sighed; it had to be said. "I'm here to rescue you."

She raised an eyebrow, grinning ever so slightly, but otherwise refrained from comment.

Noise out in the hall; moving this way. "Here they come," Dortmunder said.

Sister Mary Grace listened for a second, then nodded, and headed across the room toward the other door, gesturing for Dortmunder to follow. He followed.

30

"You notice Dortmunder takes the easy part," Tiny Bulcher said, hefting a black plastic bag filled with about fifty pounds of jade, gold, ivory and other nice things, which he then tossed over his left shoulder. With a second black plastic bag, similarly filled, on his right shoulder, he looked like the rebuttal to Santa Claus.

"Aw, come on, Tiny," Andy Kelp said, stripping rings from his fingers and bells from his other fingers to go into the next plastic bag to be filled. "You didn't want to go up there with the nun, you said so yourself."

"We bust and break and carry and schlep," Tiny said, unappeased, "and *he* drinks tea with some nun."

Wilbur Howey, holding with both hands a six-inch-tall ivory reproduction of a piece of erotic statuary from Angkor Wat, said, "Wants to keep that little nun all to himself, does he?"

"Listen, Wilbur," Tiny said, "you been holding that statue ten minutes now. You're supposed to *pack* it, so I can carry it downstairs."

"Oh, sure," Howey said. Then, as Tiny continued to gaze upon him, Howey reluctantly bent and put the statue away in the half-full plastic bag, stroking it a lingering goodbye before the black consumed it.

Stan Murch came out to the hall from Macaran Ivory Co. with an armload of netsuke, which he dumped without ceremony into the plastic bag, then looked around and said, "We knocking off now?"

"No, no," Kelp said. "I'm right with you, Stan."

"So's Wilbur," Tiny said. "While *I'm* carrying

all this stuff downstairs, and Dortmunder's up there playing footsie with the nun."

"You don't play footsie with nuns, Tiny," Kelp said.

Howey looked startled at that, but then he frowned, as though prepared to listen to a second opinion.

"Work," Tiny advised, and turned around to plod away, the bulging black bags on his back making him look as though he were on his way to Vulcan's forge.

Stan went back into Macaran Ivory, past the sagging door that Tiny had kicked open a while back. Howey followed, bright-eyed, looking for more reproductions. Kelp paused, watched Tiny disappear through the stairwell door at the end of the hall, and then skipped lightly into Duncan Magic, next door to Macaran. He was there three minutes, deeply involved in the process of turning a long black cane into a bouquet of bright-colored plastic flowers, when Stan came in and said, "Andy, we been pals a long time."

"Okay, okay," Kelp said, and put the cane down on the counter. "I'm just coming now."

"But if you come in here again," Stan said.

"No, no," Kelp assured him. "Not till we're done with everything else."

"I'm just gonna have to ask Tiny for advice," Stan finished.

"You don't have to do that, Stan, honest. Look, here I am, I'm going out to the hall. You coming?"

"Of course I'm coming," Stan said, but in fact he was glancing back at the long black cane lying on the counter. How do you turn something like that into a bouquet of flowers?

No. Don't even ask. Stan firmly turned his back on the cane and left Duncan Magic.

31

Pickens brooded, glowering. He was mad enough to eat the bark off a Saint Bernard.

"He's got to be somewhere on this floor," the head security wimp said. He was obviously made nervous by Pickens' silence.

"That's fine," Pickens said, standing there next to the assembly room door with his hands on his hips. "Why don't you show him to me, then?"

"We're working on it," the head security wimp said.

Working on it. They were all working on it; that is, the survivors were working on it. The scene in the assembly room had deteriorated badly once the lights went out. It had been a mistake to start blasting away with that Valmet. Pickens knew it full well and quite bitterly accepted the blame for the whole thing. He'd been aiming at the fellow purely as a threat—you don't kill a man who hasn't answered your questions yet—but the sudden darkness had startled him, and his finger was on that trigger anyway—no trigger guard, just as he'd pointed out to the troops—and his automatic reaction had been to squeeze.

Actually, it had almost worked out. Smith—call him Smith, that's the only name they had on the son of a bitch so far—had made a run for it out that back door, this door here, and Pickens afterward had counted seven big raggedy holes in this door, meaning he must have missed Smith by no more than inches.

But by however narrow a margin it might have been, miss Smith he had, and by firing off his weapon in that darkened room he'd set loose some of the worst instincts of the troops in his command. By the time the lights had come back on there were at least half a dozen spontaneous brawls and fistfights and wrestling matches already going on, and maybe ten handguns were out and being waved this way and that. Before Pickens had managed to restore order, the roll call was four broken jaws, three broken arms, nine hands with broken bones, and one fellow who'd been kneed so hard he might *never* straighten out again. Which reduced Pickens' forces from sixty men to forty-three, all of whom were right now out and about the seventy-fourth floor, looking for Smith.

He had to still be here, somewhere on this floor. The security wimps had checked with their comrades in the basement—which is what had brought this white-haired red-faced head security wimp hotfooting it up—and there had been no breach of security to the public stairwell since Smith had disappeared. There was no possible way he could get through Margrave's interior door to the separate stairway up to seventy-six, but on the other hand it was pretty certain by now he was no longer within these Margrave offices. Windows up here didn't open, and no elevator had come up to this level for several hours except the one bringing the head security wimp, so that meant Smith must have gone to ground in the territory of one of the other companies with space on this floor. That's where Pickens' troops were right now, doing a room-by-room search. It was only a matter of time.

"It's only a matter of time," the head security wimp said.

"I need my time for other things," Pickens told him. "And I need to know who that Smith is, who he's working for. Is he just a newspaper reporter? Is he FBI, or CIA, or Customs? That's our big worry, you know, Customs."

"Customs? What the hell have *they* got to do with anything?"

"If you mount an armed insurgency against a nation with which the United States is at peace," Pickens told him, "and if you gather and provide weapons for your forces on American territory and then transport them to the war zone *from* American territory, you are committing a Federal crime. And enforcement of that Federal crime comes under the jurisdiction of Customs. I feel you ought to know your situation here," Pickens finished.

"Not *my* situation," the head security wimp said, but he did look worried.

"You're part of it, my friend," Pickens assured him. "It's just as important to you as it is to me to catch this Smith and find out who and what he is. Maybe he's working for the Guerreran government, and they already know we're on our way. If so, I'd like to know about it."

"I suppose you would," the head security wimp agreed.

Pickens shook his head, disgusted at himself. "If only I'd winged the son of a bitch," he said, "so we could have ourselves some blood to follow."

"We've got plenty of blood already," the head security wimp said, sounding disapproving. He was still mad about Pickens having let off his weapon in the house like that, but didn't dare come right out and say so.

One of the other security wimps now approached them down the hall, his face all blotchy in red and white; angry, or scared, or maybe both. They watched him approach, and the head security wimp said, "You got news, O'Brien?"

"Some of those guys knocked out O'Toole," O'Brien said. He wouldn't look at Pickens.

"Well, um," the head security wimp said. He and O'Brien stared fixedly at each other, both waiting for Pickens to say something, but Pickens didn't feel he had anything to say. He turned instead and studied the raggedy holes in the assembly room door. Nice tight pattern. Good weapon, the Valmet. Pity Smith hadn't gone through this doorway just a bit farther to the right.

"Well," the head security wimp finally said, "how's O'Toole now?"

"Laying there," O'Brien said. His eyebrows were way up high on his forehead, expressing mute outrage, which was the only kind of outrage he was permitting himself to express.

"Well, there's probably an explanation," the head security wimp said.

Pickens went right on having nothing in particular he wanted to say.

O'Brien, voice trembling with unexpressed outrage, said, "They just knocked him out, that's all."

"Call downstairs," the head security wimp said. "Tell, uhhhh, tell O'Leary to come on up and take his place. Then tell O'Toole to go on down—"

"He's unconscious! I told you that!"

"When he gets conscious again!" the head security wimp snapped, getting mad at the messenger. "When he can listen, you tell him to go on downstairs, have a cup of coffee. Tell him to have O'Marra take a look at him."

O'Brien nodded, then shook his head. He was growing calmer, but still ached with an unresolved need for satisfaction. "I'm telling you, Chief," he said, man to man, "they just up and knocked him down."

"Message received, O'Brien," the head security wimp said, being very stern about it because he had no intention of taking any action. "But the

211

message I *want* to receive," he went on, "is that you found that fella Smith."

"Oh, we'll find him," O'Brien said, "if we're let alone to do it," and at last sneaked an angry look at Pickens, who gazed at him mildly. After a few seconds, O'Brien snorted and shook his head and marched away, very stiff-backed.

The head security wimp gave Pickens a sidelong glance. "Doesn't appear to be such good discipline in that bunch of yours," he said.

"Oh, I've got no complaints," Pickens said amiably. "Do you?"

The head security wimp thought about that. "I'll see how my boys are getting along," he decided, frowned at Pickens as though he might deliver himself of an exit line, thought better of it, and went stumping away toward the exit from Margrave to the public hall.

Which was, Pickens realized, off to the right from here. But if Smith went out the left side of this doorway here, pushing open a door that opens from left to right, with 62 millimeter slugs chunking into the wood just next to him on his right side, and if he was going out to a hallway just as pitch black as the room he was leaving, would he turn and go around that door and into the line of fire and off to the right? Or would his natural tendency be to go to the left? And if he went to the left, what would he find down there and how would he get himself back to the Margrave exit?

Pickens' troops and the security wimps had gone

212

all over Margrave first, keeping a guard on the only exit, and had found nothing. Still, what would be lost by Pickens himself trying to reconstruct the route taken by Mr. Smith?

Nothing.

Right hand casually resting on the butt of the Belgian Browning 9mm automatic in the open holster at his waist, Pickens strolled on down the hall. At the end, another hall went off to the left, with doors on both sides and a double door at the very end. Pickens went along there, opening the doors on the right, seeing a line of small square offices with windows looking out at a blue-gray pre-dawn sky. None of the offices had second exits or led to anywhere else. The door at the end of the hall opened to a three-room suite, including a large and elaborate corner office, but this too was self-contained, leading only back to its own entrance.

Now Pickens worked back down the hall, opening the doors on the other side. Smaller offices, windowless. The third of these had a door on its far side, which Pickens opened, and which led him into a large dark space. He found light switches, clicked them on, and looked at a very large rectangle divided into a lot of tiny cubicle offices, with windows down the right wall. If he had the geography of this place worked out, the left wall of this space would have the stage of the assembly room on its other side.

A straight central aisle led down through the labyrinth of cubicles, and at the end were three doors, one leading to a storage room full of stationery supplies, one to a small room containing two copying machines, and one to a narrow room, barely more than a closet, with the door to the interior staircase on its other side.

Pickens frowned. So far, he had seen no trail, no spoor, no indication that Smith had come this way at all. On the other hand, he had seen no circular route that would get Smith back to the Margrave exit once he'd turned left from the assembly room. *If* he turned left.

The door to the interior staircase was supposed to be kept locked. Pickens went over and tried it, and the lock was firm. There was no sign of forced entry. The keypad beside the door showed no indication of tampering. Pickens keyed in the four-digit number that unlocked the door, opened it, and stepped through to the bottom of a simple stairwell with carpeted steps and dark paneled walls and round ceiling globes kept permanently lit. Still no spoor.

Pickens looked up the stairs. He knew there was no entrance on the next floor, at seventy-five, where he himself now slept—whenever he had a chance to sleep—since some sort of religious fellow had been kicked out of there day before yesterday. (Good thing he hadn't been asleep up there, that religious boy, when the Valmet went off!)

Two flights up, at the top of the tower, was the private apartment owned by the boss of bosses, Mr. Frank Ritter. Pickens, having tracked down a rumor with his usual thoroughness, now knew that Ritter had a daughter locked away up there, a loony or something, that the religious fellow had been praying over or trying to exorcise the devils out of or some such thing. She was locked away and a couple of private guards were on duty up there at all times; better men than the security wimps, but not as all-out homicidal as Pickens' boys.

Was it time to think the unthinkable? If Smith turned left—that's the key point right there, *if* the son of a bitch turned left—then the narrow end of the funnel was this stairwell. Did Smith have access to the four-digit lock code? If not, how would he get through this door? And what would happen when he got to the door upstairs? And then what would happen when he got to the private guards up there?

Was Smith linked to Ritter in some way?

Double-dealing did always have to be allowed for.

Pickens stood at the bottom of the stairwell, frowning, thinking it over, and came to a conclusion. All right. If Smith turned right from the assembly room, and went straight out the Margrave exit, there's a lot of places he could be, all on the seventy-fourth floor, and we'll look in every one of them. And if he doesn't turn up . . .

Pickens brooded at the carpeted stairs. "I sure wish I'd winged you, friend," he said aloud. "I could use just one little drop of blood right now. But if we don't find you back the other way, then you damn well *had* to come this way, and I don't care if it's possible or not. And when I find you,

Mr. Smith, you can tell me yourself just how you did it."

32

"I think I'm bleeding," Dortmunder said. On the right side of his neck, just about where a vampire would get him—remembering that scary moment in the dark hall when Sister Mary Grace's hand had closed around his wrist—just about at that spot, there was a growing itchiness, and when Dortmunder touched it his fingertip came away with a drop of blood. A tiny, faint, almost invisible drop of blood, but still. Dortmunder held it out for the good Sister to see.

They were in a bathroom, a strange place to be with a nun, but she'd insisted, pushing and prodding him as though he were a big piece of furniture like a chiffonier she was trying to get through a door, and he supposed she was right. Here was about the only place in this apartment where the guards wouldn't just knock and walk in.

The bathroom was very expensive-looking, with brown-flecked white marble everywhere, and a special beige bathtub the size of a Toyota Tercel, plus a walk-in shower larger than Dortmunder's closet at home, and lots of big fluffy tan towels, and lights all around the mirrors, and a very soft tan terrycloth-covered stool on which Dortmunder sat and looked at a drop of his own blood on his fingertip.

both out of here, but things aren't— Well, this wasn't the plan."

She pantomimed shooting a machine gun.

"Yeah, those guys," he agreed. "I didn't know they were there, I figured I'd just come up through Margrave late at night, pick you up, go back down."

She folded her arms and very slowly shook her head.

"Well, I know that now," he said. "Who are those guys?"

She marched in place, saluting.

"An army. They're going down to South America somewhere, overthrow a country or something?"

She nodded.

"For your father?"

She pretended to throw up, quite realistically, over the toilet.

Dortmunder said, "Well, they're between us and getting out of here. Plus the regular security guys, plus the guards up here."

She nodded, accepting the grimness of the outlook.

"They're all gonna be looking for me," Dortmunder said, "and—" Struck by a sudden thought, he said, "Oh, boy! I hope they don't find my friends."

Question?

"Well," he said, "some people I'm working with."

She looked hopeful and eager and pointed at herself.

"Well, not exactly," he said. "I'm the only one actually coming up here to, uh, rescue you."

Quizzical frown, pointed downward.

"Well, what they're doing," Dortmunder said, hemming and hawing, "they're kind of— Well, they're doing other parts of it."

She frowned, not getting the picture, then all at once gave a big knowing nod. Holding one finger up for him to attend, she tiptoed over to the sink, sneakily looked in both directions, picked up the soapdish, held it tucked in under her armpit, and sneaked away, then stopped to give him a raised-eyebrow question.

"Well, yeah," Dortmunder admitted. "They are, uh, stealing. I mean, it's what we do. And I needed help to get into the building and all."

She waggled a naughty-naughty finger at him.

Dortmunder said, "Anyway, everybody's insured these days, right?"

She thought about that, then suddenly smiled all over.

"What's up?"

She pantomimed throwing up in the toilet, then pantomimed dealing out dollar bills.

"You mean, your father has to make good on losses in this building?"

Emphatic nod.

Relieved, Dortmunder said, "So it's okay, then."

She thought that over and did a teeter-totter motion with one hand; morally ambiguous.

Dortmunder would accept that. For him, morally ambiguous was a lot better rating than usual.

She looked alert, pointed to her own head: *Idea.* Pointed downward, then with both hands did fingers walking up steps.

"You mean, my friends will come up and get me?" Dortmunder considered this idea, matching it to the characters of his associates. "Well," he acknowledged, "they will notice I didn't come back. And they wouldn't have all this profit and everything if it wasn't for me. *And* you."

She spread her hands: *Ergo.*

"You could be right," Dortmunder said, not wanting to shatter either of her beliefs; in rescue, or in the human race. Then he said, "How about a phone? Can we make a call?"

Sadly, she shook her head and made a listening-in gesture.

"Well," he said, "that army's got to leave for South America sooner or later."

She nodded, and held a hand up. Then she looked very wide-eyed, then pretended to sleep, then looked wide-eyed again, pretended to sleep again, looked wide-eyed once more, then did flapping motions with her arms.

"They fly away day after tomorrow. Monday." Dortmunder nodded. "Of course, that still leaves building security and your private guards."

She pointed at him, then did the fingers walking up the stairs.

"Oh, sure. And my friends."

She pointed at her wrist.

"In the meantime . . ."

Covered her face with her hands, peeked out between the fingers, then pointed at him.

". . . I should hide . . ."

Fingers walked up stairs.

". . . until my friends get here."

Big wide smile, hands stretched out with palms up.

"Simple. Uh huh." Dortmunder made a smile.

33

"I'm gonna tell you one thing about Dortmunder," Tiny Bulcher said. "He's on his own."

The army platoon in camouflage fatigues and assault rifles had continued on up the stairwell now, and Tiny had caught his breath, but his face was still just as red as when he'd come tumbling back in here with a hundred pounds of precious *objets d'art* bouncing on his back. Andy Kelp looked at that face and didn't particularly want to disagree with it, but he just felt somebody ought to defend Dortmunder and it didn't look as though either Stan or Howey was interested in the job, so that left it up to him. "Gee, Tiny," he began.

"Enough," Tiny said, and lowered an eyebrow in Kelp's direction.

Kelp closed his mouth. In truth, he couldn't really blame Tiny, because what had just occurred pretty well had to be connected somehow with Dortmunder's activities up in the tower, and if

Dortmunder was going to knock over this kind of hornet's nest he really should give his partners a little bit of advance warning.

Here's what had just occurred: It was nearly six in the morning, they'd finally broken into the last store on twenty-six, being Kobol & Kobol, and Tiny was taking yet another load of booty away. He'd carried the hundred pounds' worth in two plastic sacks down the stairwell and had reached the landing at the eleventh floor when all of a sudden he heard a door clang below him, and then the sound of a lot of boots on the metal stairs, and voices, and a whole lot of people were coming *up*. He couldn't see them yet, but he knew there was a whole crowd of them, and he knew they were climbing those stairs at a good steady rapid pace, and he further knew there was absolutely no way for him to make it down to the seventh floor and out of the stairwell before those people reached seven from below.

So he did the only thing he could do: He turned around and ran back up the stairs. And because he didn't dare leave the plastic bags full of booty for these new arrivals to find, he ran from the eleventh floor to the twenty-sixth floor carrying them on his back.

And when he made the turn at the landing on the twenty-third floor was when he first heard the second group coming down from above. Two groups in a pincers movement, and Tiny in the middle. He kept going, carrying one hundred pounds up two hundred twenty-four steps as fast as he physically could go, and even Tiny Bulcher flagged under that strain and had slowed considerably by the time he reached twenty-six. The guys below were no more than two flights away by then, with the ones above somewhat farther off.

What they were doing, they were double-checking the remotest of possibilities. Security down in the basement remained absolutely one hundred percent positive no one had gone in from the stairwell to any other floor (another man was on duty now at the dial that had made trouble earlier), so if the fellow they knew as Smith somehow or other had managed to get *out* to the stairwell, he would still be there. Therefore, one platoon had gone down to the lobby in the elevator that had brought the security chief upstairs, while another platoon had entered the stairwell on the seventy-fourth floor, just outside the Margrave offices, and now they swept both up and down, looking for signs of forced entry (just in case Security in the basement had its head up its behind), hoping to squeeze Smith between them, and damn near finding more than they'd bargained for.

Tiny burst into the corridor at twenty-six, dropped the sacks in the corner, didn't even notice the long black cane turning into a bouquet of flowers in Andy Kelp's hand midway down the corridor, and hissed at him, "Everybody shut up!" Then, while Kelp hotfooted away to make everybody shut up, Tiny ran back out to the corridor, reassured himself that Wilbur Howey had left the

224

security panel neat and trim and looking undisturbed, and risked a quick look over the railing at the guys coming up. Which was when he saw the camouflage uniforms and the assault rifles, and made his guess that there were seven guys, maybe eight, in that platoon. And more coming from above.

Back into twenty-six he went, silently shut the door, and leaned against it, listening, while Kelp and Stan and Howey came out of Kobol & Kobol at the other end of the corridor and walked silently down to stand near Tiny and watch and wait and wonder.

They all heard the boots go by. Tiny opened the door a few seconds later, and they all saw the boots—paratrooper style, with bloused camouflage pants-legs tucked into them—tramping on up out of sight to the next landing. They all listened with the door open, and heard the two groups meet and talk things over, though the echo in this metal stairwell was too severe to make out any of the words. Then they heard both groups thump away upstairs, slowly fading, and that's when Tiny shut the door and faced the others and announced that Dortmunder could now consider himself on his own.

Kelp considered friendship. Then he considered reality. What could one lone man do up there against what was apparently some sort of organized army? Nothing. But if Andy Kelp on his own, without the rest of the string, were to go up and try to help Dortmunder out of this fix, what could *two* lone men do against that same army?

"It's a pity," Kelp said sadly, and turned the bouquet back into a cane.

EXODUS

34

"Lie down with wolves, you get up with tooth-marks."

Frank Ritter sat at his desk in the corner office suite of Margrave Corporation and studied this addition he'd just made to his commonplace book. Was that truly an aphorism? Possibly it was merely a low-level epigram or even, God help us, just a joke. Ritter didn't like crossing things out in his commonplace book, it made for a sloppy appearance, but this particular statement, well . . .

On the other hand, it wasn't inaccurate, as his current situation—and the inspiration for the re-mark—demonstrated. The wolves were the five dozen mercenaries he had employed to ease his irritation vis-à-vis General Pozos of Guerrera; and the toothmarks? Bullet holes in the assembly room door. Several broken seats in there as well, and sixteen men on the injured list (the kneed victim recovered). None needing hospitalization, happily, but all with broken bones and all unavailable for the punitive strike. Shattered morale among the building's own security forces, there was another toothmark. And from the grim tone in Virgil

Pickens' voice this morning, when he'd requested a meeting with Ritter, there were further tooth-marks to come.

It was now not quite nine o'clock on Sunday morning, and Ritter, as usual, had been up for hours. ("The first arrival gets the best seat.") Family business had kept him at the Glen Cove estate out on Long Island until nearly eight, when the helicopter had flown him in to the pad at East Twenty-third Street, where his car had been waiting to take him through empty Sunday morning Manhattan streets to his own tower. Here and there in high-floor windows of the office buildings along the way lights had gleamed, and Ritter felt a kinship: We are here, we are working, we are not making excuses. "The deadline," a laughing executive at a company social event had once unwisely remarked to Ritter, "is when you have to have your alibi ready." Not a Ritter-style aphorism; that executive, if he still laughed, did so with some other corporation.

One single firm rap at the door, military-style. There was no secretary available here on Sunday mornings, unfortunately, but this could only be Pickens arriving, precisely on time, so Ritter put away his commonplace book with the wolf line intact and called, "Come in." The man himself entered, burly and thick-bodied, but neat as a pin in his pressed and creased camouflage fatigues.

"Good morning," Ritter said, and gestured at the easy chair across the desk. "Have you had coffee?"

"I've had lunch, sir," Pickens said, and remained standing.

"Sit down, man, you'll give me a crick in the neck."

So Pickens sat, uncomfortably, on the edge of the chair, knees together, hands on thighs, as though waiting to see the dentist. Ignoring this overdone Spartan effect, Ritter said, "We've lost a lot of men, have we? And the war isn't started yet."

"Some limited casualties," Pickens agreed. "Nothing we can't live with."

"Sixteen men!"

"Twelve, as a matter of fact," Pickens said. "The boys with the broken jaws have all been wired, they'll be coming along."

Ritter was astounded. "With broken jaws?"

"You don't squeeze a trigger with your mouth," Pickens pointed out. "And none of them speak the language down there, so there won't be that much to talk about. And a man with a wired jaw is a fearsome thing to look at anyway; good for psychological warfare."

Could Pickens possibly be pulling his leg? Ritter peered at the man, but nothing at all flawed his military correctness. "So," Ritter said, "you'll be going down with forty-eight men instead of sixty."

"We could probably do the job with forty," Pickens answered. "We've still got a comfortable cushion. No, sir, that's not the problem, that's not why I requested this conference."

231

More toothmarks, Ritter thought, and asked, "Then what's the problem?"

"Smith."

"The interloper, yes." Ritter sat back in his swivel chair, brooding. "He still hasn't been found?"

"That's one of the worrisome parts of it," Pickens said. "But, to begin with, where did he come from? Who's he working for? Then, after that, how'd he get in? Of course, I myself let him into these offices, but how did he get to that public hallway out there at that hour of night?"

"Hiding in somebody else's office until everybody went home for the night," Ritter guessed. "We share this floor with three other firms, you know."

"Still," Pickens said, "who's he working for? But the most important thing is, where is he now?"

"Escaped," Ritter suggested. "Reporting at this very minute to somebody five miles from here."

Pickens shook his head, an unimaginative but stubborn man. "No, sir," he said. "Smith never got off the seventy-fourth floor of this building. At least, not downward. Building security says so and my men say so."

"But you haven't found him."

"No, sir, not on this floor." If Pickens were uncomfortable about the subject he was raising, it showed only in an increased stiffness and precision in his bearing. "He didn't go below this floor, and he isn't *on* this floor, and that's the situation, Mr. Ritter, as it now pertains."

"I'm not sure I follow you, Pickens," Ritter said.

"Here's the question I've been asking myself, sir," Pickens told him, "for the last few hours. Who turned off those lights?"

That's when Ritter saw it coming. But he didn't want to see it coming, and he didn't want to make Pickens' task any easier, so he said, "Some confederate of Smith's, I suppose."

"All right, then, sir," Pickens said. Those "sirs" were getting thick on the ground as Pickens neared the crux of his complaint. "So now, sir," he said, "we have *two* people mysteriously disappeared. And one of them knows these offices well enough to find the right circuit-breaker in the right circuit-breaker box without a whole hell of a lot of lead time. Sir."

"Then that's the situation," Ritter said. "Two disappearing people is no more difficult to believe than one disappearing person. It's impossible either way."

"Not impossible, sir," Pickens said. "Unlikely maybe. But I haven't yet run across anything in my experience that turned out to be *impossible*."

Damn Pickens! It was clear now that he wouldn't volunteer the next step, that he'd remain perched on the edge of that chair, well pressed and correct and buttoned up tight, until Ritter *asked* him, if it took a hundred years. "All right," Ritter said at last, reluctantly. "I take it you have a theory."

"A possibility, sir," Pickens said. "The only

thing I can think of that makes the impossible possible in this particular case."

"And it is?"

Pickens took a deep breath. "I assure you, sir, " he said, "it is never my wish to pry into any other man's personal affairs. We all have our family tragedies, family problems, and they're nobody's business but our own."

Irrelevantly wondering what sort of family problem an automaton like Pickens could have, Ritter said, "Get to the point, man."

"You have a daughter, sir, as I understand it," Pickens said, "living on the top floor here."

So here it was. "Yes, I do," Ritter said, wondering just how common that knowledge might be.

"I understand she has some sort of problem," Pickens went on. "I don't know what. It's not my business to know what. But I believe she's there."

"She's there," Ritter agreed. He spent a millisecond considering whether to explain the case of his daughter Elaine to this man, decided the fellow could go to Hell first, and said, "She's confined to that floor, for her own good, for personal reasons of my own."

Pickens showed a calloused palm in a traffic-stop gesture. "Not my business, sir. But I wonder, sir, if this daughter of yours might not have come *down* these here interior stairs into Margrave last night and had some hand in the events taking place."

"Definitely not," Ritter said. "I already told

you, she's confined there, locked in. I have private guards up there to see she doesn't leave."

Pickens was unmoved. He said, "Mr. Ritter, I'm sorry, but that's the only direction left. Smith is no longer on this floor. He didn't go down. That leaves only one alternative."

"It's simply not possible," Ritter insisted. "The security between here and the top floor is of a much more sophisticated nature than in the rest of the building, it would be far easier to go down from here than up. Have you seen the spec books?"

"Which books would those be, sir?"

Ritter got to his feet, his body full of tension, pleased at the opportunity to move, to work off some of the pressure accumulating inside. "Come along," he said.

The office containing the spec books was nearby, just down the hall, one of the small windowless rooms Pickens had looked at last night, this one lined with plain metal shelving stacked with various records, some office supplies, and shelf after shelf of ledger books filled with manufacturer's spec sheets on everything in use in this building from the heating plant to the water coolers. Among these were the two black unmarked ledger books filled with the specifications and details of usage of all the security systems in the entire Avalon State Bank Tower.

"Here they are," Ritter said, reached out for the books on a shelf just at eye-level, grasped them both with the spread fingers of one hand, lifted and pulled, and the books were so startlingly light that his hand jumped and he almost punched himself in the face. As it was, the books spurted from his grasp and fell on the floor, opening flat, face up, lying there like accident victims, spread-eagled on their backs.

And empty.

Ritter stared at the books on the floor, black cardboard covers and gleaming metal rings. Empty!

"Sir? Something wrong?"

Ritter reached out, grabbed another ledger book at random. Full. Another; full. Another; full.

Pickens said, "Sir, were those the security spec books?"

"Yes." Ritter's voice was suddenly hoarse; he cleared his throat.

"And all the information is gone, sir?"

Ritter stared again at the fallen books, and into his mind came an idea so forbidden that he refused to believe he'd even thought it: Maybe God *is* on her side.

Pickens said, "Sir, request permission to conduct a search of the top floor."

Ritter blinked at him. "Granted," he said.

35

Wilbur Howey came out of the men's room with *Scandinavian Marriage Secrets* under his arm and deep gray circles under his eyes. Nevertheless, his step was light as he hurried down the seventh floor corridor to room 712, rapped on the wood in a secret pattern—two, then one, then one, if you *must* know—heard the lock click, and was admitted by Stan Murch, who looked at him and said, "All full inside."

"Say, don't I know it?" Howey answered. "I had to come out here to shrug."

Howey squeezed past Stan, who shut and relocked the door and returned to his work, which was taking precious objects out of black plastic sacks and putting them on the receptionist's desk. Seated in the receptionist's chair was Andy Kelp, who placed the precious objects in mailers of various sizes, ranging from small padded envelopes suitable for mailing books such as the one under Howey's arm up to cardboard boxes the store would mail a shirt in. Some objects were too large even for these and were placed in a pile on the floor in the corner behind Kelp to be dealt with later, a pile that was already knee-high and steadily growing.

J.C. Taylor's office was, at this moment, a madhouse and a mess. It was a little after nine on Sunday morning, and in the two hours since they'd finished looting the stores on the twenty-sixth floor only a minimum amount of order had been brought from the prevailing chaos. Full black plastic bags were piled everywhere, the mounds reaching head-height in some precarious places, and leaving only a twisty narrow route through to the inner room, where Tiny could be heard huffing and puffing, like the Minotaur in his cave.

Kelp looked up from his packing and said, "Aren't you Wilbur Howey?"

"You just bet I am," Howey told him. "Howlin' Howey, ever ready."

"Then you're the guy over here working with me," Kelp told him. "Where've you been?"

"Mother Nature called," Howey said. He was looking around, trying to find somewhere to put the book.

"The next time she calls," Kelp advised, "tell her to leave a message. Look how much stuff there is here."

"Say, here I come," Howey said, edging past Stan and through the stacks of plastic bags and around the desk. "Your troubles are over."

"Wonderful news," Kelp said.

A certain backlog had built up in Howey's absence. It was his job, once Kelp had put each object or group of objects in the appropriate packaging, to seal it with either staples or shipping tape and then carry armloads of completed packages to the next room. Unsealed packages now towered up like a model city on the receptionist's typing table, weaving and tottering, reaching nearly to the ceiling. Dumping the Scandinavian book in the wastebasket, as being the only place around to put it, Howey went right to work, taping and stapling, and soon had enough to tote a stack of them into the next room.

Where Tiny was a one-man team all his own, surrounded by more high mounds of plastic bags, sorting and packing like mad, tossing sealed packages into the corner between the window and the piano. The great big toilet-paper carton they'd brought in with them, which had at that time contained most of these mailers, had been emptied and placed in the corner to receive the completed packages, but they now filled and overflowed the carton and were gradually turning into a jagged brown cardboard replica of an alp, its peak just under the ceiling.

Howey added his new armload to this ever-growing slope and gathered up another stack of empty packages from atop the piano. As he was going out, Tiny looked over at him, paused, and said, "Wilbur."

"Here I am," Howey told him, peering over the top of the mailers.

"When we get done here," Tiny told him, "take a look through those two books of security specs."

Howey said, "Sure thing. You want to go up look for Dortmunder, huh?"

Tiny glowered. "There is no Dortmunder," he said. "There's only us. And what you're gonna do is find us another floor with good stuff in it that we can hit tonight."

Howey gaped at him. "Tonight? Say, Tiny, you want *more?*"

"Yes," Tiny said simply.

"Well, but, say, listen," Howey said, the stack of mailers wobbling in his arms. "When do we grab some shuteye?"

Tiny grinned. "When we get to Bermuda," he said.

36

In his dream, Dortmunder walked a tightrope between two tall towers. Instead of a balancing pole, he carried a long heavy lance, tipping first to the left and then to the right. And the tightrope itself was made of long blonde hair. In the arched window at the top of the stone tower out in front he could see the girl whose hair this was, still attached to her head, long and braided and looped between the two towers; from the strained and painful expression on her face, she didn't much like what was going on.

But what could he do? Looking down, he saw a jousting arena laid out on the bare tan ground between the towers. Men on horseback tilted at one another down there, but instead of knight's armor they were dressed in green-shaded camouflage uniforms, and the weapons they jousted with were Valmets. Each pair started far apart, then rode madly together on their horses, whacking and whamming at each other with the rifles, never firing them.

Other green-clad men off to the side were setting up a catapult, and beyond them stood a company of archers. In bleachers farther away, a group of nuns silently applauded. As Dortmunder watched, the archers nocked an arrow into their bows, took a stance, and at a signal from their commander—the burly man who'd led Dortmunder into Margrave—a volley of arrows arched into the air and came straight at *him!* Yi! he tried to shout, but couldn't make a sound. He ducked and wiggled, his feet shuffling back and forth while the girl in the tower window grimaced and grabbed at her hair to ease the strain, and the arrows went whiff-whiff-whiff on by.

Thwack! A great boulder came curving up from the catapult. Dortmunder dropped his lance and fell forward onto the braids, and the boulder brushed his back as it went by.

Dortmunder clung to the braided tightrope. The archers were readying a second volley. Another big boulder was being tipped into the catapult. The silent nuns jumped up and down in excitement. The jousting men all stopped lambasting one another to point their pennant-tipped Valmets at Dortmunder. And now they were shooting! Bullets ripped through the hair-rope, breaking it, Dortmunder was losing his grip and falling, and somebody pinched his nose hard. His eyes popped open, he stared at Sister Mary Grace leaning over him, and he said, "Oh, thank you! I needed that."

Wide-eyed, she put a warning finger to her lips, then pointed a thumb toward the doorway.

Dortmunder had been sleeping in the big beige marble bathtub, the surface softened by a couple of layers of terrycloth towels and with a tan terrycloth robe thrown over him for comfort. Now he tried to sit up, bumping his elbow on bare marble and his knee on a faucet, and whispered, "Somebody's coming?"

She nodded. She pretended to open a door and look in, to raise a chest lid and study the interior, to pull a curtain aside and peer past it.

"They're *searching?*" His whisper was so loud and harsh that she made the shush-shush gesture with finger to lips again. More quietly, he whispered, "Here? Up here?"

Emphatic nod. Then she tugged at his wrist.

"Okay, okay, here I come."

He crawled and struggled up out of the bathtub, not aided by the fact that terrycloth slides on marble, and when at last he was more or less erect and on his feet he found he was just as stiff and sore as if the surfaces he'd slept on had been of more plebeian matter. "Whoosh," he commented, and pressed knuckles into his back.

She was over by the bedroom door, gesturing dramatically for him to come on. He looked around the bathroom, and said, "Uh. Do I have two minutes?"

Her face was agitated, but then she nodded briskly and hurried from the room, pulling the door shut, and two minutes later Dortmunder followed her.

A clean and simple bedroom. The twin bed stood high enough from the ground and was so unostentatiously covered that the well-swept floor beneath it was in plain sight. A small wooden chest of drawers, a modest bedside table and an armless wooden chair completed the furnishings. The closet door stood open, revealing an almost empty interior. "There's no place to hide," Dortmunder pointed out.

She was over by the hall door. She nodded agreement, touched finger to lips, and cautiously opened the door, looking out. Dortmunder heard male voices, and slid over to peek past the top of Sister Mary Grace's head.

A short hall. Half a dozen tough guys in camouflage uniforms out of Dortmunder's dream were just entering a room down to the right. They weren't carrying their Valmets, but on the other hand they didn't have to.

The instant the last of the searchers disappeared into that room, Sister Mary Grace was out the bedroom door and moving away to the left, gesturing for Dortmunder to follow. He did, both of them jogging on the balls of their feet, and she led them into the kitchen.

Large, airy, very elaborate and modern, with a big double-ovened electric stove. Side-by-side refrigerator-freezer, with icewater dispenser. Butcher block island in the middle of the room, with copper pans hanging above. Blond wood cabinets, white tile floor. Twin stainless steel sinks. Dishwasher, with a small magnetic sign on the front reading, SUCIO—DIRTY. Lots of unopenable windows letting in the morning light here a thousand feet closer to Heaven. Dortmunder opened a narrow wooden door and found a broom closet crammed with brooms and mops and buckets. There was nowhere to hide.

Sister Mary Grace had made one brisk circuit

around the room, staring and frowning at everything, then abruptly hurried to the dishwasher and
turned the magnetic sign around so it read,
LIMPIO—CLEAN. A hell of a time for tidying up.

But now what? Opening the dishwasher, which
was less than a quarter full, she started pulling out
used glasses, coffee cups, plates, forks, everything.
Opening cabinets, she stowed it all away, dirty
dishes with the clean. Not only that, she gestured
urgently for Dortmunder to come over and help.

So Dortmunder went over and helped. "What's
this for?" he asked, putting glasses with milk scum
on their bottoms on a shelf with clean glasses.

She pointed at him. She pointed at the dishwasher.

"*Oh*, no," he said. "I couldn't fit in, that's
nothing I could, no way I'm gonna . . ."

She was very good at ignoring him, when she
was of a mind to. The dirty dishes dealt with, she
pulled the lower rack out of the dishwasher,
reached in and lifted the propeller-like water dispenser out of the bottom and dropped it in the
rack, then carried the rack over to the stove. The
wide oven ate the rack as though it were no more
than a thirty-pound turkey or three pies.

Hardly believing he was doing it, Dortmunder
removed the dishwasher's top rack and brought it
over to Sister Mary Grace, who fed it to the other
oven. Meantime, Dortmunder was saying, "See,
it's this phobia, I can't, there's a phobia with
places like that."

Well, there's about a million phobias in connection with getting inside a dishwasher; about the only phobia that doesn't come into play is the fear of heights. But there's claustrophobia, the fear of small enclosed spaces; nyctophobia, the fear of the dark; dysmorphophobia, the fear of being bent out of shape; lyssophobia, the fear of going crazy; hydrophobia, the fear of someone turning the dishwasher on to rinse cycle . . .

Sister Mary Grace pointed at the dishwasher, her mouth a stern grim line. Dortmunder paused to marshal further arguments, and heard male voices out in the hall, crossing to search the bedroom. It wouldn't take long at all to search that bedroom, nor the bathroom beyond it. "I'll try," Dortmunder said. "If I can't fit in, I'll just give myself up or something."

Shoo, shoo, she gestured, and he went over to the dishwasher and tried to figure out how to get into it. If he stepped on the open door, it would break. Finally, he turned his back to the thing, spread his legs wide like a parody of a cowboy on a horse, and backed up slowly, shins brushing the sides of the door, while Sister Mary Grace held one arm to help him keep his balance.

Tight, very tight. Dortmunder sat down in the dishwasher, hit the back of his head, scrinched around, hit the back of his head, drew his left leg up inside, hit the back of his head, drew his left leg up inside, hit the back of his head, wriggled farther and farther back while his spine found an interesting curve it had never known it could make before, and then there he was, head bent down to look at his own stomach, legs tied in a granny knot, and body generally speaking doing a Lon Chaney imitation.

But he was in it, by golly, inside the dishwasher. By looking as far upward as possible, past his own eyebrows, he could see the dishwasher door closing. "Not all the way!" he said.

Not all the way. In fact, it rested gently on the top of his head just a quarter-inch from being completely closed, so there was even a bit of light in here. So much for nyctophobia. But what if I get a cramp in here, he wondered, so there's another one: crampophobia.

The dishwasher smelled of sour milk. Also something vaguely Mexican or South American. Dortmunder heard the faint rustle of Sister Mary Grace leaving the kitchen, and he spent a moment in extreme discomfort, sniffing, trying to place that somehow Latin odor, and the kitchen filled up with men talking, walking around, banging into things. "Goddamnit," one voice said, "there's just nobody here."

A voice that sounded to Dortmunder like the leader, the guy who'd been up on the stage last night, said, "He's got to be, boys. I doped it out, and that little quiet girl there has to be the one that helped him with the lights, and up here is the only place she could bring him."

"Well, she won't talk."

"I know she won't talk," the leader's voice said. "She's took a vow of silence."

"Vow of silence? Is that spreading around among

246

women?" asked another voice; he sounded hopeful.

"Mr. Pickens," said another voice, "the fella just isn't here. We've searched every room. We've left a man on duty in every room, so the fella couldn't do a flanking movement and get around behind us. He just plain and simple isn't up here."

"And yet," said the leader's voice, who must be Pickens, "he just has to be. I don't get it."

Another voice suggested, "Maybe we oughta do another sweep down on seventy-four. And in that apartment on seventy-five."

"We've *done* all that," Pickens complained, but he could be heard weakening.

Go do it again, Dortmunder thought. I can't stay scrunched up in here much longer.

A sound of water running. Now what?

"Long as we're here," a voice said, "anybody else want coffee?"

37

It was curiosity that brought J.C. Taylor back to her office on Sunday morning, but she told herself her motives were hard-headed and realistic. She wanted to be sure they weren't doing any irreparable damage to her place, for one thing, and she also wanted to be damn certain there wouldn't be any evidence on her territory linking her to whatever burglaries those plug-uglies were committing. But besides that, and at bottom, it was curiosity.

On Sunday, you had to sign in at the lectern in the lobby. J.C. knew the blue-uniformed security guard—she occasionally did come in anyway on Sundays, to get caught up with the mailing—and he gave her a happy smile of greeting, saying, "A real nice day."

So nothing's gone wrong yet with their plans, she thought, no excitement or trouble. "A very nice day," she agreed, scrawled *J.C. Taylor, 712, 10:50 AM* on the sheet, and went away to the 5–21 elevators and on up to seven.

The Avalon State Bank Tower always felt different on Sunday, huge and cavernous and echoing. There was something timeless about it then, as though it had existed forever on some asteroid out in space and human beings had just recently started to inhabit it. J.C. listened to the magnified tock-tock of her footsteps as she walked down the corridor from the elevator, and she could just *feel* the emptiness in the offices all around her.

Not total emptiness, though. Unlocking the door to 712, she stepped into the middle of a touring company production of *The Thief of Bagdad*. Inlaid chests, amphorae, statuettes, the smoothness of ivory, the glitter of jade, amethyst, alexandrite, aquamarine, drapes of necklace, bangles, armlets, anklets, pendants, gleam of garnet, jasper, peridot, heliotrope, a rainbow of crimsons and golds and fierce greens strewn about her office furniture and floor as in some Hollywood Technicolor bazaar. All it lacked was Maria Montez.

It didn't lack Sabu, however; here he came

from the inner office, in the person of Wilbur Howey, carrying a teetering stack of mailers, while the ones called Kelp and Murch worked industriously away at J.C.'s desk, sorting and stowing, like minor elves in Santa's workshop, to blur the metaphor just a bit.

It was Sabu—that is, Howey—who noticed her first, gaped with surprise and delight over the top of his stack of cardboard, and cried out, "Say, *Toots!*"

That made the elves look up. "Chicky," said Kelp, "it's the landlord."

"I guess this must be success," J.C. said. Something deeply acquisitive in her nature, something magpie-ish, some instinctive turning toward luxury and comfort and sybaritic satisfaction, some softness she invariably kept locked away so deeply she remained barely aware of its existence, made her reach out and pick up a smooth ivory bracelet, a simple oval, very delicately carved with a floral design. The fingers that typed the mailing labels gently caressed the design, the eyes that looked without emotion at the photographers softened as they looked at the soft white of the ivory. "Not too tough to take," she murmured, and cleared her throat, and put the bracelet down again before these birds got the idea she was trying to steal it. Or noticed any flaw in her armor. Looking around, she said, "Where's the rest of the team?"

"Say, I'll tell you," Howey said, dumping the empty mailers on the floor next to Kelp, "Tiny's back there," with a thumb toward the inner door.

"And the other guy? The one with the worry lines on his head."

"You mean Dortmunder," Kelp told her.

"If you say so," she said, and was becoming aware of an awkwardness in their silence when the monster appeared in the inner office doorway, glowering at her from under those throw rugs he used for eyebrows, and saying, "What's this? You come back on Monday, that's the story the way *I* heard it."

"I wanted to check on things," she said, and shrugged. Monsters didn't intimidate her, she'd worked with them all her adult life. "Where's the other one?" she repeated. "Dort-whatever."

"Munder," Kelp said.

"Gone," Tiny Bulcher said. "Like you. We'll see you tomorrow."

"Gentle down, big fella," she told him, and turned to Howey, the most malleable of them. "Where is he, Wilbur?"

"Well, say," Howey told her, and threw a worried glance at Tiny, "he's gone, you know?"

"No, I don't know."

Tiny said, "He went upstairs to get the nun and he didn't come down, so that's it."

"Nun?"

Kelp said, "It's very simple," and then proceeded to tell her a story that wasn't simple at all. For some strange reason, there was a nun imprisoned at the top of this tower. For some other strange reason, Dortmunder had to go rescue her. The whole robbery business was to pay for partners to help in the rescue of the nun. Last night, Dortmunder went away to rescue the nun, and so far he hadn't come back.

J.C. said, "And?"

Everybody shifted around uneasily. The others all glanced at Tiny Bulcher, who said, belligerently, "And nothing. He's on his own."

Slowly she looked him up and down. "So that's why they call you Tiny," she said. With a graceful sweeping gesture of the arm that she'd learned in ballet class at the age of four—J.C. Taylor was not always as we see her now—she indicated the king's ransom strewn helter-skelter around the room. "Dort-whatever brought you all this," she said, voice dripping with scorn, "and now you're going to just leave him."

38

Virgil Pickens sipped cooling coffee. "I just don't like it," he said.

The four troops sitting around the kitchen table with him were getting so bored with all this they were beginning to let him know it. "Whether you like it or not, Mr. Pickens," one of them said, "that fella Smith just isn't up in this apartment."

Pickens brooded, watching the Guatemalan cook who'd arrived just a few minutes ago—came to work at eleven, apparently—and who'd been throwing evil-eye hostile looks at the men gathered in her kitchen ever since. Wants us out of here so she can clean up, Pickens supposed, though with the number of half-dirty cups they'd found in the cabinets when making their coffee she wasn't exactly the best housekeeper money could buy.

Was that the story with the towels as well? When they'd looked through the Ritter girl's bathroom the tub had been half full of towels. Now, that could have been simple sloppiness, as everybody else suggested, but it did seem to Pickens he hadn't seen a whole hell of a lot of sloppiness anywhere else in this girl's quarters—except here in the kitchen, of course—and the alternative that had come to *him* was that somebody had used that tub to sleep in.

No, everybody said. The fella isn't here, everybody said. You can theorize all you want, everybody said, but until you have a fact or two to support your theories, essentially what you are is full of horseshit.

The Ritter daughter is closed away in her room. Every inch of this place has been searched. Smith isn't here.

"Oh, well," Pickens said, and finished his coffee. Rising, he said, "I hate to be wrong when I so *feel* that I'm right. Still . . ."

The cook, plainly in a hurry to be rid of them, picked up Pickens' cup, carried it to the dishwasher, opened it, and the dishwasher reached arms out to close itself again.

"What bugs me," Pickens said, and became aware of the cook. She had frozen in one place like Lot's wife, staring round-eyed. At the dishwasher.

Pickens frowned, trying to remember what he'd just seen. "*Arms?*" he asked.

The dishwasher sighed.

39

The public garden in the ground floor of the Avalon State Bank Tower, so green, so lovely, so productive of tax abatements, was closed on Sunday. The few passersby on Fifth Avenue on that day of rest could still look through the tall plate-glass wall and refresh themselves with the views within of slender trees and graceful shrubbery and the cafe's delicate wrought-iron white chairs, but that was all. However, on this particular sunny Sunday in spring, just a bit after eleven in the morning, a really sharp-eyed passerby might have noticed—though none did—a few shadowy figures darting through those trees, pausing behind a bush, rushing to a copse of birch and a clump of beech, infiltrating the woods like a Civil War raiding party just before Shiloh.

Howey, with the appropriate spec sheets from the ledger books in his pocket, and with Stan Murch along as bearer of his toolbag, had led the way down the stairwell from the seventh floor, out to the silent lobby, and past the broad aisle at the far end of which the security guard sat on a stool, facing the other way, leaning on the lectern where people signed in. A little past that aisle, out of the guard's sight, was a wide door labeled OPEN SLOWLY, which was not actually openable at all today, since, being the door to the garden, it too was kept locked on Sunday. Howey snickered slightly when he saw this door, passed his hand over its mechanisms, and the door gaped wide without further ado. In they went; Howey, Stan, Kelp, Tiny and J.C. Taylor herself, who had broken down the last shred of Tiny's resistance to the rescue operation by volunteering to take part.

Kelp had to lead the way through the woods, Howey not having previously seen the MAINTENANCE door which actually opened to the special elevator. Once there, while the others huddled around him, glancing from time to time through the intervening trunks and leaves and branches toward the empty sunlit street, Howey studied the door, studied the spec sheet, studied the door some more, and said, "Now they're getting serious."

"You get serious, too," Tiny suggested.

"Say, you know me," Howey reminded him. "Show me a lock, and I'll show you an open door."

It wasn't quite that simple. It took three minutes and four tools and a lot of low irritable whistling from the kneeling Howey until at last he popped up onto his feet, tossed his tools with a clank into the open bag held by Stan Murch, and said, "She's yours."

Kelp opened the door to what seemed a bare

closet. But the rear wall was a sliding door, with a telephone-style keypad beside it. Soft amber light came from a recessed ceiling fixture. "Now, *that's* gonna take a few seconds," Howey said, nodding at the keypad. "I'll need somebody to hold the light."

"Me," Stan told him.

"Fine. The rest of you fellas and gals, just wait outside there, we'll knock when we're ready." Howey winked at J.C. "Don't you go too far, Toots."

"I always go too far," she told him, and he blinked and giggled and took that thought into the closet with him.

Inside, while Stan held the flashlight—"Say, pal, not on my knuckles, you know, on my *work*"—Howey brought out a small battery-operated drill and made two holes in the cover plate of the keypad, above the numbers 1 and 3. The narrow ends of a line tester were inserted, and the line tester lit up. So did Howey, saying, "Say, there, I got it in one. Listen, am I my mama's favorite child, or what?"

"Or what," Stan told him.

"Sez you," Howey riposted.

Outside, Kelp hunkered behind a planter, watching the street, remembering a war movie called *Guadalcanal Diary* that he'd seen on TV. The American Marines were hunkered like this in their foxholes. Low thick fog cover on the ground, all you could see was the shiny dark round helmets on the Japanese, crawling toward the Marine position. Scary. Kelp peered through shiny-leaved shrubbery and tall slender tree trunks, and out on the sunny sidewalk a Japanese tourist family of four went by, in their Sunday best, taking one another's pictures.

Tiny and J.C. leaned against the wall near MAINTENANCE and near each other. Breaking a long silence, Tiny muttered, "I didn't want to embarrass him, that's all."

J.C. considered this. "Oh?"

"Dortmunder," Tiny explained. "Maybe he don't *need* to be rescued."

"He'll be glad to see us, just the same."

"Maybe so," Tiny said reluctantly. His brow was extremely furrowed. He was trying to be conciliatory, a thing he'd never attempted before. "Maybe," he said, "it was good to get another point of view. Somebody come in, see it like with new eyes."

Aware of the strain of Tiny's efforts, J.C. decided to meet him halfway. "Thank you, Tiny," she said. "I wouldn't want you to think I was just being nosy or bossy or anything."

"Aw, naw," Tiny assured her. "Like I said, a second opinion. It's good with doctors, why not with everybody?"

"That's true."

Which was as far as Tiny could carry good fellowship without relief. Moving away from the wall, he glared at MAINTENANCE and said, "What's taking that scrawny chicken so goddamn long?"

"He'll get there," J.C. said.

He was, in fact, almost there. Stan Murch's flashlight now shone on a contraption of wires messily sticking out of the two holes Howey had made, and Howey's tongue was between his teeth, poking out the corner of his mouth, as he held two ends of bare wire just apart from each other. He moved his tongue out of the way long enough to say, "Well, here goes nothin."

"I don't like to hear things like that," Stan told him.

Howey put the wire ends together. Far off, something, some machine, went *chuh-uhhhhhhhhhh.* "Say," Howey said, grinning, his relieved eyes dancing, "you like to hear things like *that?* That's our elevator coming."

40

"Straighten up when I talk to you," Virgil Pickens said.

"I can't," Smith said.

So Pickens sat down at the kitchen table, where his head was at least at the same level as Smith's. Somewhere else in the apartment, the Guatemalan cook could be heard, still sobbing, while the Ritter girl tried to console her. The ten men of Pickens' search unit were gathered in the kitchen, along with the three private guards normally assigned here, all of them studying this crumpled-up man they'd found in the dishwasher.

Smith. Still Smith, unfortunately, since he carried no identification and so far refused to give any other name. "I'll tell you, Smith," Pickens said, gazing severely at the top of Smith's head, "I hate torture as much as the next man."

"So do I," said Smith.

"So that's why," Pickens told him, "I'm hoping you're gonna cooperate with me and—goddamnit, man! I can't talk to your *head!*"

"Let's straighten him," said one of the troops. A couple of the boys picked Smith up and unbent him somewhat, but when they put him down again he slowly folded back to his former shape, like plastic after you heat it.

"Well, shit," Pickens said. "Seat him in a chair here, then. It's goddamn unorthodox, questioning a prisoner, having the prisoner sit down, but maybe— There. That's better."

It seemed to be better for Smith, too; he sighed a bit, and settled, like an old house on muddy ground. Seated on the chair, he almost looked like a normal human being, with only a slight curvature around the neck and shoulders to suggest he'd been through anything unusual.

Pickens brooded, studying this sorry specimen. There's some way or another to break any human being in the world, and from the look of this fellow every one of those ways ought to work this time around. On the other hand, there was a kind of fatalism in Smith's bearing that was maybe more than dishwasher slump. A man who's already despaired before you ever start on him can sometimes be a very tough nut to crack. Probing for an opening, Pickens said, "You've run out your string, Smith, and there's nobody gonna come help, so you might as well tell us the whole story."

Smith looked around at the troops. His expression said he'd expected to meet up with them sooner or later; he wasn't surprised. He didn't even seem particularly troubled by it all. Frank Ritter's three private guards, having elected not to deal themselves into this hand, stood to one side with folded arms and impassively watched.

Pickens leaned forward to tap a knuckle on Smith's knee, recapturing his attention. Looking Smith in the eye, speaking very softly, he said, "You're all alone with us, Smith. And you're gonna stay alone with us. And we're not your friends."

Smith sighed.

The five people crowded into the elevator stared past one another's ears at their dim amber reflections in the copper walls. All was silent, save for the hum of machinery, until J.C. Taylor calmly said, "I know that was you, Wilbur, and if you do it again, I'll ask Tiny to sit on your head when we get out of here."

"Say, Toots, can't a fella, *gunnngg!*" Howey said.

Tiny nodded, and shifted position a second time. "He won't bother you no more," he said.

"That's right," said a high-pitched voice. Everybody looked around, then realized it had come from Howey. "Say," he said, sounding somewhat more normal, "I know when I'm not wanted."

"Good," said Tiny.

Non culpar, Sister Mary Grace wrote on the notepad, wishing her Spanish were better, and underneath did it in English as well: *It's not your fault*. Gently tugging the dish towel away from Enriqueta Tomayo's eyes, Sister Mary Grace waved the notepad in front of the weeping woman's crumpled face until Enriqueta focused on it, gazing ruefully and tearfully at the words, then shaking her head, her face crumpling even more, tears running down her round cheeks. Once again the dish towel, now sopping, was pressed to that wet face.

The two women sat on the narrow vinyl sofa in the plain and Spartan reception room, where the elevator opened. To their right was the doorway leading to the combination living/dining room where most of her encounters with the departed Walter Hendrickson had taken place, and beyond that the rest of the apartment, and at last the kitchen, where poor John was now surrounded by her father's hired mercenaries and assassins.

It was my fault. I should have found a way to, Sister Mary Grace wrote, and paused, listening. Hhhmmmmmmmmmmm . . . The elevator. She gazed at its door, across the room, and wondered who this might be. More reinforcements for the mercenaries? Possibly even her father himself, who she knew was in the building? Her face stiffened, and she sat hunched on the sofa, watching the elevator door. Enriqueta, aware less of the approaching elevator than of the difference in Sister Mary Grace, slackened in her weeping, peered over the top of the dank dish towel at the girl, then followed her gaze to the elevator.

Which opened, and out from it emerged the motleyest crew this side of the yellow brick road. A man monster came first, with a face like the radiator of a 1933 Ford and two clenched fists like angry basketballs. He was followed by a skittering little dancing old man, popping up and down on his toes, eyes searching in thirty directions at once. An extremely exotic-looking woman followed, very attractive and sensual but also hard, as though one could strike a match on her; not convent material, Sister Mary Grace thought. After her came a sharp-nosed, sharp-eyed, skinny man who looked like the untrustworthy small animal in a Disney cartoon; the pack rat or weasel. And last out was a red-haired chunky man who looked around with great interest and attention, as though expecting to be given a memory test on the contents of this room later.

Enriqueta gasped, and stared wide-eyed, and clasped the soggy dish towel to her throat. Everybody looked at everybody else, while the elevator door slid shut, and then the man monster came over, glowering as though he felt Sister Mary Grace were to blame for something, and growled, "You the nun?"

Could this be—? Quickly, Sister Mary Grace wrote, *Are you John's friends?* and held up the notepad.

"That's the nun, all right," said the sharp-nosed man.

Could they be heard in the kitchen? Warningly, Sister Mary Grace put her fingers to her lips.

They misunderstood, unfortunately; the man monster said, "*You're* the one with the vow of silence, lady, not us." Meantime, the skittery little old man peeked bright-eyed around the man monster's elbow and said, "Say, there, Sister Toots. Heard any good prayers lately?"

The man monster frowned at the little man. "Wilbur," he said, "I don't need you to open any locks anymore. You go on annoying me, I'm gonna unlock your nose and watch your brains fall out."

The little man, Wilbur, blinked at the man monster, daunted for a second, but then he turned aside and gave Sister Mary Grace a surreptitious grin and wink.

Meantime, the sharp-nosed man had understood the reason for Sister Mary Grace's desire for quiet. Pointing at the doorway leading to the rest of the apartment, he said in a low voice, "They got Dortmunder back there?"

Dortmunder? Not knowing that name, Sister Mary Grace wrote on her pad, *John?* and showed it to them.

"Yeah," the man monster said, sounding very irritable. "Saint John, that's him."

Sister Mary Grace nodded, and pointed at the doorway, and nodded again.

The sharp-nosed man said, "Who else is with him?"

10 armed mercenary soldiers, Sister Mary Grace wrote, *and 3 armed private guards.*

They looked at that note when she held it up, then looked at one another, and Sister Mary Grace could see them comparing the forces arrayed against them with themselves: four extremely varied men, and three extremely varied women. No wonder everyone looked a bit apprehensive, and that the little man, Wilbur, sounded shakier than before when he said, "Well, Tiny? How strong do you feel?"

That was the man monster, oddly enough. He took a deep breath, for answer, and gazed at the doorway, clearly intending to simply march in there and do his best. Sister Mary Grace wrote fast, and held up the note:

Excuse me. I have a suggestion.

41

Dortmunder gazed at Pickens' heavy and unsympathetic face, and saw little to like there. Just what sort of story would this guy believe? It seemed perfectly clear that Pickens wouldn't for a second believe the truth, that John Dortmunder was merely a professional burglar doing some nuns a favor by rescuing Sister Mary Grace. So what sort of story might he be likely to believe?

The question had some urgency, because Pickens was talking about torture again. "It's kind of amazing," he was saying, "just how many things there are in the ordinary kitchen that can cause a fella pain, if that fella isn't polite enough to answer a decent question. That electric stove over there, for instance. Jocko, go turn on the left front burner about halfway."

One of the tough guys went over and turned on the left front burner, about halfway. Dortmunder didn't watch, because his head wouldn't turn in that direction, but he knew it was happening.

"Now, in just a few seconds, Smith," Pickens said, "you're not gonna want to touch that burner at *all*. You know what I mean?"

"Uh huh," Dortmunder said.

"But you *are* gonna touch it," Pickens said, "or you're gonna answer my questions, one or the other."

"Faucet," said a tough guy.

"That's good," Pickens said, nodding judiciously, approving of a bright student. "That's another one," he told Dortmunder. "We turn the water on in the kitchen sink and then we put some part of your head in the way. Your nose, for instance, or your mouth, or your ear."

"Hot water," suggested another one.

"That's also good," Pickens said.

"Burner's turning red," said the one called Jocko, over by the stove.

"Burner's turning red," Pickens told Dortmunder.

Dortmunder nodded. "I heard," he said.

"So now," Pickens said, leaning forward again, looking very serious, "let's start with your real—"

"Hey!" said a tough guy, and another one said, "What the—" and another one said, "Jesus!"

Pickens, slightly annoyed, looked up at his troops. Dortmunder tried to, but his head wouldn't lift that far. Cocking it at an angle like a bird, he looked upward slantwise and saw some of the tough guys, the ones who'd been facing the doorway, staring that way in astonishment. Pickens was already twisting around to look at the doorway, and Dortmunder turned his aching body sufficiently to look, too, and it was empty. Just a doorway.

"Now what?" Pickens said.

"There was a . . ." one of the tough guys said, and waved his arms, and said, "There was a woman there."

"The daughter," Pickens said. "We know about her."

"Not the daughter," the tough guy said. "I saw the daughter before and believe me, Mr. Pickens, that was not the daughter."

"Then the cook," Pickens said. He was getting really annoyed. "Don't interrupt the interrogation."

The tough guy said, "Mr. Pickens, this was a different woman completely. She was a, you know, a kind of a, she was kind of a . . ."

"Knockout," said one of the other tough guys.

"She blew a kiss," said a third.

"Mr. Pickens," said a fourth, sounding awed, "she was topless!"

Pickens glared at his troops. "What the hell is all this guff?"

Those who had seen the vision told him what the guff was, volubly, agreeing with one another. Pickens shut them with a barked, "Enough!" and turned to one of the three private guards leaning against the side wall. "Who else is up here?" he demanded.

They shifted uneasily, glancing at one another. They didn't have a leader, and hadn't expected to do anything but observe. Finally, one of them said, "Nobody else."

"Did you see this so-called topless woman?"

"Nope," the spokesman said, and the other two nodded agreement with him.

"Maybe," Pickens suggested, his jaw bunching with repressed anger, "maybe you birds ought to check out your territory."

The three guards looked at one another. They were in civilian clothing, neat jackets and ties, but their manner was semi-military, and they clearly didn't like taking orders from somebody outside their chain of command. Still, if a topless woman was wandering around their allegedly secure area, they ought to check it out, so finally the spokesman said, "Come on, boys, let's see if there's anything to it."

"Oh, there's something to it," he was assured by one of the guys who'd seen the topless woman. "There's a *lot* to it."

Carefully blank-faced, the three guards left the kitchen, and Pickens turned back to Dortmunder, saying, "Before we were so rudely interrupted, we were talking about accidents that can happen in the home to people who don't answer questions. As I remember, we hadn't even got around to the whole subject of knives."

"No, we hadn't," Dortmunder agreed.

"Smith," Pickens said, "I'm tired of calling you Smith. Tell me your name."

"Ritter," Dortmunder said. "William Ritter."

Pickens reared back to stare at him. "Ritter?"

"I'm the black sheep uncle," Dortmunder explained. "Sister Mary Grace's uncle." He wished he could remember Sister Mary Grace's other name, her family name; an uncle would be expected to know something like that.

Pickens squinted, as though trying to see Dortmunder more clearly. "You're telling me," he said, "you're Frank Ritter's *brother?*"

"No-good brother," Dortmunder said, and then just sat there and looked at Pickens, allowing his patent no-goodness to substantiate his claim.

Pickens said, "That is the most ridiculous—"

"God*damn*it!"

It was one of the tough guys who'd seen the topless woman, and he was staring at the doorway again. Pickens squinted at *him*. "You seeing things again, Ringo?"

"I saw—" Ringo turned to the guy next to him, and pointed at the doorway (it was empty). "Didn't you see it?"

"Little guy," the other one said.

"That's right. Little old geezer."

Dortmunder became very still.

"Now, goddamn, wait a minute," Pickens said. "This wasn't the topless woman? This was somebody *else?*"

"Little old geezer," said the guy who'd said it before.

"And was *he* topless, too?" Pickens asked, with heavy sarcasm.

"No, sir, Mr. Pickens. He was bottomless."

Ringo said, "He mooned us, sir."

Pickens' hands were bunched into fists on his knees. He said, "Mooned you?"

"You know, sir," Ringo said. "When a fella turns his back and drops his pants and bends over and wiggles his ass at you."

Pickens turned around and stared at the empty doorway. Then he turned back and stared at Ringo. "You're telling me," he said, "that a little old man came to that doorway and turned around and dropped his pants and bent over and wiggled his *ass* at you?"

"Bony old guy, too," said Ringo.

"Say, I am not neither!" cried a voice from somewhere else in the apartment; it had the sound of the voice of a little old geezer, probably bony.

"There he is!" cried Ringo. "Hear him?"

"I heard him." Pickens gave Dortmunder the fisheye. "What do you know about this, Ritter, or Smith, or whoever you are?"

Poker face, Dortmunder told himself; you'll never have a better opportunity to practice your poker face. "Nothing," he said.

Pickens stared at him a second longer, then turned to his men and pointed, giving out assignments. "Ringo, Turk, Wyatt, Pierce, go out there and get me that guy. *And* the topless woman. And find out where the hell those private guards got off to."

"Yes, sir, Mr. Pickens," they said, and trooped out of the room.

"This place is supposed to be secure up here," Pickens grumbled. "Most sophisticated security money can buy, and we're loadin up with *tourists*. If this is Margrave employees having fun, I'm gonna get a whole bunch of people fired." He glared around at his troops, but no one had anything to add to that sentiment, so he gave his attention once again to Dortmunder. "I'll tell you," he said. "I could phone Frank Ritter, he's just two stories down from here, in his office. I could phone him and ask him if you're his brother. But if I do, and he says you're *not* his brother, I'm gonna break both your arms and both your legs. You want me to go ahead and make that call?"

"Frank, uh, disowned me a while ago," Dortmunder said.

"Yeah, well, I don't blame him," Pickens said, and leaned back, and said to his troops, "Do you suppose we could get his hand on that burner and his nose under that faucet at the same time?"

"We could anyway try," one of them said.

"That's the spirit." Pickens nodded at Dortmunder as the tough guys laid a whole lot of hands on him. "Anytime you want to talk with me," he said, as Dortmunder was carried away toward the appliances, "just let me know."

"Mr. Pickens!"

Everybody stopped, and turned to look at the doorway, the tough guys still holding on to Dortmunder, who sagged at waist-height among them like a rolled-up rug they were throwing away. They didn't drop him, but their hands tightened on him, as they all saw their comrade Ringo in the doorway. He was naked, standing there with his hands over his crotch, and he looked utterly miserable.

Pickens rose slowly from his chair, staring. "Ringo," he said. "What's *out* there?"

Ringo didn't move. He said, "Mr. Pickens, I'm told to ask for your surrender."

"Surrender!" Pickens cried. "Never!" He sounded shocked at the idea. "Surrender to *who?*"

"Whom," said a voice from the corridor.

"Mr. Pickens," Ringo said, "these people— They say they want to avoid bloodshed, if they can."

"Well, *I* don't," Pickens said, and turned to point at Dortmunder, saying, "Put that fella on the stove. Let's let everybody listen to him holler."

The troops hustled Dortmunder closer to the stove. "Say, uh . . ." he said. He could see the dull red glow of the burner.

"Mr. Pickens, *please,*" Ringo said, and when they all turned to look at him again he was still in the same position as before, but now an arm had extended out from beside the doorway, and was pressing the barrel of a Smith & Wesson .38 caliber Official Police revolver against Ringo's right ear. Blinking a lot, but not moving his head, Ringo said, "Mr. Pickens, they got Turk and Wyatt and Pierce locked up in a room. They got those guards in there, too. They say they don't want to kill anybody, but they will if they have to."

"*Who* says?" Pickens demanded.

"These people, uh, holding this gun to my head, Mr. Pickens."

"Surrender to an enemy I can't even *see?*" Pickens took a stomping step toward the doorway.

"Oh, *no*, Mr. Pickens!" Ringo said, bobbing up and down on the balls of his feet. "If you come over here, they'll just shoot me, and then they'll shoot you, and then they'll shoot everybody!"

Pickens stopped. He pointed at Dortmunder, hanging from his troops' hands. "I've got my *own* hostage, goddamnit!" He was so mad he was punching the air with both fists, but he wasn't moving toward the doorway anymore.

"Mr. Pickens," Ringo said, "I think they're kinda getting impatient."

"They are, are they? Getting impatient, are they?" Pickens put both hands on his hips, and leaned toward Ringo and the doorway, and said, "I tell you what I'm going to do. You people *hiding* back there, do you hear me?"

A woman's dulcet voice said, "Oh, we hear you, Mr. Pickens."

"One-on-one," Pickens shouted, and started

pulling handguns out of his clothing and slapping them down on the butcher block island in the middle of the kitchen; three guns in all. "A fair fight, goddamnit," he yelled, "like the old days, like the *knights!* Send out your best man, damn you to hell and back, no guns, no weapons at all! I'll meet him one-on-one, and if I beat him you'll surrender to *me*, whoever the hell you are! But if he beats me, I'll surrender my entire company!"

Ringo moved backward, and from around the corner came Tiny Bulcher, stepping into the doorway, filling it, arms at his sides, carnivorous eyes on the blanching Pickens. "You called?" Tiny asked.

42

New York Police Department recording, 11:22:45 A.M., Sunday, a call to the emergency number, 911:

NYPD: Police Department, emergency.

FEMALE VOICE: I want to report a mercenary army.

NYPD: Your name and location, please.

FV: Hannah McGillicuddy, Seven fifty-one East Forty-fifth Street.

NYPD: And what is it you wish to report?

FV: A mercenary army. Sixty professional soldiers armed with Valmets and—

NYPD: Helmets?

FV: Vel—Wait a minute.

(male voice, unintelligible, off)

FV:*(off)* What difference does it make?

(male voice, unintelligible, off)

FV:*(off)* All right, all right, you risked your life for the information, the least we can do is get it right. Meantime, you can help clean up my office. *(into phone)* You still there?

NYPD: That was sixty soldiers in helmets.

FV: No, no, no. It's a rifle, it's—*(off)* I'm telling her! *(into phone)* An *assault* rifle, I'm informed, whatever that is. It's made in Finland, it's called a Valmet, V-A-L-M-E-T. It's like a machine gun and the idea is, they're planning to take a plane down to South America, to a country called Guerrera, and start a war.

NYPD: Where are these sixty armed men?

FV: At the top of the Avalon State Bank Tower on Fifth Avenue. A financier named Frank Ritter that owns the building is the one paying for the war. They plan to fly down tomorrow morning.

NYPD: And their weapons and supplies are in that building on Fifth Avenue?

FV: Right again. Fifty of them are hanging around the seventy-fourth floor, in the offices of something called Margrave Corporation, and the other ten are up on the seventy-sixth floor, in a bedroom there.

NYPD: And your name is Hannah McGillicuddy, of Seven fifty-one East Forty-fifth Street.

FV: That's right.

NYPD: And your phone number there?

FV: Eight nine eight, five six five.

43

"As time is the fourth dimension of space, so
patience is the fourth dimension of confidence."
Leafing through his commonplace book, waiting for Virgil Pickens to return from upstairs—
he'd phoned down awhile ago that someone had
been found up on seventy-six and the investigation
was continuing—Frank Ritter came across that
aphorism on the subject of patience, done at some
time in the past, and he considered it without
pleasure. It was too long, too many words, and the
analogy seemed strained.

Or was it merely that this was a moment when
he didn't feel like hearing patience extolled? He
wanted to know what was going on upstairs, he
wanted to hear about it, and he wanted it to be
done and over with. Skipping past his previous
wisdoms to the most recent page, just beyond,
"Lie down with wolves . . . ," he wrote, "Patience
is sloth ennobled." There; *that* took care of it.

A knock on the door. Pickens at last! "Come
in," Ritter called.

But it wasn't Pickens. It was a middle-aged
woman, the Sunday receptionist and telephone an-
swerer whose post was at the desk just within the
Margrave Corporation entrance. Ritter frowned at

her, had time to notice her worried expression, and then she said, "Mr. Ritter, the police are—"

And two uniformed New York City patrolmen came in, sloppy young men with black hair over their collars and scuffed shoes and ill-fitting dark blue trousers. "Frank Ritter?" one of them said.

Ritter got to his feet; he was used to dealing with men in livery. "Yes, officers? What can I do for you?"

"We have a report," one of the policemen said, "of a paramilitary organization assembling in these offices, armed with illegal weapons."

Ritter's spine stiffened. "I *beg* your pardon," he said coldly. "This is a legitimate business office, with some respect and, if I may say so, influence in the world at large."

"And lots of activity on a Sunday," the second police officer said, unabashed.

The first one was also unabashed. "We have to follow up a report like this," he said.

Ritter glared. "And do your superiors know you're following up such an absurd accusation?"

A female police officer, just as sloppy as the males, with blonde hair messily over her collar, appeared in the doorway (where the worried receptionist still lingered, fretfully washing her hands) and said, "Door down here to some kind of theater, all shot up."

The first policeman cocked an arrogant eye at Ritter. "Running off a few practice rounds?"

"You people can't do this!" Ritter insisted.

"Come marching in here— Do you have a warrant?"

"We have probable cause," the second policeman said.

"You most certainly do not!" Ritter still believed he could drive these interlopers out by force of will alone. "A man's office is his castle!" he declared. "You can't trample on my rights like this! Your law stops in the lobby!"

"Right now, Mr. Ritter," the first policeman said, "in this office, we *are* the law."

A second female police officer, this one with red hair curling over her collar, appeared carrying a Valmet with both hands. "There's a bunch of them," she said. "No ammo."

A third male police officer, even younger than the others, and looking flushed with excitement, appeared and said to his comrades, "This army couldn't wait to get started. A report just came in of looting in this building last night."

That last remark made no sense to Ritter, and he was too bedeviled by the things he *did* understand to think about it. He put his hand on his telephone, glaring at the first policeman, whom he had decided was in charge of this farrago. "The mayor of this city is a personal friend of mine," he said. "What do you suppose he'll say to you if I call him now and tell him what's happening here?"

The policeman grinned at the Valmet, and grinned at Ritter. "I think he'd call me sergeant," he said.

44

Stan Murch, forehead pressed to the unopenable glass in the window in J.C. Taylor's inner office, watched the activity on the street seven stories below. "There goes the last busload," he said, as another Department of Corrections bus, dark blue with barred windows, pulled away from the curb in front of the Avalon State Bank Tower, taking the last of Pickens' Army away to its final ignominious defeat.

"Hey, Stan," Kelp called from the floor, "come on back to work, huh?"

Kelp was a little out of sorts because, while J.C. Taylor had been phoning the police, he was the one who'd been chosen to go back downstairs with Howey to the special elevator and back up to the top floor, carrying one plastic bag of swag to be distributed around the apartment up there; salting the felony mine, as it were. It had been Dortmunder's idea, once he'd gotten over the personal humiliation of having been rescued *twice* by the putative rescuee, and everyone agreed it was a good one. It would distract the police, give them every reason to suppose there were no crooks in the building except the ones they already had, and suggest the rest of the loot had already been exfiltrated from the building via elevator.

All well and good. What had Kelp's nose out of joint was the fact that when he and Howey had been coming back down in the elevator, it had all at once stopped, somewhere in the middle of the vertical tunnel between the basement and the roof. It turned out later that some building maintenance man had seen the mess of wires sticking from the keypad in MAINTENANCE—what was he doing in *there?*—and echoing that Watergate guard who removed the burglars' black tape from the door latch without telling anybody, had taken away the wires, merely to tidy up.

It wasn't so much that Kelp had immediately panicked, bouncing around the stalled elevator like a neutrino in a lab experiment, loudly declaiming that they would be stuck there until Kingdom Come or, even worse, until De Police Come, while Howey methodically unscrewed the control panel plate and got them moving again. No, what really browned Kelp's toast on both sides was the fact that when they returned safely to J.C.'s office Howey had *reported* Kelp's panic, complete with piping laughter and exaggerated imitations of Kelp in full cry. Howey had continued this entertainment for some time, until Tiny closed a hand around his head and quietly suggested he stop.

That was more than an hour ago, but Andy Kelp was still to some extent a bird of ruffled plumage, which was why, rather than argue, Stan Murch simply said, "Here I come, Andy," left the window, and went back over to sit on the floor beside Kelp and return to addressing packages.

They were all addressing packages now, Dortmunder and Tiny at J.C.'s desk, Kelp and Stan

278

seated on the floor, and on the floor in the other room Wilbur Howey, with J.C. Taylor and Sister Mary Grace at the receptionist's desk out there. Some discussion had taken place as to whether it was appropriate for Sister Mary Grace to be an accessory to grand larceny by addressing packages full of stolen goods, but she had resolved the issue herself with a note reading: *I obey a higher law. It says I can address packages in a good cause.*

There were nine different convenience addresses to which the packages were being sent, various cousins and attorneys who would restrain their curiosity. Now, when each of the addressers completed a batch, he or she carried them to the table in the inner room with the scale and meter, and added the appropriate postage. Then the packages were stored here, there and everywhere, ready to start going out, some tomorrow, some later in the week. In the days to come, packages would be retrieved from those convenience addresses and turned over to one of four different fences alerted and waiting. Very soon now, in a matter of just a few weeks, everybody in these rooms—except Sister Mary Grace, of course, another of whose vows embraced poverty—would be very rich.

Not rich *rich* RICH! But not bad, either.

45

Howey didn't want to take his clothes off. "Say, listen," he protested, "do I got my dignity or what?"

"Or what," Stan Murch told him.

"Sez you."

"Try not to panic, Wilbur," Kelp said nastily.

"Look, Wilbur," Dortmunder explained. "The odds are, Sister Mary Grace's father has people out looking for her already. Including he'd certainly have a couple guys hanging around the lobby, just in case she didn't get away yet. So the thing to do is disguise her as somebody else, and you're the only one around her size."

"And you don't want those rotten rags anyway," Kelp told him.

"Say, I *like* these duds," Howey complained, looking down to admire himself in his baggy tan chinos and penny loafers and bright plaid polyester shirt. "When I got out of the big house, the state gave me that suit, you know, that suit they give you, that suit was out of style when I went *in*. I went out to this snazzy new place in the suburbs, this K mart place, I got the latest threads. I *need* these togs, I got a front to keep up."

"Keep *this* crap up," Tiny told him, "you're not gonna have any front at all. Strip."

Howey looked around at the grim determined faces ringing him about. Dortmunder, Tiny, Kelp,

Murch. These were, after all, desperate men, hardened criminals. If they wanted his grade-A best casual attire, they were going to get it. "Say, *I'm* gonna look like some fruitcake," he muttered unhappily, starting to undo his belt buckle, "going out of here in my skivvies."

"You'll get her stuff," Dortmunder assured him. "And it isn't skirts or anything, it's regular blue jeans and a shirt."

Howey thought about that. "The stuff she's wearing right now, huh?"

Stan Murch shook his head. "This man is disgusting," he said. "Don't ever cross the street in front of me, Wilbur."

"Wha'd I say? Wha'd I say?"

They wouldn't tell him what he'd said. Finally his clothing was off, and then there was a brief argument about the Coors cap—"To put her *hair* in," Dortmunder pointed out, while Tiny ostentatiously mimed the wringing of a chicken's neck—and then Dortmunder took the rolled-up duds to the closed door leading to the outer office and knocked on it. J.C. opened it partway and said, "*That* took long enough. We've been ready a long time out here."

"There was some discussion," Dortmunder said, handing over the clothing. J.C. went away and came back with another little pile of clothing, and Dortmunder closed the door again. Howey didn't like Sister Mary Grace's clothes after all. He said the shoes were too tight, and the blue jeans were too tight around the knees but too loose around

281

the hips, and the blouse was too loose around the torso but too tight around the shoulders. And he felt naked without a hat. "You could wear the wastebasket if you want," Tiny told him, so then he shut up and just stood there, looking in the high-necked long-sleeved black blouse and oddly baggy jeans like a defrocked Druid.

"Okay," Dortmunder said. "Could be worse. She could of been wearing her habit, right?"

"Say," Howey said, "I don't want to get in the habit, do I?" But his heart didn't seem to be in it.

J.C. appeared in the doorway. "Okay," she said.

They all trooped out there, Howey last, to discover that Sister Mary Grace had been less severely dealt with by the transformation. J.C. had glued some of the girl's own cut-off hair onto her upper lip, which at first glance looked enough like a moustache to pass. With the rest of her hair tucked up inside the Coors cap, and wearing Howey's shirt and chinos and loafers, the worst you could say for her was that she looked like a tourist from Eastern Europe. But male.

"It's a different guard down there now," J.C. said, "so I'll sign out like we came in together. Just remember," she told the girl, "to let me do the talking." Then she shook her head: "Sorry. I forgot."

Sister Mary Grace went over to Dortmunder, smiled up at him, and held out her hand. Dortmunder shook it, and said, "Thanks for rescuing me." She did a graceful pointing-finger-rolling-over-pointing-finger gesture: *Thanks for rescuing me, too.*

Everybody then told the sister goodbye. "Pleasure," Tiny told her, briefly engulfing her hand and forearm in his version of a handshake. "If you take a cab," Stan Murch told her, "tell him to go straight down Ninth." Andy Kelp said, "It was fun, you know?" And Howey, lingering over the handshake, said, "I gotta admit it, Sister Toots, you look better in that rig than I do myself."

J.C. said, "I'll be back around nine tomorrow morning."

"We'll probably be gone," Dortmunder told her.

Tiny said, "Listen, Josie, I'll stick around, right? Help you mail this stuff."

Josie? Everybody looked at Tiny with astonishment, but he ignored them, grinning at J.C., who smiled casually back and said, "Sure, Tiny, that'd be nice."

Hmm, everybody thought.

46

"And here's the thing," Dortmunder said. "It's over, you know? And nothing went wrong."

"John," Kelp told him, "sometimes things work out, okay?"

"But I don't understand this," Dortmunder said, looking around J.C. Taylor's now-clean outer office. It was ten minutes since J.C. and Sister Mary Grace had left, and a pleasant calm had descended

283

everywhere. In the other room, Stan Murch watched early Sunday afternoon traffic out the window, Tiny Bulcher was taking the Allied Commissioners' Course final exam (and cheating), and Wilbur Howey was trying to decide if he looked worse with his shirt—that is, Sister Mary Grace's shirt—tucked in or hanging out. "We got the loot," Dortmunder pointed out. "We saved the nun. Nobody in our bunch got hurt or killed or even caught by the law. We're home free."

Kelp said, "Well, that was the plan, wasn't it?"

"Yeah, but—" Dortmunder shook his head. "I just don't get it."

The door opened, and J.C. and the nun came in. The nun looked very pale and round-eyed, and J.C. looked grim. "Trouble," J.C. said, closing the door, and the nun nodded.

"Ah," Dortmunder said. "Now I get it."

Kelp said, bright with false hope, "What, you need carfare, something like that?"

"*Big* trouble," J.C. said, and the nun nodded hugely. She looked mainly like a deer who'd just heard a gunshot.

"Tell me," Dortmunder said. "Tell me every bit of it."

"There's policemen at the exits," she said, "checking everybody's ID. I sweet-talked the security man at the desk down there, and he told me what's going on. The police know there's a lot of stuff missing from the robbery, and they're not sure they got every one of those soldiers up there, so they're doing a sweep."

"A sweep," Dortmunder said. Tiny and Stan and Wilbur had come out from the other room to listen.

"They got a quick warrant to search the entire building," J.C. went on. "They're starting at the top and sweeping down. They figure it'll take hours."

Dortmunder looked around this little two-room suite; a moment ago, a safe haven, but now a mousetrap and they the mice. "We can't get out of the building," he said, "because they're checking IDs at the exits. And we can't stay here, because they'll find us when they sweep through."

"I'm the only one signed in," J.C. said. She looked and sounded bitter. "I could get out of the building, but what good does it do me? They'll find you clowns, and then they'll find my offices full of stolen property, and then they'll find *me*. And I never did look good in gray."

Tiny said, "Josie, if it's any consolation at all, I promise you that before the law gets here I will personally run Dortmunder through the pencil sharpener."

Kelp said, "Tiny, that isn't fair! John did every—"

"John, huh?" Tiny lowered his head and gazed without love at Kelp. "John and his *Sisters*," he said. "We had a nice simple little robbery, very sweet and very smart, we could come in, we could go out, not a problem in the world. But your *John* here, he has to go up to the tower and knock over a hornet's nest. All the trouble we got, we got it because of John and this *nun*. It's *Come to the Stable* all over again. And your pal Dortmunder's the one brought in the nun."

Kelp turned desperately to Dortmunder. "John," he said, "there's a way out, right?"

"I'm glad to hear it," Dortmunder told him. He was wondering if Tiny actually did have a method whereby he could run a human being through a pencil sharpener. Knowing Tiny, it was possible.

"No, no," Kelp said, jittering. "I mean, *you've* got a way out, right? A solution? You know what we can do?"

"We could give ourselves up, I guess," Dortmunder said. "End the suspense." He sat down at the receptionist's desk and waited to be taken away.

"John," Kelp said. "You're the one with the plans, the ideas. Come *up* with something."

"There isn't anything," Dortmunder told him. "It's all over." There was a certain relief, a kind of relaxation, in giving in to despair.

"Say," Wilbur Howey said, bobbing up and down, glinting and winking, "prison ain't so bad, once you get used to it. Maybe we could all get in the same cellblock. Say, I was with a swell bunch this last time. We all got together and subscribed to *Playboy*, read all about hi-fi sets and everything, time passes before you know it."

Tiny growled, "Wilbur, *you* are gonna pass before you know it."

"Nothing to drive," Stan Murch said. His voice was so sepulchral it seemed to have an echo in it.

"From time to time," the irrepressible Howey assured him, "we could escape for a while, the whole bunch of us together. You could drive then."

"The same cellblock," Kelp said, looking with horror first at Tiny and then at Howey. "John," he said, "think about it."

Dortmunder was thinking about it. He sighed. No rest for the wicked. "All right," he said. "I'll do it. Tiny's pencil sharpener is one thing, but forty-eight years in a cellblock with Wilbur Howey? No way."

"John?" Hope glittered madly in Kelp's eyes. "You've done it? You found it?"

"I'm thinking," Dortmunder told him, "but people keep interrupting."

"Stop interrupting," Tiny told Kelp.

"That's right," Stan said.

J.C. said, "Everybody just pipe down."

"Say," Wilbur said, "give this fella room."

"*Everybody's* interrupting me," Dortmunder said.

So then everybody shut up, and just looked at him. Dortmunder sat there at the receptionist's desk and thought. He looked at J.C., and then at Sister Mary Grace, and then at Tiny, and then at Wilbur, and then at Kelp, and then at Stan Murch, and he thought. He got up and wandered into the back room and looked at everything there, and

287

thought. He looked out the window at the carefree people driving down Fifth Avenue in their cars, going anywhere they wanted, and he thought. He went back to the other room, where twelve eyes looked at him, and Wilbur Howey shifted position, and a pin was heard to drop. "Sister," Dortmunder said. "Is there a telephone down there in that convent?"

Wide-eyed, she nodded.

"Is there somebody with a, whadaya call it, a, a, compensation, decoration . . ."

Sounding almost timid, J.C. said, "You mean dispensation?"

"That's the thing," Dortmunder said. To the nun he said, "Does somebody have one of those down there, so they can break the vow of silence and talk on the phone if it rings?"

She nodded.

Dortmunder pointed at the telephone. "Call the convent," he said.

Sister Mary Grace, holding her breath, picked up the phone and started dialing.

Tiny looked disgruntled. "*More* nuns?" he said.

Dortmunder nodded. "More nuns."

47

There was a time when Chief Inspector Francis X. Mologna (pronounced Maloney) of the New York Police Department didn't have to come into the goddamn city on a Sunday in May no matter *what* happened. That was when the chief inspector had been the top cop of the City of New York, master of all he goddamn surveyed and you'd better not forget it. But then, some little time ago, the chief inspector stubbed his toe on a case, let the object of a massive manhunt slip through his massive fingers, got mad, punched a TV reporter *on camera,* and in general behaved counter-productively. He didn't so much blot his copybook as crap all over it. He was still powerful enough to be let off with a mere slap on the wrist, but in effect he was no longer the top cop of the City of New York, and he knew it, and everybody else knew it. Until the stink faded, Mologna was on display duty, which was wearin, time-consumin and humiliatin.

This is display duty: Whenever some major crime occurs in the City of New York—not some second-rate murder or bank robbery or an arson confined to one side of one block, but a major big-time big city felony—whenever a crime occurs so large and interestin that the media show up, it is necessary to have present there a high-rankin uniformed police official with braid on his hatbrim to conduct the investigation. This display inspector or display captain is usually somebody so old and so dumb and so racked by alcohol they won't let him have bullets for his gun anymore, and for Chief Inspector Francis X. Mologna to be given such duty cut deep. Deep.

And now here it was springtime, out in his home in Bay Shore on Long Island. Mologna's motorboat was in the water of the Great South Bay, just beyond his own backyard. His tomato plants and geraniums were in their beds in that yard. The sun was warm, the days were growin longer, and today was Sunday. And here in the middle of Manhattan, in the Avalon State Bank Tower, displayin his bulk to the media (but not punchin any goddamn reporters, *oh*, no), stood the fat and perspirin Francis X. Mologna, walkin around under his hat with the braid on the brim.

A hell of a mess, this one. Mologna was just glad he *wasn't* actually conductin the investigation, because the parts of this story didn't fit. Up on the top of the buildin were a whole lot of soldiers of fortune, mercenaries enough to change the administration in Hell. On the twenty-sixth floor were half a dozen burglarized importers. Some of the burglary loot was on the top floor with the mercs, who claimed to know nothin about it. And in fact, burglary was not their MO; slaughter of the innocents was more along the lines of their trade.

While seated in his chauffeured official car, takin a break from displayin himself, restin in the open door with his feet on the curb while he brooded unhappily about the clear and beautiful and sunlit water of the Great South Bay, Mologna was approached by a young black police officer with the righteous dew of the Police Academy still gleamin in his eyes and shinin on his forehead. This whippersnapper saluted and said, "Sir, we have a woman."

Mologna never returned salutes; he just nodded and kept them. Noddin, he said, "Good for you."

"She's right over there, sir."

Mologna frowned. Was he actually expected to *do* somethin? "What is she?" he asked. "A burglar or a soldier?"

"A song producer, sir."

Mologna considered this young black police officer. He was too young to know better and too black to yell at and unlikely to be pullin even a display inspector's leg. "And just what, in the Holy Virgin's holy name," he wanted to know, "should I be doin with a song producer?"

"It's about some nuns," the young man said, blinkin rapidly. "Maybe she ought to tell you herself."

"Nuns? Why would I—" But then his eye caught sight of a woman over by the Avalon Tower entrance, and he stopped, and for a second he just stared. Years and years ago he'd met a judo instructor who'd looked like that. By the good lord harry, but that woman could contort herself! That's one of the ones Mrs. Mologna never did find out about. "Her?" Mologna asked.

"Yes, sir."

"And what would *she* be havin' to do with nuns?"

"She wants to make a record with them, sir."

"That'll be a hell of a record," Mologna decided. "That'll get into Guinness for sure. Bring that record producer over here."

"Yes, sir." The young man saluted (Mologna

nodded) and off he went, returnin in a moment with the woman, sayin, "Mrs. Taylor, sir."

The woman smiled, seductive but not coarse, and said, "How do you do, Chief Inspector?"

Mologna had already struggled out of the car and onto his feet, and now he smiled his avuncular smile and put out his hand, and she placed a card in it. He'd expected a hand, not a card, but recovered and read it: *Super Star Music—J.C. Taylor, President.* The address was this Avalon Tower here. "Was you robbed, too?" he asked.

"Not yet," she said. "I'm hoping there won't be any trouble about these Sisters coming to see me."

"They'll be in no danger," Mologna assured her. "The crimes here are all over for the moment."

"Then I can bring them in?" Mrs. Taylor smiled again, radiantly, and seemed about to end the conversation.

"Wait a minute," Mologna said. The fear of makin *another* mistake was still very much alive in his breast. "Maybe you better tell me the whole story."

"I'm an independent record producer," J.C. Taylor said, "and I'd arranged to do a demo tape today with a group of nuns from a convent down in Tribeca."

"So you want to go down there?"

"No, they're on their way here. It was arranged weeks ago. Their contact at the archdiocese offices is Father Angelo Caravoncello."

Mologna bowed his head, as though he'd heard the holy name. The New York Police Department and the New York Archdiocese tend to be pretty tight. Well, in the first place, they are after all on the same side in the war between good and evil. And in the second place they both tend to assay out at a high percentage of Irish and Italian. And in the third place, they share the same turf, so they goddamn well *better* get along. Mologna didn't know Father Angelo Caravoncello, but just hearin the name and the connection with the archdiocese offices was good enough for him. "I see," he murmured.

"The idea," she said, "is a nun's chorus doing a pop album, like that French nun who did 'Amazing Grace' several years ago. Top of the charts, with a bullet."

Mologna frowned. "Bullet?"

"Oh, that's just trade talk," she said. "When a record moves very fast, up through the sales charts, we say it's with a bullet."

"We police have trade talk like that, too," Mologna told her. "Only when we say somethin's with a bullet, it usually isn't movin at all. So when do these sisters of yours get here?"

"About half an hour."

The young black policeman piped up, sayin, "The building records show Mrs. Taylor signed in this morning, well after the robbery, and wasn't in the building at all last night."

"Well, of course I wasn't," she said, smilin

293

again, her eyes twinklin at Mologna. "I don't love my job *that* much."

"Sure you don't," Mologna agreed, smilin back. He wished they'd had an actual handshake. "A pretty woman like you," he said, "you'll be wantin a private life of your own."

"Oh, now, Chief Inspector," Mrs. Taylor said, gigglin and wagglin a naughty-naughty finger at him. "You just never mind my private life."

The woman's flirtin with me! "Oh, I mean nothin at all by it, Mrs. Taylor," he said, turnin red in the face, pleased all over. "Why," he said, "I'm old enough to be your big brother." Aware of somethin more acute, possibly even ironic, suddenly present in the young patrolman's eyes, Mologna ended the conversation, sayin, "You run along now, and when these Sisters of yours arrive we'll escort them right to your door."

"Thank you, Chief Inspector," Mrs. Taylor said, and now she did extend her hand, and Mologna happily shook it, and it was just as warm and soft and enjoyable as he'd anticipated.

An interestin walk the lady had, too, returnin to the buildin. *Exactly* like that judo instructor. Mologna sighed and gave himself over to thoughts of yesteryear, and just about half an hour later a battered old ex-school bus pulled up immediately behind his car. Still painted yellow, but with its original identification replaced by black letters readin SILENT SISTERHOOD OF ST. FILUMENA, it was driven by a large round-faced nun and contained a whole bunch more. Traditional nuns, Mologna was happy to see, still in the old black-and-white habit, several luggin satchels undoubtedly filled with their sheet music. Strugglin again out of his car, Mologna signaled a nearby patrolman and gave him orders to escort the nuns to their recordin session.

One of the nuns, a wiry little old woman with a look of holy command, came over to beam upon Mologna and show him a driver's license and a library card both givin her name as Sister Mary Forcible. She seemed too bashful to speak. "Oh, that's all right, Sister," Mologna told her, pattin her bony claw. "I couldn't doubt you for an instant. I'm an old parochial school boy myself, you know."

Sister Mary Forcible smiled and put her ID away, and off they all went into the buildin, sweet and harmless, about to give the grace of music to a dirty and unhappy world. A lesson to us all, Mologna thought, and went back to his car and his memories of the judo instructor.

48

"Tiny," Dortmunder said, "think about it. You don't want to be in jail."

"I don't want to be in this nun suit either," Tiny snarled, and turned to point a threatening finger at Wilbur Howey, warning him, "And one more stupid line from you about getting in the habit, and what *you'll* be is black and white and red all over."

"Say," Wilbur answered, shying away from that finger, "can't you take a joke?"

"No."

Some joke. Sister Mary Forcible, having accepted Dortmunder's contention that his efforts on Sister Mary Grace's behalf did make it legitimate to call upon the convent for help, had gathered together fifteen of her fellow nuns and uptown they'd come, bringing a bunch of spare habits in large and extra-large, as well as a cassette of an a cappella recording of the Vienna Boys' Choir singing Christmas favorites: "The Little Drummer Boy," "Agnus Dei," "Silver Bells." This tape was now cued up in the cassette player atop the piano in the suite's back room. The nuns were crowded everywhere in both rooms, some of them seated all unknowing on cartons of *Scandinavian Marriage Secrets*, every copy of which had been carefully stashed out of sight before their arrival. Sheet music that had been sent to Super Star Music by hopeful amateurs wanting the addition of lyrics had been distributed to everyone as props for the alleged recording session, and those of the nuns who could read music were studying these submissions with great dubiousness. And the Dortmunder gang was down in black and white.

Very strange. When nothing shows but your face, enclosed by the white oval of a wimple and the featureless black of a nun's costume, you wouldn't expect much by way of individual character to show through, but it did, it did. Sister Mary Grace, for instance, back in her own chosen garb, looked completed and radiant, while Tiny, whose face mostly consisted of knuckles anyway, was barely plausible as the kind of false nun who, in the Middle Ages, poisoned and robbed unwary travelers. Stan Murch looked like a pilgrim in *The Canterbury Tales*, probably the one with ideas for alternate routes to Canterbury, and Wilbur Howey had the look of someone whose parents had turned her over to the nunnery fifty years ago because she was a little too dangerously peculiar for life in the outside world. Kelp was surely someone whose sister was the pretty one, while Dortmunder looked mostly like a missionary nun who was already among the cannibals and headhunters before realizing she'd lost her faith.

But whatever they looked like, and however they felt about it, this was their only chance and every one of them knew it. They'd all shaved in the men's room down the hall, and fortunately none of them were wearing high heels. And now all they had to do was wait for the sweep to go by. In the meantime, J.C. had trained Dortmunder in the use of the cassette player and had explained to the nuns, both real and make-believe, how to look like a chorus. The three small microphones which were all she had here had been placed prominently around the front room. And Andy Kelp stood in the open hall doorway, looking away to the right toward the elevators, waiting for the red down-pointing arrow to light, announcing that the sweep had finally reached the seventh floor.

For over an hour they'd been ready to give their performance. How long could it take a squad of cops to search an empty building, even one seventy-six stories high? Dortmunder didn't want his people overtrained and careless when the moment finally came.

He hadn't mentioned robbery in his phone conversation with the convent, feeling it was better to let sleeping moral issues lie. After all, he wasn't asking the nuns to participate in any burglaries or to help move or stash the loot. He had gone at their request to rescue their stolen Sister, he had done so with the help of these other people here, and now the Silent Sisterhood was merely being asked to rescue the rescuers. Simple. Clean. Virtually honest.

"Here they come!" Kelp hissed this announcement, looking excitedly back at the room, and there was a great rustling of skirts as everybody reacted. "Any second," Kelp said, still looking out and down the hallway, "any second now."

"Then close the goddamn door!" Dortmunder told him. "The door, I mean. Close the door."

So Kelp closed the door, on the outside of which was taped a hand-written notice: QUIET—DO NOT ENTER OR KNOCK—RECORDING SESSION IN PROGRESS. Lifting his skirts with both hands, Kelp scurried across the room to his place. Dortmunder, in the back room, hit the *play* button on the cassette player, and the clear sweet tones of the boys' choir filled both rooms with Bach's "Jesu, Joy of Man's Desiring." The nuns and pseudo-nuns held their sheet music up near their faces—*very* near their faces, in some instances—and, as J.C. had rehearsed them, they lip-synced along with the tape. And the police, as Dortmunder had anticipated, ignored the sign on the door and the sound of singing from within and pounded on the glass for entry.

As Dortmunder peeked around the edge of the inner room doorway, keeping one hand on the cassette player while he watched, J.C. crossed the room, put an angry expression on her face, opened the door just far enough for the law to see all those singing nuns behind her, and whispered the prepared line: "Sssshhh! Can't you read?"

Dortmunder counted four cops. They looked tired, sweaty, dusty. They had started on the seventy-sixth floor and this was the seventh, and they hadn't found a goddamn thing. By now, they surely didn't really expect to find anything, but they and the other squads in the sweep had to go through the motions anyway, and had to go through them thoroughly, just in case. Dortmunder could see it all in their faces, even from back here, and could see the one cop wearily nod and say something quietly to J.C., no doubt apologizing, no doubt explaining he was only doing his job, no doubt insisting he had no choice but to interrupt the recording session for just a minute or two.

The boys' choir was coming near the end of the

pre-arranged line. Dortmunder's fingertip, touching the *stop* button, had started to sweat. How could a fingertip sweat? What if he missed when the instant came, and his finger slid off, and everybody out there stopped mouthing words while the goddamn boys' choir went right on singing? If it weren't for that goddamn vow of silence, they wouldn't all have to go through this rigmarole, they could just—

"Then we might as well stop," J.C. said loudly, sounding very irritated. She turned and made a down-chopping arm movement, and Dortmunder closed his eyes and pushed. Everything stopped. He opened his eyes, and the nuns were all shuffling around, looking at one another, rattling their sheet music, avoiding direct eye contact with the cops. Dortmunder slipped through the doorway and joined them as the cops walked in, their leader saying, "Yes, ma'am, we heard all about you people from Chief Inspector Mologna."

Mologna! Dortmunder almost jumped out of his habit at the name. He'd had a run-in with Chief Inspector Mologna himself awhile ago and had barely got out of it with a whole skin. He, John Dortmunder, was in a way kind of sorta almost responsible for some public trouble that had come to Chief Inspector Mologna around that time. As though Mologna were right there in the room with him now—awful thought—Dortmunder could hear the man's voice, threatening him that time on the telephone: "When I get my hands on you, you'll fall downstairs for a month."

300

Ugh.

Meantime, the leader of this squad of cops was still talking to J.C., saying, "We do got to take a quick look through here, just in case there's somebody hiding in the place and you don't even know about it."

"In *here?*" J.C. said scornfully, waving a hand to indicate the small, cramped, crowded quarters.

"We'll be very quick, ma'am," the cop promised.

This was the tough part, standing here amid the nuns, hoping their presence would keep the cops from believing they had to search inside every box and carton and drawer for loot from the burglaries. Tiny and Stan had both argued that they should leave before the sweep reached this floor, do a quick make-believe recording session and then slide out of the building with the legitimate nuns, but that would leave the loot still in these offices, and if this space were empty the cops would have no reason to hurry and be sloppy and take things for granted.

Still, this was the tough part, and Dortmunder was glad the cops were buying the whole nun-chorus story. They said they'd be quick in their search, and as it turned out they were. While the other three stood just inside the door, looking around, one of them, eyes modestly down, tugging respectfully at the bill of his uniform cap, worked his way through the nuns to the door to the inner room, looked around in there, re-emerged, and told his friends, "Nobody. You couldn't hide a peanut in here."

"Okay, fine," the leader said, and gave J.C. a kind of half salute, touching his cap. "I'm sorry about the interruption, ma'am," he said. "Hope you get a number-one hit here."

"Thank you," J.C. said, though coldly.

The cops filed back out again, but then the leader stopped and looked back at the nuns— Dortmunder shrunk down inside himself, so that the only thing left in the outer world was his nose—and then at J.C. He said, "One thing."

The tension in the room could have provided electric power for Cleveland for a week. J.C. said, "Yes?"

"You gonna do a video?"

"Well, uhh . . ." J.C. dithered, then shrugged and said, "We're, uh, thinking about it."

"That's what you gotta do these days," the cop told her. "If you want to reach the kids, you know? You gotta do a video."

"Good idea," J.C. said.

"Good luck," the cop said, and went out, and closed the door.

The sigh that went up from all the assembled nuns was almost audible; on the very edge of a vow-breaker. But framed within their wimples, all those faces were flushed and sparkling and having *fun;* this was a lot different from the usual Sunday down at the convent.

Dortmunder hurried back to the inner room and pushed *play* and the boys' choir took up again where they'd been so rudely interrupted. And Tiny said, "Video. I'd like a video of *that* clown, falling out an airplane."

Sister Mary Forcible was near Tiny. She tapped his forearm, and when he looked down at her she smiled at him and shook her finger disapprovingly, then quickly took a pen out of her habit and scrawled a couple of words on the back of her sheet music. She showed this note to Tiny.

He studied it, then spoke slowly: "Chris-tian cha-*rit*-y." He nodded, leaning over the nun like a landslide about to happen. "I tell you what, Sister," he rumbled, "he should fall out an airplane over water, okay? Warm, soft water, so he could land in it." They smiled at each other and Tiny turned away, heading for the inner room. Passing Dortmunder, he muttered, "Shark-infested water."

49

Displayin himself in the main front entrance to the Avalon State Bank Tower while TV lights enhanced the wanin rays of the late afternoon sun and TV cameras recorded every immortal moment, Chief Inspector Francis X. Mologna listened to the depressin news from his boys in blue. The sweep had swept through, right on down the buildin from top to bottom, and had produced nothin.

Well, not entirely nothin. An illegal horse parlor had been exposed on thirty-seven and a Virgin

303

Islands pro-independence terrorist group's bomb factory had been turned up on nine and two prison escapees from Massachusetts, the professional arsonist Matlock twins, had been found livin in a chiropodist's office on fifty-two, but none of the valuables stolen from the importers on twenty-six had been located. Also, a surprisin amount of sexual hanky-panky between people married to people other than the people they were hanky-pankyin with had been discovered, but no more mercenary soldiers had appeared, nor had any burglars. The men who had done the sweep had made their reports to their immediate commanders, and these three commanders, bein two lieutenants and a captain, were now passin the reports on to the chief inspector, leanin too close to be sure they got into the TV pictures.

"So it looks," Mologna growled, leanin back away from his subordinates, "as though we got all the mercs there were."

"Looks that way, Chief Inspector," said a lieutenant, talkin to a spot about a foot and a half to Mologna's right so the camera could catch his profile. "There isn't anybody in there now except the legitimate people signed in at the record book in the lobby."

"Except for the Matlock twins," said the other lieutenant, whose team had made that discovery.

"Except for them," the first lieutenant agreed, leanin to his left to block the other lieutenant from the cameras.

"And it also looks," Mologna went on, "as

though whoever else was in on this ruckus, they took the rest of the stuff out that private elevator into the garden over there and made good their getaway before we arrived on the scene."

It was too bad, damnit. If the men under Mologna's command—even the spurious command of a display inspector—had come up with the rest of that loot or whoever had actually masterminded the burglary, it would have gone a long way toward rehabilitatin Mologna back toward the top cop status that was rightfully his. Somewhere, he knew, there was somebody who'd put this whole plan together, somebody who knew just what the hell had been goin on here in this tower, and what a feather in Mologna's cap it would have been if he could have got his hands on that someone. I'd squeeze him till he sang "Dixie," Mologna thought.

But it was not to be.

The captain said, "Chief Inspector, I wouldn't be surprised if whoever made the telephone tip that brought us here was another member of the gang. A falling out among thieves, you know."

"The same idea had occurred to me," Mologna lied, noddin thoughtfully. That would be the ringleader, for sure, the one Mologna would love to have a little conversation with.

The first lieutenant said, "Chief Inspector, Building Security wants to know if they can take charge of the place. Are we finished here?"

The mastermind is long gone, probably out of the city entirely by now. Mologna said, "There's nothin left to— Wait, hold on. Move out of the way there."

They all moved to the side, away from the doorway, and out came the singin nuns, blinkin into the TV lights. Poor unworldly creatures, they seemed startled by all the attention. "Here, you fellas," Mologna called to the TV crews, "let these little ladies pass. Get them lights and cameras out of their faces. They're not used to all this carryin on. You," he told the obnoxious lieutenant with the profile, "escort these ladies to their bus."

"Yes, sir," the lieutenant complained, and moved away with the nuns, some of whom weren't such *little* ladies at all. Well, the pretty ones didn't go into a convent, did they? Except sometimes they did.

Mologna caught sight of Sister Mary Forcible, the head nun who'd identified herself on the way in. "Sister Mary," he said, gesturin to her, "you want some free publicity for that record of yours?"

Stage fright kept the little nun silent, with a glassy and terrified grin. Then Mrs. Taylor came along, smilin, self-confident, sayin, "Chief Inspector, that's so nice of you, but the Sisters are silent except when they're singing. But you get us some publicity when the record comes *out*, and we'll remember you in our prayers." She laughed, liltinly, very like that judo instructor of yore, and turned to Sister Mary Forcible, sayin, "Won't we, Sister?"

The nun nodded, spastically. She was still scared, poor thing, confused by the lights and the cameras and the big burly policemen all over the place. A big difference from all them drugged-out rock groups, Mologna thought, and said, "You go on along, Sister Mary," and watched beamin as Sister Mary and Mrs. Taylor—I'll remember you in *my* prayers, Mrs. Taylor—hurried across the sidewalk to join her friends in the bus. Turnin back to his team, displayin for the TV cameras both the forcefulness and the loneliness of command, Mologna said, "Well, boys, we ain't doin shit here, we might as well just—"

Bang! That was a hell of a big *crack*, like a rifle shot, and policemen and buildin security people all over the place quickly crouched down and reached fast for their sidearms. Mologna looked at them all, looked at the thick belch of dirty gray smoke comin out of the nuns' bus's tailpipe, and laughed at them all. "That was a backfire, boys," he called. "Take it easy." Shakin his head, he displayed the amused calm of command. "Scared of a bunch of nuns," he said.

50

(letter from Elaine Ritter to Rafael Avilez, Guerrera Popular Independence Party, c/o United Nations, NY—hand-delivered)

Dear Señor Avilez,
      In the next few days, you will be receiving a large number of packages in the mail, all

containing valuable objects such as jewelry. My father, Frank Ritter, has found it impossible after all to assist your revolution directly, as he had intended, because of the complications of international law and the arrest of the army he had meant to send you, but he still feels quite strongly in the justice of your cause, and has chosen a somewhat odd and indirect method of getting financial support to you. (You can understand that he can't at this moment let his own name be connected with your efforts to overthrow the tyrant, General Pozos.)

The objects you will receive were "stolen" from companies in the Avalon State Bank Tower. My father, as you know, owns that building, and arranged the apparent "theft"; his insurance company is making good all the losses. Individually, none of these objects is so valuable that it could be easily traced; nevertheless, my father thinks it would be better if you were to arrange to sell them in small lots and elsewhere; in Los Angeles, for instance, or possibly London.

My father would not want to be thanked yet; not until the tyrant has been successfully overthrown. With the money from these objects, you should be able to buy arms and arrange for international support. My father and I are both very sorry we cannot be more directly involved, but hope this financial contribution will turn the tide.

Vive la revolution!

(letter from May Walker, calling herself May
Dortmunder, to Otto Chepkoff, Tiptop A-1 Choice
Foods, 273-14 Scunge Avenue, Brooklyn, NY
11666)

Dear Mr. Chepkoff:
Enclosed please find copies of invoices from
your company to Bohack Supemarkets, Inc.
You will notice that these are your actual
invoice forms. You will also notice they clearly
demonstrate a pattern of double-billing for
shipments delivered. You will further notice
they are all more than three months old, which
means that no one will go looking for the
originals in the Bohack Supermarket files—
where the originals can be found, I guarantee
it—unless someone suggests to the Bohack
accounting department (anonymously, perhaps)
that you might have been up to some
hanky-panky.
John Dortmunder hopes not to hear from
you any more on that other matter.

(letter from Sister Mary Grace to John Dortmunder, sent via one of the convenience addresses)

Dear Saint John and your saint friends,
By now you know I did divert some of that
"loot," writing a different address on the
packages. But it was all in a good cause, I
promise, to help the people of Guerrera who

309

my father wanted to enslave. And it was only a little tiny portion, really, so please forgive me, and know that all of us in the Silent Sisterhood of Saint Filumena will remember you in our prayers always.

(enclosure from Mother Mary Forcible)

Dear John,
Thank you. We shall keep a closer watch on our little Sister Mary Grace from now on, and with God's help we shall not have to call upon your peculiar but oh-so-valuable talents again. Praying for long life to the Pope, forgiveness of the souls in Purgatory, the conversion of Godless Russia, and that John Dortmunder shall never ever be caught, I remain,
Mother Mary Forcible
Silent Sisterhood of St. Filumena

51

Dortmunder came up out of the water onto the thinly populated beach. In a swimsuit, he looked like something in anatomy class. He paused, gave the green Caribbean a look, and walked across the white sand of Aruba to where May reclined with a copy of *Newsweek* on a beach towel featuring a large picture of Betty Boop. Dortmunder dropped, as though a sniper had got him, onto the other towel (Elmer Fudd, with a shotgun), and just lay there awhile, facedown, cheek on the warm cloth, eyes studying individual grains of sand.

"Hmmmm," said May.

Dortmunder noticed that each grain of sand was alike. The sun on his shoulder blades was like honey. Some distance away, people were laughing, their voices muffled by the sun and the gentle rush of the sea.

"Guerrera," said May.

Dortmunder's eyelids grew heavy.

"You don't want to burn," May said.

This was true. Dortmunder rolled over and sat up. Now the whole world looked green, so he put on dark sunglasses, which made him look like a person with a horse he wanted to tell you about.

"This country Guerrera," May said, "it's in the *Newsweek* here."

"This is Aruba," Dortmunder said.

"Guerrera's the country where Sister Mary Grace made the contribution for the revolution," May reminded him.

"Contribution," Dortmunder said. "Huh." Two months, and that still rankled a little.

"Well, they had their revolution," May said.

"Good for them."

" 'General Anastasio Pozos, from his well-guarded estate near Miami,' " May read from the magazine, " 'assured loyal Guerrerans that he would soon return to oust the Communist-inspired revolutionaries.' "

"Uh huh," Dortmunder said.

" 'The United States has recognized the new

311

government in Guerrera. A State Department spokesperson today—' I guess that would be Tuesday, or Monday, or some time. Anyway, '—spokesman today said the United States was hopeful of a new era of stability in the region.' So that's nice."

"Uh huh," Dortmunder said.

"It's nice to know the money went in a good cause."

"*I'm* a good cause," Dortmunder said.

"John, we did very well out of that experience," May told him, and gestured widely with the magazine. "Look at the vacation we're taking. And there's still thousands and thousands of dollars left. *Years* of taking it easy. John, do you know what we have?"

"Sunburn?"

"Leisure time! Sociologists all say it is extremely important to have leisure time, to expand ourselves. When we get back to the city, we can go to museums, theaters, gallery openings, we can get caught up on our reading . . ."

"Uh huh," Dortmunder said.

May cast a suspicious glance at Dortmunder, but couldn't read his face because of those big dark sunglasses. "John," she said, "you won't be going out to the track, will you?"

"Maybe once," Dortmunder said. "Maybe twice."

May considered delivering a lecture, then calculated its probable effect, then decided not to. She said, "It's almost lunchtime, isn't it?"

"Just a second," Dortmunder said, and bent down and cocked his ear to listen to his stomach. It obligingly made a small gurgle sound. "Yes," he said.

"I like that lobster tail," May said. "I know I have it every day, but I like it. What about you?"

Dortmunder lay back on Elmer Fudd, with his hands under his head. Through the dark glasses he looked at the blue sky. The lines of his face shifted themselves around, making accommodation for a smile. "I think I'll have caviar," he said.

A note on the text
Large print edition designed by
Bernadette Montalvo.
Composed in 16 pt Plantin
on a Xyvision 300/Linotron 202N
by Genevieve Connell
of G.K. Hall & Co.